Praise for

Heavens to Betsy

"Navigating the rapids of life and love with the sexy Reverend Betsy Blessing is a hilarious and rollicking ride. If she could just get her man squared away, master walking in her stilettos, and keep her church from coming apart, then it might all turn out just fine. *Heavens to Betsy* is fresh and heartfelt. A great read."

—ANNE DAYTON and MAY VANDERBILT,
authors of *Emily Ever After*

"Thank heavens for Betsy! This laugh-out-loud funny story is such a refreshing read. Beth Pattillo does an outstanding job of showing us the womanly and definitely human side of a person we never see in novels: the female pastor. With a sharp sense of humor and a heart-breakingly honest look at the prejudices that plague these servants of God, *Heavens to Betsy* will have you crying and laughing and loving every minute of it. Thank you, Beth, for creating Betsy—from her stilettos and pink slip-dress to her shaky confidence and fear of con-frontation, she's one of the most believable and lovable characters out there."

—ALISON STROBEL, author of *Worlds Collide*

"In *Heavens to Betsy,* Beth Pattillo blends the most tender qualities of chick lit with some of the stringiest offerings of church life and some-how grills up a delicious tale of grace and redemption. Her breathing characters deserve a place all their own in the potluck supper of inspirational fiction. *Heavens to Betsy* is highly enjoyable reading, zinging with moments all of us can relate to."

—LISA SAMSON, Christy award–winning author of *The Church Ladies, Songbird,* and *Club Sandwich*

a novel

Beth Pattillo

Heavens
to Betsy

WATERBROOK
PRESS

HEAVENS TO BETSY
PUBLISHED BY WATERBROOK PRESS
2375 Telstar Drive, Suite 160
Colorado Springs, Colorado 80920
A division of Random House, Inc.

Scripture taken from the *Holy Bible, New International Version*®. NIV®. Copyright
© 1973, 1978, 1984 by International Bible Society. Used by permission of Zondervan
Publishing House. All rights reserved. Scripture also taken from the *New Revised Standard Version of the Bible,* copyright © 1989 by the Division of Christian Education of
the National Council of the Churches of Christ in the USA. Used by permission. All
rights reserved.

The characters and events in this book are fictional, and any resemblance to actual
persons or events is coincidental.

ISBN 1-4000-7044-9

Library of Congress Cataloging-in-Publication Data
Pattillo, Beth.
  Heavens to Betsy / Beth Pattillo.—1st ed.
     p. cm.
   ISBN 1-4000-7044-9
   1. Women clergy—Fiction. I. Title.
PS3616.A925H43 2005
813'.6—dc22   2004029561

Printed in the United States of America
2005—First Edition

10 9 8 7 6 5 4 3 2 1

For my sisters of the cloth,
wherever they may serve

Acknowledgments

I owe a tremendous debt of gratitude to the following people:

My husband, Randy Smith, who provides moral support and child care in equal measure.

My children, Sam and Meg Smith, who never mind being deprived of a home-cooked meal when I'm writing.

Jenny Bent, über-agent, who talked me into putting Betsy down on paper.

Dudley Delffs and Don Pape of WaterBrook Press—for their enthusiasm for Betsy and her story.

Cheryl Lewallen—cheerleader, counselor, and the reason I signed up for an unlimited long-distance plan.

My fabulous critique group—GayNelle Doll, Trish Milburn, and Annie Solomon—who provide invaluable red ink along with generous helpings of friendship.

The members of the Music City Romance Writers—for camaraderie and fun.

The Clergy Chix—Sandra, Donna, Ann, Janet, Megan, Elisa, and Jennifer—for monthly lunch and laughter.

And, finally, I want to thank three churches that have been important in my life—First Christian Church, Lubbock, Texas; Raymore Christian Church, Raymore, Missouri; and Woodmont Christian Church, Nashville, Tennessee. Please note that none of them serves as the model for Betsy's fictional Church of the Shepherd.

I swear this is my last wedding. All around me candles blaze, and the scent of roses overpowers the congregation. Men in black tie. Women in frothy hats. The vaulted ceiling of the church rises above me, its mahogany beams arching toward heaven. I drink in the scene, lingering over every detail, and my knees quiver. A deep breath does little to calm my nerves. There won't be any more after this.

Next to me, Dan stands tall and handsome. His tux fits perfectly— no sign of the slight paunch his usual T-shirts reveal. The organ swells as the pipes ring out the last notes of "The Wedding March."

It's the lifetime commitment I've always wanted. A deep connection through all the "slings and arrows of outrageous fortune." No more loneliness. No isolation. I look up to keep the tears from flowing. No time to cry.

I open my officiant's book and begin. "Dearly beloved…"

These are magic words, an incantation of love that required months of intense preparation on the part of the bride and groom. Dress fittings, repeated trimming of the guest list, bridesmaid negotiations, nagging Dan to pick his groomsmen. And that little trifle known as the ceremony.

"Who brings this woman to be married to this man?" I ask.

Stacy's father beams, despite the stiffness of his stance. Beside him, Stacy glows beneath the thin cover of her veil.

"Her mother and I," her father replies, just as we rehearsed.

Fathers of the bride come in three types. The first one's angry about the cost of the pageantry. The second is relieved that his daughter is now another man's problem. The third is shattered to part with his little princess. Stacy's father is the third kind, lucky girl. Her dad lifts her veil back over her head, murmurs words of love in her ear, and places her hand in Dan's.

Now it's just the two of them in front of all these people. And me, of course. The minister.

"Dan, will you have Stacy to be your wife, to live with her in holy matrimony? If so, please say, 'I will.'"

The Declaration of Intent always comes as a surprise to grooms. All of them look shocked, as if what they're doing at the front of the church in their penguin suits has come as a complete surprise. We're not to the real vows yet; just this spot check to make sure both parties are willing. It's the place where we used to ask if anyone objected to the marriage, but given what I know about Dan and Stacy's extended families, we decided to leave that part out. The ice sculptures at the reception would melt by the time we sorted out all the protests likely to be lodged.

"Ar…wll." Dan echoes me as if a boa constrictor has wrapped itself around his throat. Stacy beams as if he'd shouted his vow from a rooftop. I ask her the same question, and she starts to cry. Since we're not even to the vows yet, I save the tissue tucked in my book. I only hope she doesn't forget herself and use the back of her hand to wipe her eyes. I can already see she's not wearing waterproof mascara, and I've had more than one raccoon bride in the past few years.

"Marriage is a gift from God, bestowed upon us for the mutual benefit of men and women…" The familiar words roll off my tongue, even as they pierce my heart. Will I ever be on the receiving end of the wedding vows? A thirty-year-old, single woman minister lives in dating Siberia. The last time I went out with a man, he turned out to have a serious criminal record.

Note to Self: Never let one of your congregants fix you up with her grandson who "just needs the love of a good woman." The wayward grandson would have been happy to pursue a long-term relationship with my credit rating—I saw his eyes lusting after my American Express when I opened my purse to pay for dinner—but I'm not that desperate. Yet.

"Dan and Stacy, join hands and, with your promises, commit yourselves as husband and wife."

Does any couple really know what they're saying when they parrot back the words I read from my book?

"For better, for worse; for richer, for poorer…"

How will a couple who couldn't agree whether to have lamb or fish at the reception navigate the complexities of married life? Sure, I see their joy today. But in five years, maybe ten, they'll be in some other minister's office wondering where it all went wrong. And what will that preacher tell them? That it all started with Lamb v. Fish?

"As a sign of their commitment, Dan and Stacy have chosen to exchange rings. The wedding ring is an enduring symbol of the promises they make this day…"

The best man and maid of honor fumble for the rings, and I pray over those golden bands. I pray hard because my parents taught me how difficult it can be to keep vows made in a church. Somewhere between the custody battle, the divorce settlement, and my new half brothers, my parents' vows crumbled.

Now comes the tricky part of the service. The congregation holds its breath while the bride and groom light the unity candle. Even though I always check the wick before the service, I'm never confident this part will go well. At the first wedding I performed, the unity candle was a no-go. The couple divorced within a year, and when I saw the bride in the grocery store, she blamed it on the wick. I myself would have blamed it on the fact that the groom and maid of honor had yet to conclude their extracurricular relationship when the wedding took place. Fortunately, the candle behaves itself today as the bride's cousin warbles "Endless Love," so often sung at weddings in spite of the fact that it's an ode to a scorned teenager-turned-stalker who ends up burning down his girlfriend's house.

"Inasmuch as you have exchanged vows and rings this day, I proclaim you to be husband and wife. What God has joined together, let no one separate. Dan, you may kiss your bride."

The groom swoops in and proceeds to wash his new wife's tonsils. Funny, I'd pegged him for a peck-on-the-lips man, given that he ultimately lost Lamb v. Fish. For this brief moment, though, after weeks of having his wishes ignored and his preferences shunned, he takes charge.

The kiss starts to take on biblical proportions. People giggle, then squirm. Finally, the groom comes up for air, and I present the newlyweds to the congregation. The organ bursts forth, and they're off, trailed by assorted bridesmaids and groomsmen and two rambunctious flower girls. Privately I say another prayer, borne of thanks and worry, and then follow the wedding party down the aisle.

At the back of the church, the wedding coordinator gives me two thumbs up. Then she turns to hustle the bride and groom out to the Garden of Prayer for a quick photo op. Her assistant will gather the congregation outside the doors of the church for the staged departure. The bride and groom will dash for the limo while the guests release live butterflies from little triangular boxes. I look up at the fifteen-foot doors of the sanctuary and wonder how many of the butterflies will find their way inside to entertain worshipers during tomorrow morning's service.

I backtrack up the side aisle to the sacristy, where I stow my clerical robe and pull my purse out of its cubbyhole. That empty feeling in the pit of my stomach has become a regular visitor, and once again it makes itself known. Another wedding reception solo. But this is the last one. In six months I'll be free. I've learned the hard way that I don't belong in the ministry.

If I ever do find Mr. Right, I will insist on having my wedding reception at the Hermitage Hotel. It's all marble and elegance, two things that can be scarce commodities in Nashville. Even the replica of the Parthenon in Centennial Park isn't the real deal. It's made out of the same little pebbles and concrete as my grandparents' driveway.

The Hermitage, though, feels like a bit of European elegance plopped down amid country-music staples like the Ryman Auditorium and Tootsie's Orchid Lounge. I'm not ten steps inside the door before a black-tied waiter appears at my elbow to offer me a glass of wine. I decline, because that innocent little glass is two points on Weight Watchers. Besides, if I'm going to splurge, it will be on the newest wedding-reception phenomenon: the chocolate fountain.

Dan and Stacy are holding court in the lobby, and the guests are mobbing the buffet tables. I know almost everyone here, and yet I stand awkwardly on the fringes, trying to decide whether to join the sea of people around the hot hors d'oeuvre or elbow my way through to the bride and groom.

There are more delights to look forward to, of course. Eventually we'll move into the ballroom for dancing, and then all of my elderly parishioners will politely ask me to fox-trot around the hardwood. When I interviewed with my ordination committee, the white-haired men who held my future in their hands informed me that they were delighted I wasn't one of those bitter feminists. They approved me within minutes. I might not be bitter, but I definitely had unchristian thoughts about those guys. I still do from time to time, when I'm not holding the hands of men just like them as the orderlies wheel them into surgery, my not-a-bitter-feminist voice assuring them they're going to make it through the bypass/transplant/prostate procedure.

Someone materializes at my shoulder, and I jump.

"Take it easy, Blessing. People will think you're up to something."

"David!" I swat him on the shoulder. The Reverend Dr. David Swenson. Nemesis. Competitor. Confidant. Friend. The only brown-haired, brown-eyed Lutheran preacher I know, thanks to his Italian mother.

"Nice job on the nuptials. Do they let the associate do many weddings over there at Church of the Sheep?"

I'd like to correct David for twisting the name of my church, but when you're ready to resign, you don't feel like defending the people who've driven you to it. "I'm a last-minute fill-in for Dr. Black. After this, it's strictly Christian-education programs for me."

I haven't actually told David about my decision to leave the ministry. He's not going to like it. "What are you doing here?"

"Stacy's folks are parishioners."

"Well, that explains a lot."

He swats me back, and I laugh for the first time today. "That's assault, Swenson."

He grins. "So have me arrested."

"I will when you hit the dance floor. Your waltz is a criminal offense in ten states."

"Hey! Watch it, girl. I may be the only guy under seventy who asks you to dance."

This statement is soberingly true, so I change the subject.

"How'd your date go last night?"

David snorts and snags a glass of water from a passing waiter. "Great, until I was forced to reveal what I do for a living."

I wince because I've been there myself. "And after that?"

"She kept looking at me like I was a freak of nature."

"And your point is?"

"Should I hit you again?"

Mutual abuse has always been the cornerstone of our relationship.

When I fled my demonic little country church six months ago, I limped into Nashville, seeking shelter in the relative anonymity of being an associate minister of a large congregation. I was delighted to again be in the same city as David. We'd been friends in divinity school here at Vanderbilt, but in the intervening years, our jobs had taken us in opposite directions.

"Want to hit the buffet?" David is well over six feet tall and too thin for his own good. He could eat the entire kitchen of the Hermitage and not gain an ounce. I resent that.

"No swiping the shrimp off my plate," I warn, based on my past experience of dining with him.

"Would I do that?" His smile is as wide and open as the sky.

"Oh yes you would, Dr. Swenson. In a heartbeat."

David's words about my dance card prove depressingly prophetic. He's the only guy who steers me around the dance floor without my worrying that he might have a stroke from the effort. Frail Mr. Benson breaks my heart, telling me how much he misses his wife. I did her funeral three months ago when Dr. Black was on vacation, and poor Mr. Benson still hasn't stopped thanking me for my eulogy. The dutiful Mr. Sanderson whisks me away under orders from the formidable Mrs. Sanderson and remains mute throughout the four-minute ordeal. And the retired Reverend Squires is, as always, an energetic polka partner.

When David looms over me a second time, I'm grateful for the reprieve.

"Dance?" He extends his hand and winks at me. Unfortunately, Edna Tompkins sees that wink. She is the greatest gossip at the Church of the Shepherd (a title for which she beat out some rather gifted competition). I foresee my name being bandied about during the next meeting of the ladies auxiliary. They will not approve. David and his congregation are suspect because they only celebrate Communion once a quarter. At the Church of the Shepherd, we're weekly folks. I wonder if it has occurred to Mrs. Tompkins and Company that maybe we're just bigger sinners and need more forgiveness.

Here's what they don't tell you in divinity school: You will fall in love with your parishioners, even the snarky ones. Professors tell you how you'll have to teach your congregation, how you'll have to guide them and correct them and make sure they think like theology professors. But they don't tell you those folks sitting in the pew will worm their way into your heart. They don't teach you not to look at the mothers when you baptize their children, because then you'll start crying too, and there's already enough water involved. They never say what you should do in the middle of a eulogy when your throat chokes up so tightly you can't get the words out because you're already missing the bear hugs you used to receive from the deceased.

They also don't tell you what to do when a congregation turns on you. How to respond to the people who parade through your office with lengthy lists of complaints about your performance, when what they really don't like is your gender. I hadn't served in my first church for very long before I realized a group of my parishioners was out to get me. (Hey, just because you're paranoid doesn't mean they're not after you.) These folks didn't just dislike me; they hated me. Scathing verbal attacks, unsigned letters, secret meetings—Christian charity had fled for warmer climes than that icy congregation offered.

Six months after my departure and hundreds of miles away, I'm still licking my wounds. So when David offers me his hand, I take it gladly. Moments of respite are few and far between in this business, and David is one person who would understand exactly what I'm feeling—if I had the courage to tell him.

"Do you think they're laying odds yet?" He smiles over my shoulder at the interested audience our two-step has garnered.

I want to laugh, but something about this wedding has gotten under my skin, made me feel vulnerable. I came to Nashville to escape the loneliness and conflict of being a single woman minister in a small town. Yet except for David and LaRonda, my best girlfriend from my divinity school days, I've had little success in widening my social circle. It doesn't help that Valentine's Day is next week.

"I think my parishioners have moved beyond betting on my love life. They've resorted to prayer." The moment I say those words, I want to take them back. The one thing I like about David is that I never get any pity from him. Only good-natured ribbing, and lots of it.

He twirls me around and then smoothly guides me across the floor. "I wouldn't worry until they start organizing twenty-four-hour prayer vigils."

I laugh. I always do when I'm around David. I laugh a lot in general, too. I think it's one of the better aspects of my personality, although I haven't had much opportunity for laughter in the past few years. No one thinks you have a sense of humor if you're a preacher. They refuse to tell you the risqué jokes. Conversation grinds to a halt at your approach. This line of thinking is too depressing to pursue while dancing with David, so I change the subject.

"What's new at St. Helga's?" It's been a tough year for the parishioners since a tornado ripped through the sanctuary. They've been worshiping in their activity center for months while the debris is being cleared away. Currently, David is refereeing the design of the new "worship center"—apparently sanctuaries are passé.

He grimaces. "The vestry has formed a subcommittee to hold listening conferences about rebuilding."

"I'm in prayer for you, friend." We shake our heads over this development. Church committees move at glacial speed. Listening conferences (also known as gripe sessions) progress at the speed of geological epochs. At this rate David will be preaching from underneath a basketball goal for the next twenty years.

He shrugs. "This too shall pass."

I admire his stoicism. He twirls me around at the far end of the dance floor. "So, what are you up to after this?"

I sigh. "Quality time with my remote control. A pizza with everything if I'm feeling truly dangerous."

"How about a movie?"

I'm immediately on my guard. Action flicks are David's secret vice, his guilty pleasure. "Not if it involves Schwarzenegger, Vin Diesel, or Will Smith."

"What do you suggest? Romantic comedy?"

"How about *Pride and Prejudice* meets *The Matrix*?"

Laughing with David is *my* guilty pleasure. And one I sorely need tonight.

"Okay," I concede. "I'll go watch a couple of testosterone-challenged men blow things up—if you're paying."

"Deal." He grins, and I'm reminded that he is, in fact, a nice-looking guy. I could do worse on a Saturday night.

But shouldn't I be doing better than a movie with an old friend? What if it's not the clerical robe? What if it's me?

I lower my eyebrows and shoot him a meaningful look. "Let's be clear about one thing. If you want popcorn, order your own. No mooching off me."

David spins me around and dips me until I'm so off balance I expect to feel my head make contact with the parquet. He snaps me back up, and I'm pressed against his chest. He grins down at me— half boy, half man. "Would I do that?"

"Hah!" I push him away. "Of course you would. And I have the scars to prove it."

"Reverend Blessing, you're a harsh woman."

"Yeah, well, don't you forget it."

His expression suddenly sobers. "Believe me, I won't."

Ouch. Where did that come from?

"David?"

But in the blink of an eye, he's his usual self. He playfully punches me on the arm. "Gotcha."

"Mooch."

"Shrew."

"Shall we?"

"But of course."

He offers me his arm, and we make our way off the dance floor. A quick good-bye to the bride and groom, and we're tumbling out of the hotel into the cold February night. Two preachers trying to pass for normal people.

Chapter 2

I know what you're thinking. *What about David? Isn't he perfect for her?*

Well, I'll tell you up-front: There's no way I'd marry another minister. I had several clergy-couple friends from divinity school, and without exception, they were all divorced within five years. It wasn't that they didn't love each other. But that's what total immersion in church will do to a relationship. You have to have something outside the four walls of the sanctuary. So, while David makes a perfect movie buddy on the odd Saturday night, he's not husband material. Really.

Besides, because of David I'm trapped in Auditorium 11 of the Green Hills Cinema 16 watching a musclebound macho man blow up bad guys of indeterminate ethnic origin. It's unclear exactly who these creeps are supposed to be—Colombian drug lords? Arab terrorists? Indonesian revolutionaries? Their deliberately vague identity means the movie studio can market it all over the world without offending anyone.

David's hand sneaks toward me in the darkness, but I know what he's up to. "Stop it," I hiss and slap his fingers away. I move my popcorn as far to my left as I can, and he sulks. Don't feel sorry for him. You heard me tell him to get his own.

"Come on," he wheedles. He's slouched down in the seat, making puppy-dog eyes at me in an attempt to divest me of my popcorn. He should know by now that this cheap ploy will not work. At least not for another fifteen minutes.

"No." I scoop up a big handful of popcorn and stuff it in my mouth, chewing with gusto to show him how delicious the stuff is. Actually, it's stale and has the bitter, metallic taste of popcorn that's been in the warming thingie too long.

"You've had that stuff for an hour. Come on, share."

"Nope."

The woman in front of us turns around and shoots us a disapproving glare. I, too, sink down in my seat.

"Troublemaker."

"Scrooge."

Before I met David, I underestimated the value of being comfortable enough with someone to insult him on a regular basis. Now I find it comes naturally. Especially when he's once again sneaking his hand across my lap to get to my popcorn.

Except that this time David's hand rests on my thigh for a moment. A sharp rush of sensation emanates from his palm, jumps through my skin, and races along my spine. A sudden sweat breaks out along the back of my neck.

Dear lord, I'm embarrassed. More so than when I presided at the communion table with toilet paper stuck to my shoe. Or when I fell down the chancel steps during the recessional on Easter. Those were public humiliations. This one is intensely private—and ten times worse. I'm such a desperate old spinster, I'm getting my jollies from incidental contact with old friends.

"Here." I jam the bag of popcorn into his midsection. I don't care about making my point, don't care about losing face, don't even care about the carefully calculated Weight Watchers points I'm sacrificing.

David looks at me with surprise, enough that I can make it out in the darkened theater.

"Blessing?"

"Just take the stupid popcorn."

Wasn't it freezing in the theater just a moment ago? It's usually like a Frigidaire in here.

"No." He tries to put it back in my hands. "It's yours."

I cross my arms and shove my clenched fists under my armpits. "I don't want it."

The woman in front of us turns around again. This time she puts a finger to her lips and shushes us as if we're a couple of school kids. David looks quizzically at me but falls silent.

For the rest of the movie, we sit facing straight forward. I pretend to be engrossed in the defeat of the indeterminately ethnic villains. And when the closing credits roll, I leap to my feet and make a fuss of gathering up my purse and empty soda cup.

"Okay, Blessing. What's up?"

David just stands there, waiting for an answer, and I know I can't give him one. What would I say?

Instead, I play innocent. "You won, so quit gloating. I hate it when you gloat."

The best defense is a good offense, right?

He straightens up to his considerable height. "I'm not gloating. You gave me the popcorn."

"Nag," I say.

"Greed-head," he shoots back, and we both smile, relieved the awkwardness is gone.

"You owe me a chick flick." We move out of the row of seats and make our way down the aisle steps. Movement is good. Conversation is good. Remembering the feel of David's hand on my leg is bad.

"Wanna go for ice cream?" We reach the escalator that takes us from the bowels of the theater back up to the main level, and I hop on with alacrity.

"Nah. I'm preaching tomorrow, remember?"

David grins. "Ah yes. Dr. Black's golf injury. How goes the recovery?"

I smile, even if I shouldn't. "He's actually feeling much better, but his wife told him she was leaving him if he didn't stay in bed. Doctor's orders." Mimi Black is the classic preacher's wife—disarmingly kind, has a lovely singing voice, and is a tiger when it comes to protecting her husband. I wish I could have a wife, but that probably wouldn't go over well with the congregation, huh?

"All right," David concedes, "but next week we get ice cream."

His easy assumption that at this same time next Saturday night we'll be leaving the theater together irritates me, especially since next Saturday is Valentine's Day. Since I moved back to Nashville, David takes me for granted. It never bothered me before, but tonight is different. Tonight I don't feel like being a foregone conclusion.

"Not next week. I'm busy."

"Busy, Blessing? What's up? Hot Valentine's date?"

"Yep." I lie blatantly, instinctively, without the least bit of remorse. Yet.

"All right!" He raises his hand, and I realize I'm supposed to high-five him. "Go, Betsy!"

David rarely calls me by my first name. He likes the irony of my last name far too much to deprive himself of the pleasure of using it as often as possible. He says it's as much fun as addressing Dr. Butcher, the surgeon, or Ms. Swindle, the accountant.

We reach his car—the same beat-up Volvo he drove in divinity school. "So, who's the lucky guy?"

I'm momentarily speechless. Why did I lie? But I know the answer to that question. Because of what I felt when David's hand touched my leg. Because a girl's got to have some pride.

"He's no one." I try the dismissive approach, even though I know David will never go for it. Besides, it's the truth, since my date doesn't even exist.

He unlocks the Volvo, and we slide inside. Well, I don't slide so much as scooch, really, given the rips in the leather of the passenger seat. David turns toward me as he starts the car.

"Hmm. Must be pretty serious if you won't spill the details." In the low light of the parking garage, it's hard to read his eyes. They're usually such perfect mirrors of his thoughts, but tonight their message is clouded.

"I don't want to jinx it." I wrap my seat belt around me and try not to look at him.

"Betz, it's not one of your parishioners, is it?"

I can read his eyes now. He's dead serious.

"No! No poaching sheep from my own flock."

He sighs and leans back in his seat as he puts the car into reverse. "Just checking."

What he doesn't know, though, is that I've broken another cardinal rule—the one about mixing friendship with romantic feelings. And I know in this moment, as we pull out of the garage and head for home, I can never let him know how I feel. Because I won't risk losing his friendship. But mostly because I'm afraid of what I felt in that theater tonight.

♤

I had a professor in divinity school who taught us that the opposite of faith isn't doubt; it's fear. When she said that, my whole world shifted into place like puzzle pieces sorting themselves out and interlocking with neat precision. Don't get me wrong; I have my doubts. But they're nothing compared to my fears.

One by one I've tackled a lot of things that scare me. That's why I can stand up in the pulpit and preach to five hundred people on a Sunday morning. I can even plumb a toilet when the third-grade Sunday-school class decides to see how many paper towels can be stuffed down it before it backs up.

But some of the deepest fears, well, they're still down there, lurking, waiting to swallow me. Conflict. Loneliness. Rejection. A twisted Garden of Eden from some evil parallel universe. I'm not sure I have enough faith to face those babies.

Like a lot of people, I've discovered that if I keep very busy, I don't have as much time to think about those fears. Still, they creep in, and sometimes they jump up and snag me by the throat at unexpected moments.

Like at coffee fellowship the next morning.

I'm standing in the middle of the fellowship hall between services, the classic cup of church coffee in hand. It tastes like it was filtered through an old rubber-soled shoe. Mix that with the wax on the paper cup and a packet of Sweet'N Low (the church hostess refuses to order Equal), and you get that bitterly potent mixture that has powered the spiritual life of the mainline Protestant church for the past thirty years.

Mrs. Tompkins, the gossip queen, makes a beeline for me. Before I can escape, she's pinned me down.

"So, you and Dr. Swenson? Are you an item?" She has a crazed gleam in her eye, and I can't tell if she'd rather I said yes or no. From where she stands, she's a winner either way. She can spread the news of a budding romance, or she can revel in my inability to attract a man.

"David and I are just friends." They say dogs can smell fear; Mrs. Tompkins is nine-tenths canine.

"Hmm. That's what celebrities always say in the tabloids, and then they turn around nine months later and have a love child."

My fear disappears. It feels good to laugh. "I can assure you, Dr. Swenson and I are in no immediate danger of having a love child."

Her look of disappointment is priceless. I store that tidbit away to share with David later. At least, I *think* I'll share it with him later, but the way things have gone in the past twenty-four hours, I'm not as sure as I once would have been. Maybe it was the pre-Valentine's wedding. But I've done lots of weddings, and they haven't hit this close to home. Not in a long while. Maybe it's the law-school acceptance letter that's still in my purse. The one I haven't told David and LaRonda about because I don't want to see the identical looks of disappointment on their faces when I tell them I'm finally going to be just like my perfect sister and go to law school. At least my dad will be happy. He won't have to send me money every month to help cover my rent. And at least I won't have all these pesky parishioners making my life a nightmare. Just rows and rows of leather-bound books to stand between me and the outside world. Surely in the logical, rational world of a law firm, I won't have to navigate all these treacherous emotional waters.

Mrs. Tompkins sniffs. "Well, I'm relieved to hear there's nothing serious between you. It simply wouldn't do."

How do I respond to *that* pronouncement? My first impulse is to tell her in a precise, yet slightly profane way, that my love life is none of her business. Yet the strange reality of being a minister is that your life does become the business of your congregation. They have a stake in you. If you mess up, it reflects on them. Your errors hurt them. So you go through your days in a sort of behavioral straitjacket that keeps you from traumatizing yourself or anyone else. I'll be so glad to leave that behind.

"Have you signed up to work in the community soup kitchen yet?" I decide to turn the tables on her. At the prospect of communing with homeless people, Mrs. Tompkins melts away like snow in July. She's gone, but her words remain to stoke the embers of my fear. What if I told David how I feel? Would he laugh? withdraw? I couldn't stand it if he shuffled his feet, ducked his head, and made a beeline for the nearest exit. Like a boy I once asked to dance at a junior-high social.

Still, the seed's been planted deeply enough in the fertile soil of my mind where it might actually take root. Perhaps it would be better to know. Maybe that frisson was a freak incident; maybe if he touched me again, I wouldn't feel a thing.

Of course, I have one tiny problem. I told David I have a hot Valentine's Day date next weekend. I don't want him to know I lied, don't want to look that desperate. So first things first. I'll find a date for next weekend. And after that I'll tell David about what happened while the indeterminately ethnic villains were plotting to blow up the world. Surely I can scrape up enough courage for such a simple act. Yeah, sure. And after I'm done, I'll bungee jump from the Jefferson Street Bridge.

Church of the Shepherd is your typical graying, dying downtown congregation, which is one of the reasons I chose it when I fled my first church. How demanding could it be to serve a relic? These days we can count on our fingers and toes the number of members under thirty.

We hold two services on Sunday morning. The early service at eight o'clock attracts the eldest of the elderly, the golfers, and those headed to a Tennessee Titans game. Most Sundays you could shoot off a cannon in the huge sanctuary at that service, and no one would be harmed.

The later service at eleven o'clock is the main event. But even then you don't have to come early to get your favorite pew, unless you like to sit in the back row. No matter what the size of the congregation, the seats furthest from God always fill up fast.

I like the early service better when I'm preaching, although in some ways it's harder to stand in the pulpit and proclaim a Great Truth to thirty people scattered about such a huge space. But somehow my sermon feels more like an offering to God at that service.

Now, though, it's time for the late service, and the pressure to perform increases with the size of the congregation. I'm also feeling the burden of stepping into Dr. Black's pulpit for the first time since I've been on staff at Church of the Shepherd. Can I measure up?

I'm a one-woman show this morning. The lay liturgist didn't show up, which means the whole service is mine. That makes it tough on my voice, which is more on the soothing end of the spectrum than the booming one. In my old church, folks who liked to nap during the sermon loved my preaching.

It's winter, so I'm wearing my clerical robe. Dr. Black puts his away during the summer months, which strikes me as a very Southern thing to do, like not wearing white after Labor Day. For a woman minister, the blessing of a clerical robe is that it saves you from helpful fashion advice from your parishioners. If I stick to my navy suit, I hear that I need to be more stylish. If I wear a dress instead, I'm not properly professional. And God forbid I should wear pants on the chancel, even under my robe. The steeple would probably crack down the middle and fall into the parking lot.

Today I'm in my navy suit. After the David incident last night, I'm repressing any hints of sexuality, robe or no robe. If it wouldn't make me look like a flight attendant from the eighties, I would have tied a little bow in the scarf around my neck. Instead, it's discreetly tucked inside my jacket. My only jewelry is a pair of small pearl earrings. If I were any more vanilla, I'd be in a tub at Baskin-Robbins.

The last notes of the opening hymn die away, and I ascend the steps to the pulpit. It's a tricky moment because I have several things to accomplish. First, I need to not trip or stumble, which is an iffy proposition for me on a good day. Second, I must remember to bring with me everything I'll need while I'm up there: Bible for reading the Scripture text, sermon manuscript, worship bulletin, and a cup of water. If I forget any of these, I'm toast. At my first church, I used to put them up in the pulpit before the service, until the Sunday one of the deacons who was preparing the communion table helpfully decided my essentials were leftovers from the previous week. He dumped the water, threw away the sermon and the worship bulletin, and apparently sent my Bible to the Island of Lost Things because it's never been seen since. Oh well. It was just my study Bible from divinity school—with three years of intensive notations scribbled in the margins.

Today I make it safely into the pulpit. Before the service I did a sound-check on the microphone, adjusted the height of the pulpit with the nifty little hydraulic switch, and turned on the library lamp below the microphone. Now, as the congregation settles back in the pews, I spread the first two pages of my sermon across the podium, stow the worship bulletin on the little shelf below, and open my Bible.

"Hear these words from the gospel of Mark."

Mark's my favorite gospel. Short and to the point. Matthew, Luke, and John have lots of bells and whistles, which can be quite entertaining and illuminating, but Mark keeps his focus. I try to show my congregation the same consideration.

Today's passage is full of lost things. Sheep. Coins. And a shepherd and an old woman who go looking for them until they're found. I can identify with that lost sheep and the coin that fell between the cracks somewhere, and I figure if I can identify, my parishioners can too.

When I finish the Scripture reading, I set my Bible on the shelf on top of the worship bulletin. I swallow, take a deep breath, and begin.

"When I was a child and I'd lost something, my mother always told me it would be in the last place I looked…"

I'm off to a pretty good start. Few people, though, really listen to the sermon, and I can't say I blame them. Most sermons struggle to attain mediocrity, and today I notice several people watching the butterflies from last night's wedding flitter from one side of the sanctuary to the other. Once in a while, though, I get a live one—someone who looks at me from his or her spot in the pew—and I know that person's connecting with what I'm saying.

Happily, today is such a day.

She's an older woman I've never seen before—a visitor maybe or someone's Aunt Ruth who happened to be in town this week. She frowns at the challenging parts of the sermon, smiles at the funny parts, and even takes a few notes in the margin of her worship bulletin.

Bingo.

That's when the fun really begins. The words roll off my tongue as if I've said them a thousand times before. And they're words from my heart.

"God never quits looking, never gives up on finding us no matter where we've wandered off to. No matter what cracks we've slipped between…"

I hope the woman will speak to me before she leaves today. I'd love a more substantial comment on what I have to say than "You have such a sweet speaking voice."

The sermon peaks on the next-to-last page of my manuscript.

"Are we really willing to be found? to let God lead us back to the fold? Maybe it's easier to be lost than to be in the care of the Shepherd, because when we surrender to God's care, we're relinquishing our lives to a higher authority."

I try to leave time for some denouement, a bit of quiet reflection

before the "Amen." In that small space of time, you know whether
you've succeeded or failed. If it's quiet, you've been heard. People are
chewing on what you've said. If there's a lot of rustling with worship
bulletins and fussing with purses, you missed. If you preach every
Sunday, the misses aren't so catastrophic. There's always next week.
Now, as an associate minister, the misses hurt more because I have
fewer chances to hit the target.

I pause before the last paragraph to gauge the mood of the congregation. It's mostly quiet. A sweet sense of satisfaction starts in my
midsection and spreads outward. When you use a gift God has given
you and use it well, there's nothing comparable. At least, I didn't think
there was until last night in that movie theater.

"Thanks be to God. Amen."

And it's done. Next week Dr. Black will be back in command of
"his" pulpit, and if I'm lucky, I'll get to do some of the liturgy. That's
another reason I'm leaving the ministry. Being an associate is too much
like being Tantalus from Greek mythology, the guy who hungers in the
underworld with food eternally just beyond his reach.

The rest of the service runs smoothly, and before I know it, I've
pronounced the benediction, recessed down the aisle behind the
choir, and am shaking hands at the church doors. The visitor, the
older woman, comes through the line to shake my hand. I hold my
breath. Her fingers are warm in mine.

"That was well done." Her smile is warm and genuine. "You have
such a lovely speaking voice."

My smile freezes on my face. *Come on, woman. Give me something
better than that.*

She squeezes the fingers of my right hand, then reaches down and grabs my other hand. She looks at the ring finger on my left hand. "A lovely girl like you ought to be married by now."

Tell me something I don't know, honey.

"Aren't you sweet," I say. No hint of my frustration shows on my face, and she disappears into the Sunday-morning sunshine.

Eventually, the line of people dwindles, and I set about the business of closing up the sanctuary, not sure whether to laugh or cry.

I find myself in that situation a lot these days.

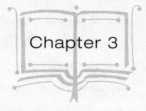

Chapter 3

"You want me to set you up with my brother for Valentine's Day?" My best friend, the Reverend LaRonda Mason, sips her Frappuccino and eyes me with skepticism. It's Monday morning, and we've met at Starbucks for a Sunday postmortem and coffee klatsch. I'm wearing jeans and a sweatshirt, and my hair is jammed into a ponytail as befits my day off. Ronnie's short-cropped hair is perfectly styled, and she's wearing a gray trouser suit with pearls. Her brown eyes are highlighted with carefully applied eye shadow. LaRonda never takes a day off. She learned that from her father, the founding pastor of Mt. Moriah Church. In a manner of speaking, LaRonda inherited the family business.

She rolls her eyes. "Honey, do you want to lose your job? 'Cause I know you don't have a thing for my brother, and unless it's true love, it ain't worth it."

I twirl my half-caff-nonfat-two-Equal-latte between my palms and try to appear nonchalant. "Well, I find your brother…interesting."

"Interesting? He's Phi Beta Kappa. Of course he's interesting. What about sexy? hot?"

Truth to tell, LaRonda's brother is all of the above, but he's too much of a brainiac for me. He's a resident over at Vanderbilt in ob-gyn. So he's sexy and smart, and he probably has a greater working knowledge of my anatomy than I do. But as intimidating as he may be, he's not David, and that's my main criterion for any date material for the coming weekend.

"I wouldn't lose my job." Not since I'm planning to resign in a few months anyway. "C'mon, LaRonda. Help me out here."

LaRonda is nobody's fool, least of all mine. "What's this about?"

"I need a date for Saturday night."

"For what? Wedding? Fund-raiser?"

"No, just to prove a point."

Her eyes narrow. "So you want to use my brother to prove a point?"

I sigh. "Not a political point. A personal one."

"Which would be?" Her generous lips are set in a thin line, and I know what it feels like to be one of her parishioners caught with a hand in the cookie jar.

"I didn't mean to offend you."

"Then don't ask me if you can use my brother."

"I guess it did sound like that."

"Uh-huh."

LaRonda waits patiently for me to cough up the truth. Around us conversation buzzes in the back room of the Green Hills Starbucks, where the Volvo and BMW moms congregate after spin class. I'm not sure LaRonda and I fit in, but when do we ever? And if being a white woman minister is an uphill climb, being a black woman minister is like hauling yourself up Mount Everest with your feet tied together. With the help of her upbringing as a preacher's kid, LaRonda has always made it look like a cakewalk.

"Look," I confess, "I need to save face here."

"Well, your face is going to have to find someone besides my brother to save it."

"But who? Do you ever meet any men besides your parishioners?" I casually scan the round room tucked in the back of the coffee shop. This space was a dry cleaner when I was in divinity school, but now it's a collage of wood and tile permeated with the aroma of burned coffee beans.

"What about David?" LaRonda swirls her straw to catch the last of her Frapp.

"David's why I need a date."

"What?"

"It's a long story."

LaRonda puts down her drink. "Which you are going to tell me right now."

I look away. "I'd rather not."

"Betsy, there's no way you're not telling me what's going on. What happened Saturday night? I thought you guys just went to the movies."

I set my empty cup down next to hers. "He touched my thigh. In the theater."

LaRonda coughs, pounds her chest, and then coughs some more. "He did what?" she chokes out.

I blush. "Not on purpose. He was going for the popcorn."

"And?"

"And…well, I felt something."

"What kind of something?"

"A zing."

"A zing? You felt a zing?"

I nod and then bow my head.

"Hallelujah," LaRonda sighs.

"What? How can you say that?"

She leans back in her chair. "I've been waiting for this since the first week of div school."

"But, LaRonda, it's *David*."

"You mean smart, tall, funny, kind David? The kind of guy we'd give our eyeteeth for?" She looks me straight in the eye. "If you think this is for real, not some biological fluke, you have to tell him."

"I know, I know. And I will. But first I have to go on this date."

She rolls her eyes. "Why?"

"Because I told him I had a date Saturday so I couldn't go to the movies with him."

LaRonda massages her temples. "Let me get this straight. You turned down a date with a man you're attracted to so you could go on a date with a man who doesn't exist?"

Well, when you put it that way, it does sound a bit ridiculous.

"But David wasn't asking me on a date. He was taking me for granted, assuming I didn't have plans for Valentine's Day."

"Girl, that's your fault. You didn't just give him a license to take you for granted. You printed it, signed it, and had it laminated."

"I know." Even my ritual latte can't straighten out my head. "But I don't want to look like a complete idiot. Where am I going to find a man by Saturday?"

"What about one of the baristas?" LaRonda nods toward the bar. "There's some nice eye candy back there."

I laugh. "I'm not about to endanger my daily caffeine source."

LaRonda taps her manicured nails on the café table. "Zing from David aside, when are you going to quit finding reasons not to date?"

"What?" My heart rate increases noticeably.

"Face it, Betsy; it's not that there aren't men out there to date. You just rule them all out before they even ask you."

The latte in my stomach turns sour. "No one's asked me out in months."

"And why is that? Could it have something to do with your wardrobe?"

"It's my day off. What's wrong with my clothes?"

"At the best of times, you dress like your mother."

That hurts. "I do *not* dress like my mother."

LaRonda laughs. "If I called your mom right now and asked her what she was wearing, what do you think she'd say?"

"I think she'd call you a pervert and hang up."

We both laugh, and that feels better. "Are my clothes really that bad?"

"Not unless you mean to put the *m* in *matron*."

"Are you telling me I'm frumpy?"

"You're the Queen of Frumpy."

"And if I dress differently, I'll date?"

"You will if you agree to do that segment for Tricia."

Now the caffeine rushes to my brain. "No way, Ronnie. I refuse to be humiliated on local television."

LaRonda's been after me for weeks to do a makeover segment for her cousin's new local morning show. She says it will empower me. That I'll be a new woman. I'm more worried that I'll be the first failure in the history of makeovers.

"What makes you think you'll be humiliated? Everybody wants a makeover," LaRonda says.

"Do we need to broadcast my unattractiveness to the whole city?"

"Once the men of Nashville see the new you, they'll be lining up at your door."

I don't believe her. But I'm a thirty-year-old single woman with all the attendant insecurities. Desperation can be a great motivator. I wanted to change my life. Maybe my appearance is the place to start. "Okay," I say with a dramatic sigh worthy of an early Christian martyr being thrown to the lions. "But you better be there. I don't want to be left alone to Tricia's tender mercies."

LaRonda beams. "Don't worry. I've got your back. You won't regret it."

Of course I will. But at least it will take my mind off all my other problems.

LaRonda doesn't let any grass grow under my feet. The next day we meet a camera crew waiting at the entrance to Green Hills mall. LaRonda's cousin Tricia hosts the local morning show for the new affiliate of a fledgling network, which would explain why someone would be desperate enough to put me on television.

Tricia is tall, thin, coiffed, and plucked. She looks like a finalist in the Miss America pageant, only without the evening gown. She smirks when she sees me. "Excellent, Rond. When I'm done with her, the *Queer Eye* guys will bow their heads in reverence."

I don't know about the Fab Five, but I feel my head sink lower on my neck. Am I that bad?

The camera lights go on, and I'm blinded. Tricia shoves a microphone in my face. "So, Reverend Blessing, are you ready to be transformed from holy to hottie?"

I mumble some inarticulate reply that Tricia takes for a yes, and we're off. If I didn't know I was leaving the ministry, I'd think this was a stupid career move. The camera stays on me the whole time, even while we're riding the escalator down to the lower level. Tricia comes to a stop in front of a store with the frightening name of Oh Là Là! "Here we are."

The mannequins in the window look like hookers with some cash to spend. The clothes do not look like they were made for a woman who can sing "Jesus Loves Me" in three languages.

"LaRonda—" My protest is cut off by the shove she gives me, propelling me into the den of iniquity. The camera swings to Tricia, who details the travesty that's about to be perpetuated on me. A perky sales assistant pops up on cue and starts groping me.

"Hmm. Size 10?"

I wish I could argue with that assessment, but I'll be lucky to squeeze into anything less than a 12.

The sales assistant looks pensive. "Normally, we don't carry anything in double digits…" She looks at me with obvious distaste. "Perhaps monochromatic, all black…"

I snap. "Something in a burka, perhaps?"

She stares back at me without comprehension. "Is that a new kind of halter?"

Mercifully, LaRonda intervenes. "How about these?" She thrusts a pair of leather pants into my arms. The sales assistant adds a see-through chiffon blouse, and Tricia shoves me toward a dressing room even as she continues to give a running commentary of my flaws to the camera.

"A bit broad in the hips, but a flare leg can balance those saddlebags—"

I slam the dressing-room door behind me, grateful to be alone, and sink to the little pink tuffet wedged into the corner. Three full-length mirrors occupy all the available wall space. I peep upward to make sure the cameraman hasn't shoved the thing over the top of the door to film this, too, but there's no sign of him. Thank heavens for small mercies.

I should put an end to this right now. I've been humiliated enough in the past year, and I know that something as superficial as my looks isn't what's truly important. But a tiny part of me wonders if it would help. If my appearance improved, would my life? Besides, Tricia will never put this on television. No amount of clothes and makeup could make me into a Glamazon.

I discover the leather pants will zip if I give up breathing. I beg LaRonda for a camisole to go under the blouse, and Tricia grudgingly consents. I refuse to look in the dressing-room mirror. LaRonda yanks me out into the shop and forces me to the even larger monstrosity magnifier out there.

"Open your eyes."

"No."

The cameraman follows my every step.

"Hmm. Not bad." From Tricia, this is a ringing endorsement.

"Come on, Betsy. Open your eyes," LaRonda says.

"Is the salesgirl gone?"

"Yeah." LaRonda laughs. "I think she was afraid of guilt by association."

"Okay, then." Reluctantly, I open one eye the tiniest bit.

Three-way mirrors are like God. You can't escape anything about yourself when you're standing in front of one. Shoot, they're worse than God—they don't forgive a single flaw. I'm still me, but… Dare I say it? I look semihot.

"Yes, I think that will work." Tricia sounds more convinced now that she's had some time to study me like a bug under a microscope. "She needs heels, though, to give her legs a longer line."

LaRonda slips out of her mile-high sling-backs and hands them over. "Try these."

Why not complete my humiliation? But as I bend over to slip them on, I discover tight leather isn't conducive to reaching your feet.

"Here." LaRonda kneels to help me into the shoes, and I turn back to the mirror. The addition of three inches to my height does perform a wonder akin to the parting of the Red Sea. The pants hang properly, and the blouse falls to just below my waist, mercifully short of my hips.

"Wow." Suddenly I'm voluptuous. The cameraman whistles, and I blush.

"Excellent." Tricia turns to the camera. "Now, for the next step…"

"Next step? There are more steps?" Isn't this enough humiliation for one day?

Tricia frowns. "Hair. Makeup. The works."

"But I took a vacation day!"

LaRonda puts an arm around my shoulders. "And what better way to spend it? What better way to get a certain lanky reverend to sit up and take notice?"

My blush could be seen by the astronauts on the International Space Station. "Ronnie!"

Tricia's ears perk up like a Yorkshire terrier's. "What's this? Is there a potential romance we could exploit…er, I mean, nurture?"

"No." The whole thing has gone far enough. I'm not the leather type or the chiffon type. Or the David type. "That's it. I'm done."

"No, you're not." LaRonda has a look of steely determination in her eyes. Tricia looks bewildered. The cameraman zooms in for a closeup of my answer.

I cave.

"New hairdo, then?" I squeak and slink back to the dressing room.

Next, Tricia drags me to a salon where an eyebrow wax costs more than I spend on a shampoo, cut, and blow-dry. Granted, I usually walk into the nearest Cheap Cuts and have the next available stylist whack away at my hair. But at Exquisite, I'm swept into a den of luxury, as opposed to the previous den of iniquity where leather and see-through chiffon carried the day. In the dressing room I leave behind my faded black twill pants and gray sweater set. The salon's terry robe barely closes in the front, and the huge embroidered E sits squarely on my generous left breast. I emerge with all the enthusiasm of a back-slider returning to church.

"First, exfoliation." Tricia presses her palms together like the high priestess in a pagan temple. "The key to beautiful skin."

I've never exfoliated any part of me, at least not voluntarily. Though I suppose falling on the sidewalk outside the post office and taking the epidermis off both my knees might qualify.

Tricia pushes me down a beige hallway and through a door into a room that looks like my dentist's office. I look around for any sign of a drill.

"Sit." Tricia doesn't spare many words for me, but she has plenty for the camera.

"Years of neglect and outright abuse have left Reverend Blessing with the skin of a woman almost twice her age."

Twice my age! I rear up out of the chair, but a large woman appears from behind me and presses me back down.

"Velcome to Exquisite, dar-link." And with that exotic greeting, she attacks my face.

Cattle are treated more humanely at slaughterhouses than this behemoth treats me. Wrap, slap, pain. It's like hell's version of lather, rinse, repeat. Exfoliation is akin to having your skin scrubbed with boric acid and a Brillo pad.

"You're glowing," Tricia enthuses.

"I'm not glowing. I'm bleeding."

"You'll live," LaRonda pronounces. She's in the corner having her nails done. That's the last I see of her, though. Hefty Gal drags me off for a massage.

"You vill like zis. Make a new voman uf you."

"I like the old woman."

Wait a minute. That didn't sound right.

I have to admit, though, the massage feels pretty good. And the bruises should heal fairly quickly.

"Zere." Hefty Gal slaps my backside. "Now you are ready for Antoine."

"Antoine?"

"Your hair shapist."

Shapist?

"He vill shape your hair."

Into what? Triangles? "Do you mean cut my hair?"

The look of horror on her face is a bit of recompense for the punishment she's inflicted on me. "Here at Exquisite, vee do not butcher zee hair."

Somehow I doubt that.

Once I meet Antoine, I miss Hefty Gal.

He spins my chair away from the mirror so I can't see myself. Antoine's hair has been "shaped" by nature, but he's fighting it with a bad comb-over. This is the man who will make me look like a supermodel?

"*Tsk, tsk.*" He fingers my hair as if dead eels are hanging from my scalp. "I can do nothing until the color is fixed."

"It's my natural color."

"That is why we must fix it."

A new woman appears at my shoulder. Her hair is at least three distinct colors, none of which normally occur in nature. Where do they get these people? Central casting?

"Hey, girl." She pops her gum and joins Antoine in fingering the dead eels on my head. "Tricia got you here just in time."

I had no idea my hair was terminal, but apparently my very life has been in danger. That's why twenty minutes later Nancy, the tri-colored colorist, is painting my hair with a smelly concoction and then wrapping it in tinfoil. When she's done, I catch a glimpse of myself in the mirror. I look like E.T.'s less attractive cousin. LaRonda appears, admiring her new manicure.

"Ronnie, is this normal?"

She takes one look at me and bursts out laughing. "Well, it is for some people, but apparently not for you. Quit looking like you're about to face a firing squad. Most women would enjoy this."

"Most women would have had enough sense of self-preservation to run away when all this started."

"Here." Ronnie thrusts a cold diet drink into my hand. "Have some caffeine to take the edge off."

I comfort myself with the diet cola while a strange wheel rotates around my head, heating up the tinfoil until my scalp feels like it's being stir-fried. Just when I think I'm about to spontaneously combust, Nancy rescues me.

"Excellent." She pulls the foil from my head with brisk efficiency. "Now you're ready for Antoine."

But is anyone ever really ready for Antoine? He spins the chair around twice, again so I'm not facing the mirror, and pulls his scissors from a velvet-lined case. No kidding.

"Now, we will bring out your cheekbones." He takes a big hunk of hair from the side of my head and slices through it with the scissors.

I bite back a scream. It's too late now. I'll have to let him do his worst. Maybe they can fix it at Cheap Cuts.

Tricia has been interviewing Hefty Gal and Nancy the Color Girl. Now she swings back to me. "So, Reverend Blessing, how does it feel to be a work in progress?"

"It's great." If my smile was any more wooden, they'd use me to build a bonfire at church camp.

"And what about the special guy? What do you think he'll think of all this?"

"There's nobody special," I bite out. My jaw is now as wooden as my smile.

"Now, Reverend Blessing, isn't it a sin to tell a lie?"

If I hurt this woman, will the cameraman get it on tape?

"What's next, Tricia?" I ask brightly to divert her.

"Makeup. The finishing touch."

"Oh, goody."

Once I've let them paint me up like a strumpet, I can escape. I have plenty of Pond's Cold Cream and Suave shampoo at home. And lots of baggy sweats.

Antoine still won't let me see my hair, even when he's done scalping me. Judging from the piles of curls on the floor around me, I'm going to look like the topiary in *Edward Scissorhands*. He dries my hair and uses a flat iron to straighten out any resistant natural curl. Then I'm off to another room in this warren of beauty, where an exotic Middle Eastern woman proceeds to smooth, pat, and powder a new face on top of my old one.

"This will look heavy to you, but that's for the cameras. For everyday, just use a lighter hand."

Since my hand is already featherweight when it comes to makeup, that shouldn't be a problem.

Makeup applied, I'm shoved back into the dressing room to shed my robe and don the leather/chiffon combo. Somewhere they've rounded up a pair of leather boots with four-inch heels for me to wear. The fact that they're a size too small doesn't seem to trouble anyone but me.

"Come on, Betsy," LaRonda calls through the door. "We want to see you."

Despite my resistance, I want to see myself. There's no mirror in the dressing room (how odd is that?), so I'm going to be as surprised as everyone else.

"Drumroll, please!" Tricia requests with a flourish, and I bravely step into the hallway.

Stunned silence. I've heard it before, most notably after I preached my first sermon—possibly the worst homily in the history of Christian worship.

"Is it that bad?" I hate the whimper in my voice.

When I look at LaRonda, she has tears in her eyes. "Oh, Betsy."

Sweet Mary, I guess it *is* that bad.

Slowly, I walk toward the mirror at the far end of the corridor. It takes a minute for me to absorb what I see.

It's me. Only it's not. What I see in the mirror is a better version of me. What I could look like, with regular help from the modern miracle of cosmetology.

My hair is three luscious shades, varying from blonde to brown. It falls in saucy layers, framing my face. Or is it my face? My eyes have new depth, new sparkle, and my skin glows. The clothes give me the attitude of a woman on her way to the hippest New York night club.

And then I realize who I look like. Barbie. And suddenly I'm crying too. Because I both love and despise this image in the mirror. It's every dream and every fear I've ever had, all rolled into one scary package.

"Don't cry!" shrieks Tricia. "You'll ruin the makeup!"

Who cares about ruining the makeup? These people have ruined my life. Because there's no way, left to my own devices, that I will ever again look like the hottie I see reflected in the mirror. If I wanted to be reminded of how I always fall short, of what a disappointment I am in normal life, I could have called my mother so she could grill me about my marital prospects. I don't need Tricia and her makeover to know that I'm only good enough if I'm someone other than the real Betsy.

Chapter 4

"I miss my sweater set," I pout to LaRonda as we head for our cars. It's easier to be petulant than honest with myself. "And leather pants chafe."

"Beauty is pain. Deal with it." LaRonda gives me a quick hug. "Be ready Saturday night at seven. And be wearing that outfit."

"Why?"

"Because that's when your date will pick you up."

"So you're loaning me your brother?"

"I think I owe it to you," she says with sudden solemnity.

I blink back tears. "No, Ronnie. You don't owe me anything."

She frowns. "I thought a makeover would make you happy. Boost your confidence."

"It did. It did." I always repeat myself when I'm telling a lie, an unfortunate verbal tic. "And you don't have to drag James into this."

"He owes me. Besides, I think you two will enjoy each other."

"You're sure?"

Instead of answering, she gives me a quick hug. "I love you, Betz."

I hug her back. "I love you, too, Ronnie. Thanks for trying."

We wave to each other as we get into our cars, and I'm thankful to have a well-intentioned, if a bit misguided, friend who cares.

So it's Saturday night, Valentine's Day, quarter till seven, and I'm stuffing myself into the leather pants. I briefly consider wearing my Doc Martens for comfort but decide that clunky man-shoes will draw LaRonda's ire if she finds out about them. I work the zipper of the pants up, allow myself to breathe out, and go in search of a pair of black stilettos I once wore to a costume party. Naturally, they're at the back of my closet. I wriggle my way past the solid wall of bland clothing hanging from the rod, pawing my way through the closet equivalent of leftovers at the back. I can't breathe when I bend over in the leather pants. By the time I fish out the stilettos, my ears are ringing from lack of oxygen.

No, that's not my ears ringing; it's the doorbell. My date is early. I sneak a quick peek in the mirror, fluff my new hairdo, slip on the stilettos, and teeter to the front door.

My apartment is on the ground floor of a 1920s bungalow in a half-seedy, half-trendy neighborhood near Vanderbilt University. The old hardwood floors slope a good bit, so I decide to blame my unsteadiness on the tilt of the floor and not on my lack of skill with high heels. I reach the door, flip on the porch light, and pause with my hand on the knob. Even though I've met James a couple of times before, I'm nervous. I turn the knob and open the door.

There, blinking in the bug-zapping yellow glow of my porch light, is David.

"Whoa, Blessing. Check you out." He's laughing.

"What do you want?" He's always dropping by to use my DSL to surf the Internet because he's too cheap to upgrade from dial-up.

Maybe he forgot I told him I was busy tonight. Yeah, right. And maybe Mrs. Tompkins is my guardian angel in disguise.

"Oh yeah. You have a date. I forgot about that." Did he really? He looks über-cool, not at all concerned about my plans for the evening, but how weird is it that he would turn up like this?

"He'll be here in a minute. Did you want something?"

I step back into the living room, and David follows me. He looks at his watch. "Are you running late?" He gives me the once over as impersonally as if he were selecting a pork chop at the grocery store. "You look ready to me."

A flush creeps up my neck and spreads across my cheeks, but it's not embarrassment. I feel hot from head to toe, but not in a sexy way. In a volcanic way.

"That's all you have to say? I look ready?" My voice skips up a good third of an octave.

David swallows, the universal signal from a male of the species when he realizes he's messed up. "So, you're not ready?" he asks cautiously. "You look fine to me."

"Fine? I look *fine?*" I am standing here in heels that a streetwalker would envy. I'm wearing leather pants, a see-through shirt, fashionably cropped and tousled hair, and discreet but helpful makeup. And the man whose casual touch has sent me into this torment says I look fine? Not fine as in "Hey, babe, you're *so* hot," but fine as in "Well, you're no Gwyneth Paltrow, but you'll do."

"Well, to be perfectly honest, you look weird." David has apparently decided to go for broke in the compliment department.

"Weird?"

"Yeah. Not like you. You're all…sexy and stuff."

From his tone of voice, I perceive this is not a good thing. Why do I not just take out my ego and spread it on the floor so he can more conveniently stomp on it?

I toss my hair back, which I can do now thanks to these new layers, and remember that I look hot. The good kind, not the temperature kind.

I take two steps toward David until I'm standing an eyelash from him. With these heels on, I have a shot at looking him in the eye, tall geek-man that he is. He's still wearing his clerical collar, which only emphasizes that he's swallowing again. Hard.

I lick my lips, and I swear to God it's not intentional, but some primal female instinct I never knew I had.

"Would it amaze you, David, to discover that some men actually find me attractive?" Before he can answer, I place a finger on his lips. Every part of me feels as if it's been wired to an electrical outlet and switched to high voltage. "No, don't answer. I don't think I want to know."

We're standing in the middle of my living room, frozen like that for what's got to be the longest moment of my life, when the doorbell rings a second time. I look over David's shoulder, and there, standing in my doorway, is LaRonda's hunky brother, James, who bears more than a passing resemblance to Denzel Washington.

"I think my date's here," I whisper to David. "You have a key. Lock up when you're done with the computer."

"LaRonda is a genius, and I will never doubt her again." I dutifully repeat her words into the phone. It's the next afternoon—Sunday—

we've both finished our church duties for the day, and she and I are in full postmortem mode.

"I told you the makeover would be worth it." She's crowing in triumph, but I don't mind. It was well worth those few moments of makeover misery to see the expression on David's face when I walked out the door with James. And my evening with James was the cherry on top. He was funny and gallant, and he treated me as if I had a brain. He also took me to the Melting Pot, a fondue restaurant I adore. David will never go there. He says if he's going to pay that much for dinner, he wants someone else to do the cooking.

"I'm never wearing leather again." I wince and tug at my jeans.

"If you play your cards right, you shouldn't have to."

"So what am I supposed to do now?"

LaRonda sighs into my ear that particularly resonant sigh of the long-suffering. "Do you think you prefer James to David?"

"Well, don't be offended since he's your brother and all, but, no."

"No problem. James said you all had a friend vibe going, but nothing beyond that."

For the first time in my life, I'm relieved a guy just wants to be friends. "So what do I do now?"

"You call David and ask him out."

The warm flush of social success disappears as quickly as teenagers cutting Sunday school to head to the Donut Den.

"Just like that? Out of the blue?"

"Look, Betz, you have him off balance. Now's the time to move in for the kill."

For a preacher, LaRonda has excellent predatory instincts. She knows just when to pounce, which is how she gets her congregation to do things they didn't think they could do. Like build a fifteen-hundred-seat sanctuary. Or partner with a sister church in South Africa to build a school for AIDS orphans. Then again, maybe those predatory instincts are why she's flourished as a solo pastor while I've collapsed under the weight of conflict and criticism. She knows how to go in for the kill while I would rather not witness the carnage.

"Okay, so I call him. What kind of date are we talking here? What if he doesn't realize I'm asking him out?"

LaRonda's laugh is like buttercream icing on warm cake. "He'll know you're asking him out."

"How?"

"'Cause you're going to tell him."

I don't know if I can. That would be putting it all on the line, no holding back, free-falling. "So I just say, 'Hey, David, I've recently developed the hots for you. Wanna have dinner?'"

"That's a start."

"I don't know if I can do it."

"Well, no one else is going to do it for you."

LaRonda continues to half-scold, half-coach me for the next twenty minutes. I dither, doing my best to keep her from hanging up. Finally, though, she shuts me down.

"Call him. Now. Bye."

Call David. I've done it a million times. I know all his numbers by heart—home, church office, cell phone. I know his address, his birthday, his shoe size, even his IQ. What I don't know is whether he'll laugh, cry, or scream if I ask him out.

I haven't felt this stupid and awkward since junior high. The only place I've ever found courage is in prayer, so I climb into my favorite overstuffed chair, cross my legs, set my hands on my knees, palms up, and hope for a little divine inspiration.

I wait. And wait some more. I try to clear my mind, to wipe away the words and simply sit in God's presence. The words, though, don't want to leave. Neither do the images. Passing notes to David in Intro to Theology. The two of us doodling caricatures of the disciples in New Testament Exegesis. His hand on my thigh exactly eight days ago.

I abandon contemplative meditation and decide to cut straight to the chase. *Well? What do you think, Big Guy? How about a little divine intervention here?*

If you attended a liberal divinity school as I did, then you know it's completely improper, politically incorrect, and otherwise *verboten* to refer to God in male terms. But I grew up talking to "him," and it's a little hard to change pronouns at this late date. Maybe if I have a daughter one day, she'll talk to "her" the way I talk to "him."

I close my eyes and hope for an answer. Nothing. I don't know if that means God doesn't approve or he doesn't want to get involved in something as irredeemable as my love life, opting instead for something easy. Like peace in the Middle East.

My breathing has slowed, and I do try to focus. Breathe in, two, three, four. Breathe out, two, three, four. *Grant me faith, O Lord.*

The warmth starts in my midsection and then gradually steals up into my chest. Over the next few minutes, it spreads through my limbs and up the back of my neck until my scalp is tingling. *Grant me faith.* The words replay in my mind. When every part of me is bathed in that warmth, I slowly open my eyes. Then I reach out and pick up the phone.

I punch in David's number, digit by digit, as deliberately as if I were a preschooler learning how to dial a phone. The receiver is still warm from my long conversation with LaRonda. Each ring seems to echo in my ear. *One. Two. Please, God, let me get the machine. If it rings four times, I'll get the machine.*

Three. Just one more.

"Hello?" It's not the machine. It's David, breathless and sounding perturbed.

"Hey, David. It's me."

He hesitates for a millisecond. "Hey, Blessing. What's up?" he asks, as casually as if last night never happened.

What's up? My hopes. My blood pressure. The likelihood that I'm about to crash and burn the most precious friendship I've ever had.

"Nothing. Just trying to unwind from church."

David doesn't understand why Sunday mornings wear me out. Every time he leaves his church and climbs into his beat-up old Volvo, he's as charged up as an addict on speed.

I clear my throat. "What are you up to?"

There's a muffled noise and some rustling on the other end of the phone. Then his voice comes through, loud and clear. "I just got out of the shower."

The rustling is probably him toweling off his hair. I decide I'd better not speculate what the other muffled noises might be.

"Want to head over to Radnor Lake for a walk?" The words fall from my lips before I even know what I'm doing. I hadn't meant to say them, and yet they feel so natural. It's what I might say to David anytime I call him on a sunny Sunday afternoon.

But it sure doesn't qualify as asking him out on a date.

David is quiet for a moment, and suddenly it's awkward again, like it was last night. I can hear him swallowing over the phone.

"Betz…"

"Yeah?"

"Well, I just figured you'd be doing something with the guy from last night."

"With James?"

"Yeah. You two looked pretty tight."

"Oh."

"Listen, I assumed you'd be tied up, so I went ahead and made other plans."

"Other plans."

"Yeah."

My stomach feels as if someone punched me in the solar plexus. I can tell from David's tone of voice that these plans involve a female.

"That's cool. We can do Radnor another time." I hate the slight catch in my voice because I know David will hear it. He knows me too well not to.

"Look, Betsy, about last night…"

"Yeah?"

"About what I said…"

"What you said?" Babies in the church nursery couldn't look as innocent as I sound. As if every word he'd uttered wasn't burned on my brain.

"About…you know…about your outfit and stuff."

Where is he going with this? Is he apologizing, or is he going to tell me again that I looked ridiculous?

"I didn't mean it to sound like it did."

"Did it sound like something?"

I'm doing it again. Ducking for cover. Emotionally cutting and running. Here's a chance to get real with David, and I'm lying through my teeth to avoid it. It makes my prayer seem as false as it felt. *Grant me faith,* indeed!

"I was afraid I'd insulted you."

My laugh's as empty as the chalice at the communion table on Sunday morning. The presiding minister always lifts up the silver cup as he says the Words of Institution, but the truth is, in our tradition that cup is flat empty. All the juice is in the trays of shot glasses the deacons pass through the pews.

"David, I never expect you to find me attractive. We've been friends too long."

That lie cuts my tongue like a shard of glass. Why can't I be honest? This is the time. I know it. It's never going to get any easier than it is right now. And I can't do it.

"Oh, well, good. That's good then." He hesitates for a long moment. "Look, Blessing, I'd better go. I have to pick up my date in twenty minutes."

"Oh, sure. Have a good time. And don't wear that Dave Matthews Band T-shirt. Wear a real shirt, with a collar."

David sighs. "I don't ever go anywhere without a collar, one way or another." He sounds as tired and as empty as I feel.

"Bye, David."

"Bye, Betz."

I hit the Off button on the portable phone and toss it onto the coffee table. It lands with a clunk next to the remote and the Pizza Hut coupon I clipped from the Sunday paper. I'm glad I have caller ID because LaRonda will call before the evening is out for a full report, and I can't bring myself to tell her that despite her excellent coaching, I've failed at Asking-Out-Your-Best-Friend 101.

The phone rings five minutes later. To my relief it isn't LaRonda. It's Ed Newman, chair of the personnel committee at the church and twin brother of my nemesis, Edna Tompkins. Weird, because I never think of older people as being twins.

"Betsy? It's Ed."

"Hi, Ed. What can I do for you?"

"We need to talk."

That's odd, because I haven't hinted to anyone about my plans to leave the ministry. And Tricia's "Holy to Hottie" piece hasn't aired yet. After last night's fiasco, I banished the leather, hair gel, and heavy cosmetics to the back of my closet. At church this morning I was my usual average Jane.

Our conversation doesn't take long. Turns out that any notions I had of a dramatic exit next August have been upstaged. Dr. Black has just announced his immediate retirement, and Ed's calling to tell me I've been appointed interim senior minister.

"It won't be any more money, of course, and you'll still need to see that all your Christian education programs keep running. But we have faith in you, Betsy. We know you can do it."

Faith? A slow flush creeps up my neck and heats my cheeks. This isn't about faith. It's about being too cheap to pay a real interim minister.

"Look, Ed, I'm flattered—"

"'Course you are. Most churches wouldn't trust a woman with this kind of thing. But we're progressive at Church of the Shepherd."

"Yes, I know, but—"

"Thought we'd better have an emergency meeting of the personnel committee tonight to iron out the details."

I sigh. The church steamroller is fully engaged and running in high gear. "What time?" I'll have to go and figure out how to head all this nonsense off at the pass.

There's a moment of silence, and not the prayerful kind. "Um, well, Betsy, you don't need to be there."

"Doesn't the senior minister serve on the personnel committee?"

"Well, yes, but you don't need to worry about that. We'll take care of everything."

I'm quite sure they will. Just like my last church took care of everything, including running me out of town. "But I wouldn't want to shirk my duties before they've even started, Ed. What time did you say the meeting was?"

"Um, seven. In the boardroom."

"Great. I'll see you then."

For a second time I toss the phone down next to the pizza coupon. I will not answer it again today; I don't care who calls.

So much for a pleasant Sunday afternoon. I'm avoiding my best friend, torturing myself with imagining exactly how Paris Hilton–like David's date is, and I have only a few hours to prepare for escaping the personnel-committee steamroller.

I see now why God said we shouldn't work on the Sabbath. That would leave us at least one day a week when we couldn't ruin our lives.

Chapter 5

The boardroom at Church of the Shepherd is aptly named, though not correctly spelled. It should be b-o-r-e-d. A heavy mahogany conference table, harvest gold upholstered chairs, and generic framed artwork provide the perfect setting for the long-winded, self-aggrandizing speeches that consume most of the oxygen in the room.

I'm late for the meeting, thanks to a last-minute panic over pantyhose. I ran my last pair of taupe—a color that would appall the sales assistant at Oh Là Là!—which necessitated a mad dash to CVS. By the time I arrive at church, looking smartly professional and completely un-madeover in my aforementioned navy suit and crisp white blouse, the personnel committee has assembled. Hunched over the conference table, they remind me of a row of buzzards on a dying tree branch.

They've also occupied all the chairs, leaving me with no place to perch.

"We've already started," Ed informs me as I wrangle a straight-backed chair from the reception area through the doorway. I sink into it and gasp when the pointed corner of the conference table catches me squarely in the midsection.

"As I was saying—" Edna Tompkins casts me her customary look of disdain while completely ignoring her twin brother. She gets away with this behavior because it's an open secret that she's the largest contributor to the church's budget, even though that information is technically kept in confidence. Even from the pastors.

Edna looks around the table like Queen Elizabeth addressing her household staff. "I feel it is a mistake to ask Reverend Blessing to take on the role of senior pastor."

Like one of Pavlov's conditioned dogs, I feel my stomach sink and beads of sweat break out along my forehead at the prospect of conflict. I arrived prepared to inform the committee I have no interest in becoming the interim senior minister. But this time, despite the sweat and the sinking stomach, Mrs. Tompkins's clear disdain for my ministry raises my hackles. Maybe it's my frustration with my feelings for David. Maybe it's the chemicals from the makeover. Or maybe I've just finally had enough of these kinds of meetings.

"In what way, Mrs. Tompkins, would that be a mistake?"

The other committee members shoot me a nervous glance. They know that the financial consequences of standing up to Edna could be fatal.

"Now, dear, I'm only looking out for your best interests. You're far too young and inexperienced. Besides, taking on these responsibilities would leave you with no time for what little social life you do have." She pauses. "Oh dear, I mean—"

"Thank you, Edna, but this decision has nothing to do with Betsy's social life." Thin, balding Ed looks around the table too, eyes narrowed and lips pursed as if he's checking temperature gauges at fifteen paces. He's the only one who would dare contradict his sister. "The bottom line is that Dr. Black's contract gives him the right to retire on short notice. It also requires us to pay his salary through the end of the year."

Pay his salary through the end of the year? My jaw drops, and I have to tell the muscles in my face to pull it closed. I knew senior ministers had a little more butter on their bread, but this is the whole cow.

Gus Winston, the chair of the stewardship committee, clears his throat behind the restriction of his bow tie. "We don't have the reserves to pay three ministers for that length of time. Our debt load on the new activity center is too high." He's referring to the addition we built in a last-ditch effort to attract some members not eligible for AARP. It's now shuttered and silent, and it isn't even paid for.

Ed nods. "That's why Betsy's the perfect solution. She can fill both chairs. In the meantime, we'll start a search committee. We can have a new senior pastor in place by next January."

I snort with laughter, and their vulture-like heads swing my way. "Um, sorry, it's just that a search process normally takes at least a year. Sometimes eighteen months. Isn't it a little…um…ambitious to think a new minister would be in place by January?"

Ed frowns at me. "That's really up to us, Betsy. We just need you to hold the fort through the end of the year. It's not that much to ask, really, considering what we've done for you."

What they've done for me? He's got to be kidding, but there's not a hint of humor in any line on Ed's face. This is the church that put me up in a Motel 6 when I came to interview, refused to pay my moving expenses unless I rented a U-Haul and carted all my stuff myself, and makes me pay the church hostess for any leftovers I take home from fellowship dinners.

"I don't think—"

I never get a chance to finish the sentence. Judge Blount clears his throat in preparation for rendering a decision. As the chair of the elders, he represents the spiritual leaders of the church. On cue, the others swivel their heads toward him and wait in respectful silence.

"We don't need a real senior minister for this interim. Just someone to preach and make hospital visits. Betsy can do that, which leaves our bottom line intact."

I wouldn't be surprised to see steam coming out of my ears. If these people valued me any less, they'd have me typing up the Sunday-morning worship bulletins and sticking address labels on the weekly newsletter.

"I'm not sure—"

Marjorie Cline, who's sitting next to me, sets her knitting down on the table and reaches over to pat my hand with her gnarled fingers. "I'm sure our Betsy will be delighted to do what we ask. She knows we couldn't get along without her." Marjorie says it so sweetly, with such trust, that I can't do anything but stammer.

"That's settled, then," Ed says. He nods at me. "Betsy, we'll have to ask you to excuse yourself so we can talk about starting the search process. Thanks for coming."

Just like that. In less than ten minutes, they've decided my fate, and all I've managed to do is splutter out a few half-formed sentences of protest.

I try to form the word *no,* but my lips won't move. Not because I don't want the job and I'm afraid, but because suddenly I *do* want the job. And I'm very afraid.

I love preaching. I love visiting people in the hospital. It's why I took a small country church in the first place. And why it devastated me to leave in disgrace. I despise the routine tasks of Christian education—finding Sunday-school teachers, reviewing curriculum, running to Wal-Mart for markers and tape. But to dangle something like the senior-minister position in front of me—even temporarily—when I'm headed to law school is just not fair. Why put this temptation in front of me when I've already acknowledged I'm inadequate for the demands of the ministry?

The Judge steeples his fingers under his chin. "Perhaps you'd best begin work on next Sunday's sermon, Miss Blessing." He always calls me "miss," even though he knows my correct title is "reverend."

"Perhaps I should." I stand up, and my spine finally locks into place. Maybe I'm not a victim here. Maybe these people have just handed me my golden opportunity to prove myself. I'll give them the best senior minister they ever had. I might not be in it for the long haul, but at least I can leave for law school in a blaze of glory.

On the other hand, it could be one last chance to make a fool of myself in every possible way.

"If I can assist in the search process, let me know." With as much dignity and professionalism as I can muster, I turn toward the door.

"Oh, Betsy," Mrs. Tompkins calls as I leave, "would you be a dear and brew us some coffee before you go?"

I slowly turn. I know what I should say. I should point out they'd never ask Dr. Black to make coffee. I should rail against patriarchal practices that treat women as capable of little more than fixing refreshments. But I don't want to lose my golden opportunity before I climb into the pulpit next Sunday. I'm going to preach the steeple off this church.

"Regular or decaf?" I choke out, and Mrs. Tompkins glows with triumph.

"Decaf, please, dear. And perhaps some of those little cookies left from coffee fellowship."

Hello, my name is Betsy, and I'll be your server this evening.

"Of course."

Somehow I make it out of that room and to the church kitchen. And while the coffee brews, I try to figure out how my life got so complicated so quickly.

You see, in the ministry there's a fine line between leader and serv-ant. The minute you stand up for yourself, a parishioner is quick to remind you that Jesus washed the disciples' feet. But nowhere in the scripture does it say the disciples asked him for a pedicure while he was down there.

While the coffee slowly drips, I replay how I struggled for five years in my previous church to find the right balance. In a small con-gregation with fewer than one hundred people in worship and a tight budget, everyone pitched in wherever there was a need. So I didn't mind when I wound up cooking the fellowship meal or running the vacuum in the sanctuary after a wedding late on a Saturday night.

At Church of the Shepherd, though, where we're staff heavy and cash poor, lots of members never lift a finger. That makes Mrs. Tomp-kins's passive-aggressive command for coffee all the more irritating. I'm tired of feeling like a hired hand who's supposed to be grateful for a bed in the bunkhouse.

And as the Bunn-O-Matic spits out the last few drops of brown goop, it occurs to me that when I take the coffee and cookies into the boardroom, I don't have to leave. As the new interim senior minister, I could simply sit down and stay.

Do I want to fight that battle? A scene from my previous church flashes through my mind—the chair of the board and the chair of the elders sitting down in front of me after the service one Sunday.

"It's for the best," they said.

"If you leave today, we'll pay you for four weeks…"

It hurt so much I was sure I must be bleeding. Their message was clear. I wasn't good enough.

No, I wasn't male enough. Or was it the same thing?

I might have thrown in the ministerial towel right then if, when we stood up to leave my office, I hadn't noticed the chair of the board go beet red. His fly was unzipped.

They were human. Wrong, but still human. And Jesus would have loved them anyway. Just as he kept on loving the disciples, clueless wonders that they were. I hate that part about being a minister. That compassion you feel for parishioners even when you'd like to run them over with your car.

So now, armed with a thermal carafe of coffee and a tray of stale cookies, I gird my loins—emotionally, not literally, because the taupe pantyhose have taken care of that—and march toward the boardroom. I open the door, and the first thing I hear is The Judge saying, "We have her over a barrel after the way she was run out of her last church. You know we'd never have hired her in the first place if it hadn't been for the regional office insisting."

The tray of cookies rattles in my hand. "Coffee, anyone?" My smile tastes like the paste it must be stuck on with.

Kind Marjorie has the grace to blush. Ed coughs and shuffles some papers. Gus won't meet my gaze. Edna looks as if she's just feasted on canary. Meow.

My knees wobble so hard I'm sure they're going to start knocking together. To cover the surge of adrenaline flashing through my body, I scurry to the cabinet at the end of the room and retrieve some Styrofoam cups. Church of the Shepherd may be edging toward political correctness by hiring a woman minister, but they've not made much progress on the environmental front.

Cup by cup I move around the table pouring coffee. The committee doesn't say much. At least they're able to pass the cookie tray by themselves. Refined carbohydrates are a great motivator in the mainline church.

When I'm done, I pour myself a cup and pull my chair up to the table. Apparently The Judge's faux pas is big enough that no one's going to ask me to leave again. Shame is another great motivator in your average congregation.

"I'll oversee the custodial staff," Gus, the chair of the property committee, offers into the silence.

"Isn't that Dr. Black's responsibility?" My voice sounds unnaturally loud, but I'm afraid I won't be heard from down here halfway under the table. "I can see to that."

The Judge splutters a protest, but Ed waves him off. "That's great. I'm sure you can manage to see the building is kept clean."

"Thank you." I beam at him.

"Yes, dear," Mrs. Tompkins adds. "After all, housekeeping is a woman's province, isn't it?"

I have two choices here. I can challenge her or ignore her. Since my hands are shaking in my lap, I choose the latter. Because what I really want out of this meeting is not a fight, but every ounce of authority I can extract from these people to see me through the next six months.

A preemptive strike might be more effective than a defensive challenge. "I'll also oversee the administrative assistant. And I can supervise the interns from the divinity school. The stewardship committee can meet next week as planned. I'll make sure the bookkeeper has the end-of-the-month statement done. And, Gus," I turn to the property chair, "if you'll follow up on the estimates for the new carpet in the sanctuary, we can make a decision before the end of the month. Also, we're hosting the Middle Tennessee Ministers' Conference in a few weeks, so we'll need to ask the ladies auxiliary to bring baked goods for the coffee break. Mrs. Tompkins?" I smile with all the sweetness of battery acid. "Can you arrange that with the ladies?"

I'll give her "a woman's province."

All of them look bamboozled. Well, good. They'll collect their wits soon enough and pile some more obstacles in my path. But for this moment, I'm in the driver's seat.

Have I made the congregants of Church of the Shepherd sound more like a coven of devil worshipers than a group of faithful Christians? That's the problem with an inside view. You're likely to focus on the flaws and miss the good. And there's plenty of good here. Elderly ladies like Marjorie hug my neck at every possible turn. Little notes of encouragement show up in my staff mailbox in the office on a fairly regular basis. Folks are willing to spend their Friday nights hosting a group of homeless men overnight in the church basement during cold weather. Love and grace live here, too, at Church of the Shepherd, but like all human institutions, it has its share of greed, pride, and power-mongering.

Now, for the next six months, it's my institution to serve and to lead. For good or for ill. If nothing else, perhaps this sudden turn of events will take my mind off David. And that telltale moment when his hand moved across my thigh.

I'm going to have to call him, of course, and let him know what's happened. If I don't call, he'll know my denial about being upset with him is as false as my new hair color.

The complications just keep on coming!

By Monday morning I've discovered that as the new interim senior minister, I'm going to be too busy to take my regular day off. Because when you're trying to be all things to all people, you can't afford to lose a whole day on frivolities like grocery shopping and having a personal life.

By Monday morning I've also worked up the nerve to call David again.

"Yo, Blessing. What's up?" David sounds reassuringly nonchalant, which means my nervous dialing of his number at the church didn't transmit itself through the phone lines.

Remember to breathe. In and out. In and out.

"You'll never guess."

"Aliens have invaded?"

"No."

"They found WMD in Iraq?"

"You were closer with the alien thing."

"Spill."

"Dr. Black resigned yesterday. Effective immediately."

"No kidding? So what sucker are they getting for an interim pastor?"

There's what you might call a pregnant pause.

"Betz?"

"Well, they're getting me, actually."

The pause gestates, gives birth, and cuddles its offspring.

"How much?"

"How much what?"

"How much are they paying you?"

I swallow. "The same."

David sighs. "Did it hurt?"

"Did what hurt?"

"When they tattooed *welcome* on your forehead?"

Tears prick my eyes. "I'm not a doormat. C'mon, David, I need some support here."

"No, what you need is an intervention. What were you thinking?"

I feel the blood rushing to my head. One long deep breath to center my energy, and I let him have it.

"I'll tell you what I was thinking. I was thinking that for once I'd like to have the privileges you take for granted every day. I'd like to be the one in the pulpit. I'd like to be the one who gets called when someone important dies, instead of doing the funerals for the hangers-on." My throat tightens, and I have to swallow hard. "For once I'd like a starring role instead of being a bit player."

"Whoa." I could picture David making a staying motion with his hand. "Down girl."

"Don't 'down girl' me! I'm not a dog. And I don't need to be judged. I need advice. Can you do that for me? Can you be helpful instead of judgmental?"

"Yeah. Sure." He was quiet for a moment. "Why don't we meet for lunch?"

"Okay. Where?"

"At 12th and Porter?" To appease me, he suggests one of our favorite haunts.

"Noon?"

"Yeah. And Betz?"

"What?"

"Just because I said I'd help doesn't mean I think this is a good idea."

"I know. Bye."

LaRonda's response is less tempered than David's, once she's finished castigating me for losing my nerve about asking him out.

"You are the biggest fool in Christendom."

I laugh. "Are you sure you want to award that honor so hastily? There's a lot of competition out there."

"You know they're using you, right?"

"Yep."

"You know they'll never consider you for the permanent position?"

"Uh-huh."

"You deserve better."

"Yeah, but what if this is the best I'm going to get?"

And that's the $64,000 question, isn't it? This may be my only chance. This belittling offer to lie down so the congregation can wipe their feet on me. This rare chance to do the thing I have the gift of doing.

LaRonda makes an irritated noise, somewhere between a growl and a groan. "We need to strategize."

"I'm meeting David at 12th and Porter. Want to join us?"

LaRonda's nobody's fool. "Did you call me for advice or because you wanted a third party at lunch?"

I have the grace to feel ashamed. "All of the above."

"You have to face him, Betsy, without help from me or anyone else."

"Please, Ronnie."

"Nope. You're a big girl. Go deal with it."

Some friend. There are two things girls should always do together. One is going to the restroom. The second is providing backup for awkward lunch dates.

So I'm having lunch with David, alone, and I have no idea what I'm going to say to him. Except that it probably won't be even a reasonable facsimile of the truth.

Chapter 6

Five minutes after I hang up with LaRonda, my first Serious Crisis as interim senior minister erupts. I should have anticipated this showdown because I've known for a while now that Dr. Black was not the most powerful man in the congregation. No, that title belongs to another member of the church staff.

The head custodian.

"The dang fool thing is leaking something fierce," Jed Linker drawls as he sags against the door frame of my office and shoots me a challenging gaze, as if he's Wyatt Earp at the OK Corral. Jed is the longtime custodian of Church of the Shepherd, rising through the ranks to become the building manager and supervisor of three other custodial workers. In fact, he predates every other employee and most of the members. If you want to know the truth about anything around Church of the Shepherd, Jed's your man. And if you want to be history yourself, then you only have to get in his way.

I know Jed's none too happy with having a woman for a boss, especially since he and Edna Tompkins have been thick as thieves since the Nixon administration. It briefly occurs to me that he might have sabotaged the baptistery himself, just to test me.

"Can't you patch it?" I ask in the vain, foolish way of a woman who has little actual knowledge of plumbing.

"Nothin' left to patch," Jed says around the toothpick protruding from the side of his mouth.

"So what do we do?" I know what he's going to say, but I want him to be the one to say it. A new baptistery. The size of a couple of hot tubs stacked on top of each other. For a brief moment I wish that when it came to baptism, we were "sprinklers" instead of "dunkers." It'd be far more cost-effective if we just needed a pitcher and a bowl instead of a tank that holds several hundred gallons.

"New one's gonna run in the thousands," Jeb says without inflection, but we both know the church budget is stretched as tight as Mrs. Kenton's new face-lift.

I straighten my spine, not willing to let Jed see me wilt in the face of a challenge. "Do we have any baptisms on the calendar?" Since the normal age for baptism by immersion is eleven or twelve, we haven't had much call to fire up the baptistery of late. In fact, I'm not sure it's been used in the six months I've been here.

"Nothing on the calendar."

Then a question occurs to me. "If we haven't done any baptisms, how do we know it's leaking?"

"Oh, *we* haven't done any baptisms." Jed looks at me as if this is my personal failing. "It was some folks from that new church in Williamson County," Jed says, referring to the affluent southern suburb of Nashville. "They're meeting in a school, and it's too cold to use somebody's swimming pool this time of year. Dr. Black told them they could have the service here."

And there's the sad truth slapping me in the face. The farther away prospective church members move, the grimmer the future for Church of the Shepherd. People would rather worship in a school cafeteria than drive the thirty minutes to downtown to enjoy the Gothic arches of our sanctuary. And I can't really blame them.

"I'll have to call Gus and get the property division working on it," I tell Jed, hoping this is the right answer. There goes the new sanctuary carpet we'd all been dreaming of since a deacon fell down the chancel steps while carrying a tray of communion cups brimming with Welch's Grape Juice.

"If you think that's best," Jed drawls around his toothpick. He knows I'm passing the buck, and he doesn't approve.

"On second thought, I guess I'd better take a look for myself," I say and stand up to follow Jed from my office to the sanctuary.

I've learned in the past few years that I missed a few necessary courses in divinity school. Plumbing 101. Introduction to Catering. Basic Accounting. I thought that all I was going to need was a working knowledge of the Bible and systematic theology. Turns out there's a lot more call for the ability to make meatloaf for a hundred or to replace PVC pipe.

Jed leads me through the baptismal dressing-room area and then down behind the baptistery. It's a large tiled tank at the back of the chancel with steps leading down into it from both sides. If you were sitting in the pews, you wouldn't necessarily know it's there. Behind the baptistery is a small passageway that allows the ministers and the organist to move from one side of the chancel to the other without being seen. A small door in the passage wall leads to the baptistery's innards, so to speak.

Jed opens the door, hands me a flashlight, and motions for me to crawl inside. "You can see for yourself."

I'm sorry now I took his bait. At least he has the good grace not to smile. With a grimace, I survey my clothes. I made something of an effort to keep up the makeover this morning—black pants, high heels, even a blazer. I run the flashlight around the crawlspace and shudder at the dust-and-cobwebs interior decor.

"Um, I bet I could just take your word for it."

"No, no," Jed says with false politeness. "I wouldn't want you to doubt me."

So I'm caught. With a sigh, I sink to my knees and crawl inside. Quick as I can, I run my flashlight around the plumbing, and that's when I see the problem, big as day. Everything around the drainpipe is crumbling. Jed's right. There's no way to patch something to nothing.

With a resigned sigh, I switch off the flashlight and attempt to inch my way out of the crawlspace. Only I keep getting stuck. First my blazer gets hung up on a pipe. Then my hair gets caught in some wire mesh. By the time I finally extricate myself, I know I look as if I've been dragged backward through a hedge.

Jed doesn't so much as crack a smile around the ever-present toothpick.

I brush my palms together to try to rid them of the dust and dirt. "You're right, Jed. It's hopeless."

A twinkle appears in his eye. "No, Reverend. Not hopeless. Just in need of some male know-how."

And I know he's not talking about the baptistery. He means Church of the Shepherd.

Well, my first encounter with Jed as interim senior minister didn't go exactly as planned, but I'm definitely the wiser for it. I'm also the filthier. I figure I'll pop into the restroom and freshen up, but to get there I have to cross the waiting room in the office area. And when I do, I find some folks waiting for me. The personnel committee, to be exact. Ed. Edna. The Judge. Even Marjorie, who's the only one smiling.

"Miss Blessing, there you are." The Judge frowns, his jowls hanging down in parentheses around his displeased expression.

"Good morning, Judge. Everyone."

I fight the urge to reach up and smooth my hair.

"Is that dirt on your face?" Edna asks, aghast.

"Well, um, yes. Just a bit of a problem with the baptistery—"

Ed frowns. "I'm afraid we have bigger problems than the baptistery, Betsy."

Great. And here I thought the day couldn't get any worse.

"What seems to be the trouble?"

Edna's eyes flash with disapproval. "We have all seen *it*."

"*It?*" I ask, baffled.

Ed shifts from one foot to the other. "The television piece. This morning."

My makeover misery. I'd forgotten it was going to air today.

"'Holy to Hottie' indeed," Edna sniffs. "I've never been so embarrassed for this church in my life."

The flush starts on my cheeks, drops to my neck, and eventually suffuses my whole being. "I didn't think—"

"Apparently not," The Judge booms, and I suddenly feel like I'm twelve and my father's caught me sneaking off to school wearing eye shadow and lipstick.

Ed won't meet my gaze. "It just puts the church in a bad light, Betsy. Not the image we want to project."

"You looked like a harlot," Edna snaps.

"Oh no, Edna." Marjorie finally finds her voice. "She just didn't look like our own sweet Betsy."

God bless Marjorie.

I swallow past the lump of anxiety in my throat and muster up a response. "I'm very sorry if I embarrassed the church, but I don't think it's that big a deal. I doubt many people saw it."

"You doubt many people saw it?" Edna snaps. "I've been fielding phone calls from members of the Women's Club all morning. We're the laughingstock of Nashville."

The Judge eyes the current state of my hair and clothing. "Well, apparently it was a one-time thing. I feel sure it won't happen again."

And that comment lights a flame of anger in my belly. "That what won't happen again?"

He scowls. "We'd better not see any more getups like that one on television, Miss Blessing. At Church of the Shepherd, we know how to behave, and so do our ministers."

There it is. The threat that always emerges when the minister upsets the status quo.

"Are you saying you'll fire me if you don't like the way I dress?"

"We're saying," Edna interposes, "that we won't stand for you making a spectacle of this church."

Ed looks at least a little embarrassed by what's being said. "We just need you to be careful, Betsy. To not do any damage until we can get a real minister in."

And there's the truth, once again slapped right across my face. They may have given me the responsibilities, but in no way are they going to grant me the authority to be the senior pastor of this church.

I'm nothing but filler.

"Will you promise not to do anything else like this?" Ed asks in a conciliatory tone. "Otherwise, we may need to make some changes."

In other words, if I do anything that upsets them, they're going to fire me. And I need a paycheck until August when law school starts. If I were stretched any further over the proverbial barrel, I'd be seven feet tall.

"I'm very sorry if I embarrassed anyone," I say, but I don't sound convincing, even to my own ears. "It won't happen again."

But it will. It has to. Because ministers are human and because what kind of minister would I be if all I ever did was rubber-stamp whatever the congregation wanted? That's not a pastor. That's a whipping boy. Or, in this case, whipping girl.

"That's settled then," Edna purrs, triumphant. She looks at Ed and The Judge and ignores Marjorie. "I told you a firm hand was needed."

And since Edna's the biggest contributor in the church, we don't have any choice but to let her hand be as firm as she wants it to be.

I'm delighted when they turn and leave. And I'll be twice as delighted when it's my turn to leave. Feeling older than Ed and Edna combined, I return to my office, pull a calendar out of my middle desk drawer, and cross through another day with my red pen. Only 189 more to go.

"How do you do it, Ronnie?" I lasted all of ten minutes after the confrontation in the reception area before picking up the phone and calling her.

"Do what?"

"Be a woman and a minister at the same time."

She chuckles. "I guess some of your parishioners were watching Tricia's show this morning, huh?"

"Apparently everyone in Nashville was."

"Good. Then your phone should start ringing off the hook."

"Yeah, with irate parishioners. Not with eligible men calling to ask me out."

"O ye of little faith."

"You keep saying that."

"Wonder why?"

Argh! "You're not helping."

LaRonda laughs. "Actually, I *am* helping. You just don't care for the way I'm doing it."

"Conflict is the last thing I need right now."

"Conflict is exactly what you need right now. You're afraid of it after your last church. But conflict isn't always bad, Betz. Sometimes you need it. Sometimes it helps you grow."

"I don't want to grow! I just want to get through—" I stop myself just in time, because I've yet to tell LaRonda about the law-school acceptance letter that seems to have taken up permanent residence in my purse.

"You can't play it safe in the ministry, Betz. Security means you're not doing your job."

"Doing my job means I'll lose my job."

LaRonda's rueful chuckle acknowledges the truth. "It's a delicate balance."

"I'm no good at that delicate balance stuff."

"Yeah, well, you're about to learn."

LaRonda sounds confident of that, but I'm not so sure.

"You have to trust it, Betz."

"The last time I trusted a church, I got fired and humiliated."

There's a pause. And then LaRonda says, "I know you want guarantees, but there aren't any. You can't expect them."

Which just reaffirms my decision to leave. How can anyone live without at least a few guarantees of some kind? How is that possible?

LaRonda knows she's not getting anywhere with me and changes the subject. "Isn't it about time for you to meet David for lunch?"

I look at my watch, and my heart trips into overdrive. "I can't go looking like this."

"Looking like what?"

I give her the thumbnail version of my encounter with Jed and my climb through the inner workings of the baptistery.

"You can't dodge David forever, Betz. Get a comb and some lipstick and hit the road."

"Yes ma'am."

"I mean it."

"I know."

"Don't make me come over there."

She's not going to let me duck and run. "Okay. But only because you're forcing me."

"Well, somebody's got to."

Now it's my turn to pause. "Listen, Ronnie, thanks. I appreciate your advice, even when I don't like it."

I can sense her smile. "I know, hon. Now get your booty in gear and go meet David."

"Okay. Bye."

I set down the receiver, fish my purse out from underneath my desk, and head for the restroom to see how much of the damage I can repair.

I hate it when LaRonda's right. I really do. Because it usually means I'm going to go do something I don't want to do. All in all, I'd rather eat dirt, but I don't think it's on the menu at 12th and Porter.

Chapter 7

Whenever I want to have lunch or dinner away from the watchful eyes of my parishioners, I head for 12th and Porter. My congregants wouldn't be caught dead in this art deco/funky/retro temple. So I can gorge on Pasta YaYa without each calorie noted and each sip of my rare glass of wine observed and judged.

David's already there when I arrive. He's poached our favorite table by the window. Just the sight of him makes it hard to breathe. When did *that* happen? When did he start messing with my most basic functions?

My sexy heels feel six feet long, so I endeavor not to trip over the step beside the hostess station as I make my way to the table. David's smile holds a hint of wariness, but he stands to give me a hug. For the first time in forever, I don't want him to hug me. All those other times his touch didn't matter. It was as comforting as tomato soup and grilled cheese. But all that changed in a darkened movie theater, and if he puts his arms around me, if I feel the strength of his chest against the softness of my own, I won't have enough wits about me to get through this lunch.

So, instead, I stick out my hand. "Hey."

David looks at me as if I've sprouted antennae. He looks at my hand, and then his gaze rises to meet mine.

"Are you that mad at me, or are you too glamorous to hug now?" Hurt lines his forehead.

"Don't be stupid. Why would I be mad at you?" Call me Cleo, Queen of Denial. I slide into my chair and stow my purse underneath. "I guess you saw the makeover segment."

He grins. "One of my parishioners taped it and brought it over first thing this morning."

"They couldn't wait to rat me out, huh?"

"Apparently it confirmed his opinion that letting women into the ministry was tantamount to asking strippers to do a pole dance during worship."

I hate myself for it, but I have to ask. "Well? What did you think?"

David rubs his chin. "Now I know why you were so dolled up last week." His gaze drops from mine. "Took me a minute to figure out it was you." He tilts his head and looks at me as if he's seeing me for the first time. "Looks okay, but I miss the curls."

I make a move like I'm going to stab him with my fork. "Do you never learn?" It works to cover up my disappointment. I really thought the makeover might at least get David to acknowledge I'm a female of the species.

"Don't get mad. It's just that it's so…stylish."

"And that's a bad thing?"

"It's just not you, Betz."

Well, at least it's not me in David's eyes, and I'm suffocated with the realization that it never will be. He just doesn't see me as girlfriend material.

LaRonda's always saying I should clarify my goals. Well, given the state of things, here are my goals for this lunch with David:

1. Convince him it's a good idea I took the interim senior-
   minister job.
2. Convince *myself* it's a good idea I took the interim senior-
   minister job.
3. Don't let on to David I have the urge to lean across the
   table and nibble on his neck.
4. Don't actually lean across the table and nibble on his neck.

There's also the small matter of not letting the whole law-school acceptance thing slip out. Or talking about the rather disturbing phone call I received last night at 2:00 a.m., which consisted of heavy breathing and muffled pounding. Muffled pounding? What's that all about? An enigmatic pervert is all I need to make my life complete.

Our smiling waitress appears tableside. Like the restaurant, she embodies art deco/retro/funky. Her eyebrows, nose, and lip are pierced. Strangely, her ears are not. "Can I get you something to drink?"

I'd like a single-malt scotch straight up, but that's not going to happen. "Diet Coke, please."

David smiles in that boyish yet charming way of his. "Iced tea."

The waitress smiles back at him, and I resist the urge to take her out at the knees. Fortunately for her, she disappears as quickly as she came.

"So." David lounges back in the chair, his lanky frame sprawled everywhere. If it weren't for the clerical collar, you'd think he was a dot-com whiz or a struggling artist. Amazing what a symbol of re-spectability will do for someone.

I unroll my silverware from my napkin and make a good show of arranging it in front of me. Then I take my time placing my napkin just so in my lap.

Finally, I have to look up at him. "Well."

In eight years we've never been awkward with each other. I don't know how to smooth it over, how to make it like it was. Before, I wasn't hiding all these secrets. Now I feel as though every guilty transgression is inscribed on my face.

"Betz, what are you doing?"

"I'm arranging my silverware. It's a common dining custom in many nations."

David curls forward, languor gone. He puts both elbows on the table and clasps his hands. "I'm serious, Blessing. Why are you doing this?"

"So I can consume my food when it arrives?"

Of course, I know perfectly well what he's talking about, but I can't tell him I need the senior-minister job for six months and that they have me over a barrel. I have to lie to him, and I've never lied to David before. I don't really know how to do it. Not with confidence, anyway.

"I told you on the phone. I just want a shot at being the top dog. I want a little bit of what you get every day."

David frowns. "This isn't the way to get it. You're a convenience to them, not a real senior pastor."

How can he not feel the heat that's coursing through me just sitting here looking at him? I've never noticed his hands before. Have they always been that large? And his forearms. Did they always have those little ropes of muscles running from his wrists and disappearing into his shirt cuffs? Pounding a hammer on Habitat for Humanity houses all the time must be better than Nautilus.

What was he saying? Something about being a convenience. Oh yeah. I need to defend my choice here.

"It's not the conventional way to step into the pulpit, no, but maybe I have to take it by any means I can get."

"Are you saying you want the position permanently?"

The waitress returns with our drinks. I'm grateful for the pause so I can figure out how to answer the question. Maybe I can be truthful about this part.

"I don't know if I want the permanent position. But I don't know that I *don't* want it, either."

The waitress lurks tableside, so we have to order. Even after we've asked for two plates of Pasta YaYa, she seems reluctant to leave. In fact, she's flirting with David! What kind of shameless hussy flirts with a man in a clerical collar? And he's certainly not shutting her down, either. The sight of David smiling at another woman is worse than his disapproval of my recent career choice. Beneath the table I wipe my clammy palms on my artfully arranged napkin and resist the urge to kick David in the shin.

Eventually, the multiply pierced hussy leaves.

David turns his attention back to me, and I'm both alarmed and ecstatic. "Betsy, you deserve your shot at a healthy pastorate. This isn't it. Not when you go into it at a disadvantage."

It doesn't help to know that David is absolutely right. "I can overcome disadvantages. I've had to every day of my ministry."

"You can't change a sick system, Betsy, and that's what you're trying to do. Codependent no more, babe."

"David, I've made the decision. I don't need you to question it. I need you to help me live with it."

He frowns. Who knew he was adorable when he frowned? How could I have known him for eight years and not noticed this?

"Okay, if you're hellbent on doing this, you need to know a few senior-pastor secrets."

I straighten my spine in righteous indignation. "There are secrets? You never told me there were secrets."

He grins. "You didn't need them. You weren't a senior pastor."

I bristle. "I was too. I was a senior pastor in my first church."

"Nope. You were a solo pastor. That's different. I mean the secrets you need to know when you have to supervise other church employees, other ministers. When you're in a significant congregation."

That smarts. "As opposed to all the insignificant congregations out there?"

A faint blush rises in his cheeks. Good. Every once in a while, I have to call him out when he develops symptoms of SPS—senior-pastor syndrome. At least I'm not the only one uncomfortable here.

"I can't believe you've never told me there were secrets." Suddenly, I feel normal with David again. Evidently, equal discomfort means equilibrium. We could be back in the student pub processing the divinity-school mantra of "minister as theologian" over endless cups of coffee.

David leans forward and lowers his voice. "Information like this is shared on a need-to-know basis only."

I lean forward too, liking the conspiratorial aspects of this conversation, as if someone's giving me the secret handshake for the Old Boys' Club. As I lean forward, though, the waitress appears and slides my Pasta YaYa in front of me so my nose almost wipes across it. The steam stings my eyes.

"Thanks." David smiles at the waitress, and she more or less melts. What is it with women and their attraction to men in clerical collars? There's probably some deep psychosexual explanation courtesy of Freud. *Ew.*

David twirls some pasta around his fork. "Okay, Secret Number One."

I wish I could pull a pen and paper out of my purse, but I feel stupid enough already. "Yes?" I'm not even paying proper attention to my pasta, which tells you how much I want to know this stuff.

"At least once during each sermon, hold the Bible up in the air and wave it around."

My fork falls from my fingers. "I thought you were serious." David teases me all the time, or at least he used to, but I'm too raw right now to cope with it.

He laughs. "I'm not kidding. Congregations want someone who will 'preach the Scripture.' If you give them the image of you holding your Bible up in the air, they'll think that's what you're doing."

I'm impressed. And also appalled. "How'd you learn that?"

"Same way you are."

"Over Pasta YaYa?"

He twirls more pasta on his fork. "No, you dope. Another minister told me."

"Okay, wave the Bible around. What's next?"

I think I can eat now. I dive into my food and wait patiently while David chews.

"Secret Number Two is pretty easy too."

"What is it?"

"Visit anyone who goes into the hospital within twenty-four hours."

I snort, and the pasta goes down the wrong way. After I finish coughing, I say, "Oh, come on. Who wouldn't do that anyway? That's no secret."

David nods sagely. "You'd be surprised. I've heard horror stories about my predecessor at St. Helga's that would curl your hair."

I lift a hand in a staying motion. "Please don't. I'm already using six different styling gels to keep my new hairdo straight as straw."

David eyes my hair warily. "It certainly is strawlike. I'll give you that."

"Okay, flatterer, what's Senior-Minister Secret Number Three?" David's indifference to my looks would never have bothered me a few weeks ago. Now it cuts to the quick.

"Number Three. Never drive a better car than your parishioners."

I almost choke on my Pasta YaYa, and I have to make a dive for my napkin. Once I clear my throat, I laugh. "No problem there." My ancient Honda Civic would make anyone else feel like the owner of a Bentley.

Then a thought occurs to me. "Is that why you haven't traded in the Volvo?" Poor car. It deserves a mercy killing.

David taps the side of his nose. "Exactly."

I set down my fork and push my plate away. "David, none of this stuff is going to help me be accepted as the senior minister at Church of the Shepherd."

David waves his fork at me. "Don't underestimate this advice, Betz. It's golden."

"And that's it?"

"Well, there's one more thing."

"Which would be?"

"Don't date a parishioner."

"Not a problem."

"Yeah, well, you'd be surprised."

"David, this is the second time in a week you've warned me off. What's going on?"

"Look, Betsy, when you're the top dog, people project all sorts of stuff onto you. But it's not really about you."

I think of the waitress. And then I wonder if that's what I'm doing. What if I'm not immune to this phenomenon? What if what I'm feeling for David isn't real at all but some sort of head trip? Am I just another senior-minister groupie?

"David, none of this will help me get Mrs. Tompkins off my back or convince The Judge I can lead the congregation."

"Try waving the Bible around next Sunday. You'll be surprised."

"It doesn't change my gender."

"No, but if you act like a male preacher, people won't be so threatened."

"I can't believe you just said that." He sounds like the grievance committee that confronted me this morning. Can you want to kiss someone and clobber him at the same time? "I thought you were one of the good guys."

"I'm just saying you should give people what they expect to get. At least at first. At least in the short term."

But I've tried that already. I did that at my first church. I was the model pastor, a "man of God" in every way but the one that counted to them most, apparently—the biological way.

"David, I can't believe you're telling me to sell out."

He pushes his plate back too. "You asked me how to make this choice of yours work until they hire someone else, and that's what I'm telling you. Church of the Shepherd is not interested in your remaking their collective expectations of a minister. They just want you to behave yourself until the right man comes along."

Oh, heavens. He's right.

I'm stupid to hold on to the slightest hope that this situation can be transformed. It's only a paycheck until I can check out and go to law school. I can't let myself be seduced by the idea that it could mean more.

"Okay, so what you're saying is wave the Bible around, make a beeline for the hospitals, keep my old Honda running awhile longer, and no romancing parishioners."

"That's pretty much it."

"I could have figured that out myself."

David looks at me sideways. "Betsy, you have a habit of not figuring things out until quite a bit after the fact."

It's not fair. The clammy palms. The scrambled brain. Fear that feels this good. I hate the symptoms of infatuation, and I especially hate that David is the cause of them. Except I don't really hate it at all. I leave 12th and Porter no wiser about how to proceed with revealing my feelings to David.

Okay, let's review my goals for my lunch meeting with David and evaluate how I did.

1. Convince David I did the right thing to take the interim senior-minister position. Nope, didn't meet that one. In fact, he pretty much convinced me of the opposite.

2. Convince myself I did the right thing. Hmm. I think the jury's still out on that one.

3. Don't let on to David that I wanted to lean across the table and nibble on his neck. Oops. Did I play it cool enough about the waitress?

4. Don't actually lean across the table and nibble on David's neck. Hallelujah! That's one goal I *did* achieve.

The drive back to my office at church isn't a long one, but it gives me time to compose myself. What did David mean by the comment that I don't figure things out until after the fact? I'm a very perceptive person, and he knows it. I'm always eyes-wide-open, and just because I've been blindsided a few times doesn't mean I stick my head in the sand.

Like, I knew David wasn't for me within thirty minutes of meeting him.

These days not as many people go straight to divinity school right out of college. But a few years ago, the economy wasn't great, and everyone I knew was going to grad school instead of trying to land a nonexistent job. I chose div school by process of elimination. Nothing else felt right. Maybe that's a bad reason to think about serving God as a profession, but sometimes the "right path" is the only one that unfolds in front of you.

I arrived in Nashville with all my worldly possessions in the trunk of my ancient Olds Cutlass. Thus began a life of what I like to call "divinity school chic." My first apartment was an efficiency studio in a less-than-reputable part of town. I heard gunshots in the night fairly often and learned to appreciate gangsta rap.

Orientation for first-year div students began at the end of August when Nashville swelters like a Southern belle in three layers of petticoats and a corset. I'd already discovered a few anomalies about my new town. Barbecue was pig, not cow. The pronunciation of many street names had little to do with their spelling. And for the first time in my life, I was in a place where I literally didn't know a soul.

Until David.

I arrived for the first orientation session late and overdressed, sweat dripping from the end of my nose. My graceful entrance consisted of using the wrong door—thereby walking into the room directly in front of the dean of the school who was giving a welcome speech—and tripping over a pair of rather large Nikes before half-sliding, half-falling into a desk.

The owner of the Nikes chuckled and pulled his feet back under his desk. I shot him a look of disdain in my best grrrl-power manner. He chuckled again.

"Klutz."

I couldn't believe he said that. Without thinking, I responded, "Oaf." He grinned back at me, and the effect was like mainlining caffeine. Thus our friendship was cemented.

After the orientation we went for coffee in the common room. He told me about his fiancée, Jennifer. I told him about my apartment in the war zone. We commiserated about the cost of textbooks and the prospect of taking five graduate courses while working a menial job. If we could find one.

I didn't meet Jennifer for a week or so. When I did, I was appalled at David's judgment. Jen was the poster child for high maintenance. He didn't exactly dance attendance on her, but you could tell he was willing to go to great lengths to placate her. Jennifer looked like Cindy

Crawford, dressed like a New Yorker, and talked like a sweet Southern belle—none of which I ever had a prayer of pulling off.

David and I established a regular routine of repairing to the student pub after Old Testament class three days a week. Over innumerable cups of coffee, we picked apart our classes, our professors, and each other.

Why didn't I fall for him then? Maybe because I had a strict policy about stealing someone else's man ever since the time a girl stole mine. Maybe I recognized he was far too besotted with Jennifer to see anyone else. Mostly, it was because I'd finally found a friend who understood everything about me and liked me anyway. No way was I going to mess with that.

And I never have. Until now. Eight years after the fact, I'm faced with the truth. I had feelings for David from the moment I tripped over his feet, but I buried them when I found out about Jennifer. Only now there is no Jennifer. There's just this looming pit of an opportunity to go after what I want.

Before I can lose my nerve, I reach for my cell phone and dial David's number.

It barely rings before he answers. "Yes?"

"Want to go bowling Saturday morning?"

"Will there be chili dogs?"

"Do they make bowling alleys without them?"

David recognizes this invitation for the olive branch it is, because in all the years I've known him, I've never agreed to go bowling with him before. I hate bowling, I hate putting my feet in shoes other people have worn, and most of all I hate chili dogs.

"Pick you up at ten." I can hear the smile in his voice. He thinks he's won, but he doesn't know yet what the game is. On Saturday he's going to find out.

"Okay. See ya Saturday." I hit the End button and, heart racing, pull into the church parking lot. Maybe David's right. Maybe I catch on a little late sometimes. Fine. He wants after-the-fact? On Saturday I'll show him "after-the-fact."

Chapter 8

When I return to my office, I find a long white florist box resting on top of my desk. Or rather, it rests on top of piles of old sermons, flyers for evangelism aids, and various biblical commentaries. I've never seen one of these boxes in person before, just in the movies. The red ribbon is crisply tied into an opulent bow.

"Go on, open 'em." Angelique, our administrative assistant, is hovering in my office doorway. "I'm dying of curiosity here. Who do you think they're from?"

I have no idea, so I walk over to my desk and slip the little envelope from underneath the ribbon. The simple typed message reads: From an Admirer.

"It's not signed."

Angelique squeals. "A secret admirer? That rocks!" Her eyebrows shoot up in delight, which only accents their piercings. Matching silver doodads make her look like a pale version of some native tribeswoman. Yes, Angelique was once a waitress at 12th and Porter before she came to Church of the Shepherd.

I find the long white box disquieting rather than exciting. My only date in recent memory was with the penniless ex-con, so I doubt he's the source. And it couldn't be David because—well, just because he doesn't see me that way. I remind myself of this rather sharply to avoid disappointment.

With trembling fingers, I slip the ribbon from the box and lift the lid. A dozen dead black roses lie nestled in white tissue paper.

"Ayyy!" Angelique's scream makes mine unnecessary, but it doesn't prevent the icy shiver that shoots down my spine.

My knees threaten to give way, and I sink into my desk chair. "At least they're not rats." You see this kind of thing in the movies, but you never really expect it to happen to you.

Again, *ew.*

Angelique approaches the box cautiously. "Who did you tick off?"

Angelique came to us through a Welfare-to-Work program. I knew her at 12th and Porter forever, and then she showed up one day for a job interview through a Women in Transition Program we support. Spaghetti tanks with bra straps showing turned out to be the least of our worries. Dr. Black and I've been working with Angelique on her professionalism, but clearly we have a ways to go, and with Dr. Black gone, it's up to me now.

"Who delivered these?" I ask, not quite prepared to give Angelique a lecture in verbal office etiquette.

Angelique shrugs. "No clue. They were propped against the office door when I got back from lunch."

I retrieve the small envelope and card from the detritus on my desk. "There's no florist imprint. Nothing."

Angelique grimaces. "Some special delivery."

"Yeah. My sermon must have been worse than I thought."

"Reverend Blessing?"

"Hmm?"

"Do you think you're being stalked?"

I don't think I'm being stalked, at least not until I check my voice mail. Three heavy-breathing phone messages later, my skin crawls like a sinner coming back to church.

Weird occurrences are a part of any ministry, and if you're a woman, you get your own special brand of inappropriate stuff. I regularly receive letters from prisoners requesting I pray for them—and would I mind sending them a pair of underwear I've worn recently? More than once a male parishioner has approached me and expressed a wish to discuss the sexual feelings he's been having for women other than his wife. I've learned the Woman Minister's Secret Handshake. When a man approaches, you extend your right hand and place your left hand on his right shoulder. This demonstrates your warmth and interpersonal skills but also keeps him from getting too close. All that is normal stuff. These dead roses, though, are another thing entirely.

So I do what I always do when I want to run away and hide. I head for the nursing home.

Okay, that's a little strange, I'll grant you. A place that smells of disinfectant and rubber-soled shoes isn't most people's first choice for sanctuary, but most nursing homes don't possess the secret weapon they have at Hillsboro Health Care: Velva Brown, a five-foot-tall resident who's a cross between Yoda and Mother Teresa.

I was drawn to Velva the first time I met her. Maybe it's the glow that emanates from her weathered face. It could be the zinnias she grows in the flower beds so she can make floral arrangements with her gnarled hands. She carries them to patients who can't get out of bed. Most important, I think, I seek her out because Velva, too, is ordained. Not that she generally admits to the fact. When she was young in the 1920s, churches ordained women mission workers so they could get the clergy rate on train fare. Velva worked in the Philippines for a few short years, and then came the stock-market crash of 1929. Mission funding disappeared, and she was called home. She spent the next fifty years of her life working in the denominational offices, typing and filing and waiting for her chance to go back overseas.

Every time she had a chance to return to her beloved Philippines, something intervened. She had back problems. Her mother fell ill. Finally, when she was almost eighty, she went back for a two-year mission stint. Now she lives at Hillsboro Health Care with only a niece in New Jersey to see about her and her memories of the people of the Philippines to make her smile.

Velva's room reflects her spirit. It's crammed full with a lifetime of memorabilia. Tibetan prayer drums. A tidy stash of tea bags and a porcelain teapot. Books, books, and more books. Her roommate, Dottie, is usually comatose. She spends her days mumbling. I finally figured out she was counting. "Dottie refuses to die until she turns one hundred," Velva once told me. So that's how Dottie passes the days, and Velva happily works her into the ambiance. Every morning she brushes Dottie's hair and puts lipstick on her with the same diligence she employs when she dusts the tops of the furniture and neatly makes her bed.

Today Velva sits in a chair by the window with her Bible open in her lap. I don't think she's reading it so much as communing with it. No doubt she has most of it memorized anyway.

When Velva hears my footsteps in the doorway, she turns. I know the aura around her is only backlighting from the sun streaming in the window, but she still looks as if she's seen the face of God. That's a glow no makeover in the world can give you.

"My dearest Betsy." The lines around her mouth emphasize her smile. Her bright blue eyes sparkle. "Such a treat."

Okay, one of the reasons I love Velva is because she adores me just for showing up.

"Hello, friend." I cross the room and kneel beside her chair. It's too hard for her to get up and down, so I adjust to her. She puts one hand on the top of my head, as if she's giving me a blessing. With the other, she tilts my chin toward her.

"What's all this?" She looks concerned. "When did you start wearing war paint?"

I flush, which only emphasizes the war paint. "I got a makeover."

"A makeover? What was wrong with you before?"

"I was frumpy."

Velva sighs. "According to whom?"

"According to me." I take her fingers from under my chin and very gently squeeze them. With someone as old and frail as Velva, you have to be careful with physical affection. Fortunately, the most minute of touches can convey the deepest feelings. "How's your arthritis today?"

"Still here." A conspiratorial light glints in her baby blues. "Did you bring what I asked?"

I cast a quick glance back over my shoulder to make sure no nurses are lurking in the doorway. "Yep." I reach into my purse on the floor beside me and withdraw a small vial of pills. I slip them into her fingers, and she quickly tucks them under her Bible.

"You're a dear girl."

"I feel like a drug dealer."

"They're only herbal supplements."

"And strictly banned in this place."

Velva smiles. "Let me worry about that." She motions me to sit in the chair opposite her.

"How is Dottie today?" I look over at her roommate, who lies motionless in the bed.

"She's tired. We stayed up too late reading last night."

"What kept you up so late?"

Velva draws a book from the seam of her chair where it had been tucked. She turns it toward me. *Lady Chatterley's Lover.*

"You wild woman." I laugh and she joins me.

But, as always, Velva knows I've come with something on my mind. "What's troubling you, Betsy?"

I sit in the chair opposite her. "Dr. Black resigned. They've asked me to be the interim senior pastor."

Our lighthearted mood quickly evaporates. "Did you agree?"

"Yes."

Her brow furrows. "Why?"

"Because I want to prove I can do it."

She adds a frown to her furrow. "That's not the reason."

Velva sees into my soul even more deeply than David does. Maybe it's her greater years of experience.

"No. It's not the reason." I'm quiet for a long moment, and Velva just sits with me, waiting. She's good at that. Just being a companion, not pushing or prodding, but waiting as if she has all the time in the world. Why is it that a woman of ninety-four, who probably has very little time left, can be far more patient than a woman of thirty who has a lot of years ahead of her?

"I'm leaving the ministry." There. I've said it. It's out there, named, floating around in the ether.

Velva reaches out and takes my hand in hers. Her fingers are twisted and weak, but her touch conveys strength. She doesn't say anything for so long I feel compelled to speak.

"I'm going to law school." The words ring with a harsh belligerence I hadn't anticipated.

Velva cocks her head like a little bird. "Has God called you there?"

As usual, Velva cuts straight to the heart of the matter. Tears gather in my eyes, and my shoulders slump. "I don't know. I don't know what God wants anymore."

Since my parents split up when I was fifteen, church has been my refuge. I found comfort, affirmation, opportunities for leadership. When I was a senior, the pastor told me I should think about ministry. The seed seemed to grow of its own accord, and until the day my first church fired me, it always felt like the right thing.

"I've tried to do what I thought was right," I tell Velva, "and look where it's gotten me. I thought the Big Guy said 'ministry,' but maybe it was 'misery.' I don't want to—" I stop myself just in time.

"You don't want to what?"

But I can't say it—not to her. I can't say I don't want to spend my whole life waiting for a chance that might never come.

"It's too hard, being so close to what I want and knowing it will never be mine. That's why I agreed to the interim job. It's the closest I'll ever come to getting what I want, even if it's only temporary. And I have to have a job for the next six months until school starts."

Velva's hands caress the pages of the Bible in her lap. "Is it what God wants for you, Betsy? Or are you like Jonah, running away because things aren't going according to your plans?"

I know the answer, but I can't say it. Velva's right, though she probably won't actually offer her opinion. No, she'll ask supportive, nonthreatening, and open-ended questions and in the process make every point she wants to make.

I sigh. "I can't cut it in the church, so does it really matter?"

"You know the answer to that."

"I'm not sure I do anymore."

"That's fear talking."

"Yes, well, fear has a lot to say these days."

In the bed by the wall, Dottie snorts and snuffles. Velva releases my hand. "How long would you be willing to wait for God to lead you to the right place? What's your limit?"

I have the grace to lower my head. I know what Velva's saying. God works in the Divine's own sweet time. I've read enough Bible stories to know that. Fourteen years for Jacob to finally get the right bride. Forty years of the Israelites' wandering in the wilderness. But doesn't God know the world moves at a faster pace these days?

"I've reached my limit. I can't wait anymore."

With great difficulty, Velva rises from her chair and shuffles to the counter that runs along one side of the room. She plugs in her electric teakettle and begins to lay out the tea things. It's a familiar ritual I've come to rely on over the past six months.

And, as always, I feel compelled to fill her silence with words. "I thought you would understand better than anyone."

"If you've come for a blessing, I can't give you one. But I suspect you knew that before you got here."

We're both quiet for several minutes. The kettle whistles, and she shakily pours the water into the teapot. "You made a commitment to God. You're the only one who can give yourself permission to unmake it. Have you done that?"

Once again, Velva's nailed my problem perfectly. Because, of course, I haven't done that. Even though I've decided to leave, I haven't let go.

"Can you walk away under your own power?" Velva places the teapot, cups, and sugar on a tray. That's my cue. I leave my chair and go to her side. It's my job to carry the tray to the little table by the window.

"Until two minutes ago, I thought that's what I was doing." Coming face to face with your own self-delusions is never a pretty prospect, as the knot in my stomach indicates.

"If you truly wanted to leave, wouldn't you just turn in your resignation today?"

"It's more complicated than that."

"Is it?"

Velva slowly sinks back into her chair and smiles with bliss as she settles into the cushions. I pour the tea and hand her the little china cup on its matching saucer.

We both sit quietly for a few minutes as we sip our tea. Dottie mumbles something from her bed, and it blends with the birdsong from the tree outside. Velva had the maintenance men hang several feeders outside her window, and she cajoles and shames the staff into keeping them filled.

"Sometimes things aren't complicated. We just make them that way." Velva looks into her teacup as if the answers to all my questions can be found in its contents. "Honestly, Betsy, what's keeping you from leaving the church?"

I can lie to myself all day long, but lying to Velva is another matter. I grimace. "Because hope won't die. No matter how hard I try to kill it. I keep thinking something will happen to make it all work out somehow."

Velva smiles and sips her tea. "I know, my dear. I know."

Fifty years of waiting for two years of ministry. The longest advent season ever. Velva was woman enough to manage it, but I don't think I am.

"Thank you." I set my cup aside and reach out to squeeze her hand again. "I'd better go."

"You haven't finished your tea."

"That's okay." I get up from the chair and reach over to kiss her papery cheek. "Sometimes it's not the tea you need. It's the tea ceremony."

Velva smiles. And so do I, in spite of my tears.

I return to the church more confused than when I left it. Angelique is waiting to pounce the moment I walk through the office door. She clutches a fistful of pink phone-message slips in her fire-engine-red acrylic talons.

"The Judge called, and he wants to vet your sermon before you preach it Sunday."

"Great. My own personal critique service. What else?"

"Mrs. Tompkins wants you to make a run to Kroger for salad dressings before the next ladies auxiliary meeting."

"I wasn't aware I was her personal shopper as well as her minister. Next?"

"Um, some lawyer. I didn't quite catch his name. He says the Longworths are suing the church over their wedding."

"Suing the church? For what? The wedding was perfect."

"Mrs. Longworth is upset there was a lady minister in all the wedding pictures. Says it ruined the whole thing. She wants money for her pain and suffering."

"Tell her to get in line." I start walking to my office, but Angelique follows. "Don't tell me there's more?" I ask over my shoulder.

"Just one."

I stop and turn. Knowing Angelique's penchant for drama, I'm sure she's saved the best for last.

"Yes?"

"Mavis Carter's son called. She passed away."

"God finally gave in and took her, huh?"

Okay, I know that sounds harsh, but if you'd known Mavis, you wouldn't blame me. Her favorite pastime was causing misery and suffering. Mostly for the ministerial staff at church.

"Her son says the funeral is Saturday at 11:00 a.m."

Smack in the middle of my date with David.

"Who's doing the service?"

"He didn't say. It's at some little country church. Here's the info."

I take the slip of paper from Angelique and stuff it into my purse, and what's left of the Pasta YaYa in my stomach turns to lead. That's one of the realities of ministry. All your best-laid plans count for nothing when duty calls. Normally I'm philosophical about it. Doctors have it worse. But the closer I get to leaving the ministry, the more I resent its demands.

"Okay. I'll adjust my schedule." Don't I always?

Having dropped all the proverbial shoes, Angelique evaporates back to her desk and her nail file. She's supposed to be practicing her keyboarding skills, but I'm not sure she's even figured out how to turn on the computer yet. On the other hand, parishioners love her because she always has time to chat with them.

I head straight for my office and close the door firmly behind me. It's a risk, that closed door. The parishioners of Church of the

Shepherd seem to take it personally if their ministers aren't constantly available. I find this compulsory open-door policy ironic. When exactly am I supposed to have time for prayer and contemplation, not to mention sermon preparation?

Fortunately, my voice mail doesn't contain any more heavy breathing. Just the usual stuff. A salesman from a video company who wants me to buy a series of tapes on dealing with divorce. His take on it is that if the woman would just submit to the man as it says in the Bible, the divorce rate would drop dramatically. I hit the pound key and delete him without further ado.

E-mail is the same old, same old. A few quick notes from friends across the country. Some spam for a service where you can download prefab sermons. And something from David.

My heart picks up its pace.

I double-click, and the message opens. It would be nice if it was a declaration of undying love, but it's a joke he's forwarded to me.

How many women ministers does it take to change a light bulb?

Only one, but if she messes up, they'll never hire another woman to change a light bulb again.

How true.

I click Reply and type in the painful words that delay our bowling date until Saturday afternoon. And, like Scarlett O'Hara, I invoke God as my witness—once I'm out of the church, I will never again let my professional life interfere with my personal life.

Chapter 9

The last place I want to be today is the Mt. Carmel Community Church in Podunk, Tennessee. I'm supposed to be meeting David at the bowling alley. The fact that I'd rather be lacing my feet into stinky bowling shoes tells you how I feel as I race into the tiny parking lot. Of course I ran into a traffic snafu on the way here. The service begins in five minutes, so there's just time to sign the guest book and slip into the back row. I wonder what poor schmuck Mrs. Carter's son roped into doing the service. Thankfully, I'm not the schmuck du jour.

The funeral director, easily identifiable in his dark suit, waits at the entrance and swings the door open for me as I approach.

"Reverend Blessing?"

Uh-oh. I guess my reputation has preceded me. Matt Carter has resented me since I objected to his attempts to get his mother to sign a new will while she was still under the influence of anesthesia.

"Yes, I'm Betsy Blessing."

His furrowed brow relaxes. "I'm Fred Brown. We were worried you weren't going to make it."

A shiver starts at the base of my spine and works its way heavenward. Either this man is the most hospitable funeral-home director in the history of mortuary science, or I've been had.

"Waiting for me?"

He chuckles. "Well, we can't exactly start without you, now can we?"

I will not allow my knees to give way beneath me. My fingers curl around the strap of my purse.

This is what's known in the business as The Irate Relative's Revenge. And here I thought I'd learned all the tricks. Matt Carter made a practice of ignoring the calling cards I left when his mom was out of it and then telling her the "lady preacher" never bothered to visit. As I mentioned, he did his best to change his mother's will when he found out the church was among the beneficiaries. But hood-winking the preacher at the funeral service is a new low. How many people would be willing to ruin their mother's memorial service to get payback on the preacher?

I swallow, blink twice, and smile. "So sorry. There was a wreck on Charlotte Pike." I have nothing with me. No notes. No Bible. Just a head full of Scripture and a depressing familiarity with funeral liturgy. Fortunately, in our denomination, when it comes to funerals, we make it up as we go along. But we usually make it up the night before instead of on the spot.

The taped organ music is wailing "The Old Rugged Cross" as the funeral director, relieved to have lassoed a pastor for the service, leads me up the aisle of the church to the thronelike chair behind the podium. It's ironic they give the best chair to the one person who will be standing for almost the entire service. For the moment, though, I'm grateful for the next three minutes I'll have in that chair to collect myself and plan Mavis Carter's funeral.

Deep breaths. Deep breaths. My insides rumble ominously, not liking the sudden onset of adrenaline pumping through my veins.

All too soon the tape shuts off with an audible *click,* and silence descends. I rise and step to the podium to look out on the twelve folks scattered among the pews. A lifetime of meanness, and the old biddy still managed to draw a dozen people to her service. Nice work, Mavis. Mrs. Tompkins and The Judge, our professional mourners from Church of the Shepherd, are seated together on the second row, no doubt rubbing their hands together in glee at my situation.

"Friends, we are gathered here in the sight of God, to celebrate the life of Mavis Jewel Carter…"

So far, so good. I can reel off the introductory remarks by heart. Or at least by mouth, even if my heart's not in it. Which it isn't; not today. Resentment, frustration, irritation—did you know sometimes that's what ministers are feeling when they're standing up in front of you preaching about the love of God? Fortunately for those of us of the clerical persuasion, God can use us anyway—even when we're as recalcitrant as a six-year-old being forced to swallow medicine.

The Scripture readings flow as easily as the introduction. The "in my father's house are many rooms" part of John 14. A bit from Revelation about no more crying and God wiping away every tear, not that anyone here is shedding a tear for Mavis, the old harridan. Even Mrs. Tompkins and The Judge aren't that good at playacting.

"Even as we come together to mourn," I say, "we also gather to celebrate the gift of life that comes from God—"

And then, as I'm mouthing the words, something twists in my midsection. The twist that happens from time to time when I'm doing my thing in the pulpit. One moment I'm a competent-if-uninspired preacher, and then—grace happens. The truth of the words I'm saying resonates through me, and suddenly my voice is not my own. Is this how all those Old Testament prophets felt? Maybe that's why they compared their calls to having a burning coal pressed to their lips.

The prayer flows so easily I'm practically singing it. This is why I chose ministry in the first place, this experience of leading and yet being led. "Use these moments of remembrance, O God, to open our hearts to you. Amen."

I look out at the dozen mourners to see if they can tell the difference. Do they know the minister is having a "moment"? Hard to tell. Mavis's son is scowling. Guess he hasn't caught on to the spiritual depth I've tapped into. One older woman with bluish hair and Coke-bottle glasses is blowing her nose, but that's not unusual in Middle Tennessee, where allergy season lasts from January to December. Mrs. Tompkins never changes her expression, and The Judge is using the end of his penknife to clean under his fingernails.

The eulogy presents a bigger challenge. My mother raised me to believe that if you can't say anything nice, you shouldn't say anything at all. That dictum doesn't apply when you're delivering the eulogy of a woman who didn't like anyone and who wasn't liked by anyone in return.

"Mavis Carter was faithful to her church…" Okay, that'll work. She was faithful to tormenting her fellow parishioners. But that one statement's not going to be enough. I rack my brain for some memory, however fleeting, of Mavis engaging in any act of compassion or genuine feeling.

For several long moments, the chapel is dead silent. No pun intended.

And I realize I can't talk for the next ten minutes about Mavis. Not without exposing her, me, and Church of the Shepherd. So instead of a eulogy, I say what I know to be true. I talk about the gift God gives to us when we find a community of faith. How much it means to be part of one, even under the worst of circumstances. How we struggle. How we fail. How we shine. In the midst of my eloquent delivery, I realize this is my chance to address Mrs. Tompkins and The Judge when they have no chance for rebuttal. So I say everything I've always wanted to say about church life. How we mistake showing up for being faithful. How power in church should be used to build one another up, not tear one another down. And how our life together in churches ought to be measured by a standard of love, not a standard of condemnation.

At the end, I say a brief prayer and sit back down on the preacher throne.

The funeral director looks shell-shocked. Matt Carter has steam coming out of his ears, but, then, when doesn't he? The Judge has put away his penknife, and Mrs. Tompkins is pursing her lips as if she's sucking the world's sourest lemon.

And I realize that in dying, Mavis Carter may have finally contributed to the betterment of her church.

Preaching a funeral service on no notice turns out to be far easier than meeting David that afternoon. Normally after I do a funeral, I receive an honorarium from the family. It's not usually a large amount, but in a low-paying profession like the ministry, it's always a blessing. I give ten percent to the church, and then I use the rest to splurge on fun things like rent and groceries. Today, to no one's surprise, I receive no honorarium. In fact, Matt Carter refuses to speak to me after the service.

So I arrive at the bowling alley later than originally planned. We're lucky to get a lane. The folks in the Saturday-afternoon leagues are filing in, and a smoky haze drifts over the well. The sharp crack of pins against the hardwood and the jeers and cheers of serious bowlers punctuate the eighties rock music blaring from overhead speakers. The pungent aroma of stale beer and greasy chili dogs assures me that David will be in hog heaven.

In fact, he's already there and looks as if he has been for some time. I stop at the top of the steps to admire his form. I mean his bowling form! He looks so competent as he squares up to the lane, strides forward while arching his left arm back, and then in a pretzely kind of way, twists his body and releases the ball with swift, deadly accuracy.

The pins at the end of his lane crack with a satisfying resonance. His spine straightens, and the fist at his side clenches with satisfaction. He's not the type to pump his fist or high-five, my David. Just that clenching of his fingers to show his satisfaction with what he's done. And the fact that I know the meaning of that gesture speaks of an intimacy born of long years of friendship. Can I really risk that for a little romance?

David turns, sees me, and smiles sheepishly. "I couldn't wait," he confesses, nodding toward the lane. His ball reappears in the return with a hiss and a thump.

I look at him, standing there in jeans and a long-sleeved Rugby shirt, and to me he looks better than James Bond in a tux. And I know I'm a goner. Whatever happens, I can't go back to pretending he's only my friend.

"Got your shoes?" he asks.

Weakly, I hold up the fashion-challenged green and red lace-ups.

"Great." His smile takes on a teasing slant. "I knew you'd love the shoes."

How can I not laugh and smile back? I sink into one of the plastic chairs and change my shoes while David looks for a ball I can actually lift. The only bowling balls I can use are the kid-size ones, but my fingers don't always fit into the holes. By the time I'm laced up and ready to go, David's secured a lightweight ball that will work.

"You go first," I suggest, and he agrees. He bowls a strike and tries not to look too triumphant.

"Come on, Betz. Your turn."

I'd rather have lunch with Edna Tompkins at a Daughters of the Confederacy meeting where they discover I'm a Yankee by birth. But I'm also no coward. So I grab the ball, march to the little arrows on the floor, and try to imitate what David did. Only I'm right-handed instead of left, and my ball doesn't quite fly from my hand with the precision of a cruise missile as his does. Instead, it drops to the lane with a *thunk!* and bounces into the gutter.

My shoulders slump, and I decide to pout. "Can we get them to put the gutter guards up?"

David looks horrified. "Gutter guards are for kiddie birthday parties." He frowns for a moment. "Okay, let's try this." He grabs my ball from the return and steps up to join me on the platform. "You just need to quit overthinking it and let your natural rhythm take over."

Natural rhythm? The only thing rhythmic about me is the accelerated pounding of my heart when David spins me to face the lane and stands close behind me, one hand on my left shoulder and the other on my right arm just above my wrist. The weight of the bowling ball in my hand is nothing compared to the sudden leadenness of my feet.

"Let me guide you," he says in my ear, and his breath tickles. "Okay, now take three steps and then release."

Steps where? Release what? My brain is mush, and my body is completely liquid. David's hands propel me forward, and I scramble not to trip over my own feet. The ball drops from my fingers and almost lands on my toes. It rolls like a tortoise up the lane, and for a blissful eternity I stand there watching it with David pressed against my back. I can feel his breath as clearly as my own. We're frozen in time, or at least the time it takes my pathetically thrown ball to meander to the end of the lane. It delicately brushes against a pin, which slowly tips over like a drunk slithering to the floor.

David stiffens and then steps away. "Well, that's an improvement," he mutters as he walks toward the scorer's table. His words are like a razor across my soul, even though I'm sure he didn't intend me to hear them.

I join him at the table, wedging myself between the chair and the sharp Formica edge. "David, if you'd rather, I can just watch you bowl." The tension between us is as thick as the smoky haze.

"Don't be ridiculous." He punches my score into the computer without looking at me. "I never bowl alone."

"Me neither," I say, deadpan.

He laughs and slumps back in his seat. Just like that, the tension diffuses, and it's simply me and David hanging out, like always.

Ten frames, then ten more. Time flies. David consumes two chili dogs and, ever mindful of my Weight Watchers points, I settle for diet soda.

We're shucking our rented shoes when David suddenly turns serious. "Betz, are you okay?"

We've avoided talking about my decision to accept the interim senior-minister position, but clearly it's the elephant in the living room. Or bowling alley, as the case may be.

"I guess."

"I know you wanted me to be more excited for you."

My chest tightens. "Yeah, I did. But it's okay."

David reaches over and squeezes my hand. "Not really. That's why I asked if you're okay."

It's the moment. It's the absolutely right time to broach the subject of my newly discovered feelings for him. I take the deepest breath ever. "It's just that…"

I can't go on. A long silence.

"Just that what?"

I study my socks, not daring to look at him. "It's not really about the church. It's more about me."

"Yeah?" He's studying me, not his socks. I both love and fear being the focus of David's scrutiny.

"I guess you could say I've been lonely lately."

Okay, that'll work as an entrée.

"What about that guy?" He's suddenly focused on unlacing his shoes.

"That guy?"

"From Valentine's Day. The one who picked you up that night you looked so…" He doesn't finish the sentence. He doesn't have to. *Weird* was, I believe, his exact word for my appearance on that occasion.

"Oh, James. That was just LaRonda's brother. He's a friend."

"I'm a friend, and you never dress like that when we do stuff together." He actually sounds the slightest bit jealous.

"I was just trying out the new me. From the makeover."

He slips from the bowling shoes to his Merrells, flipping one shoe in his hand like Mister Rogers. "Betz, there's nothing wrong with the old you."

No, nothing at all. Except that the old Betsy can't attract the one man she wants to notice her as more than a friend.

"The male population of Nashville would not seem to agree with you on that issue."

"You don't need a man. You just need a friend."

"I have plenty of friends, thanks."

Tell him, tell him, tell him.

Suddenly, David snaps his fingers. "I know what you need."

My heart leaps. "Yeah?"

He stands up, bowling shoes in hand. "Come on."

Now he's a man on a mission. He grabs my hand and tows me out of the bowling alley, stopping only long enough to turn in our shoes. We head for the Volvo, and he opens the passenger door. "Get in."

"What about my car?"

"We'll come back for it. First, we're going to solve your problem."

My heart starts knocking louder than the Volvo's engine. I didn't even have to say the words! David has figured it out. Where are we going? Back to his place? to my place?

He pulls out of the parking lot. "Where are we going?" I ask.

He grins at me from the driver's seat. "You'll see."

A fish. The man took me to PETsMART and bought me a fish. A betta, to be exact. A fish that can't be put in the same tank with any others because it will attack and kill them.

"Now you won't be lonely." David's so pleased with himself I can't bear to rain on his parade. He sprang for the whole thing—the bowl, the food, the gravel, and, yes, the fish.

"How could I be when I have Simon Peter for company?" My smile feels as watery as the fishbowl is going to be when I get home and fill it up. Only David could buy me a fish and name it after the world's most famous fisherman.

David takes me back to the bowling alley and shifts all of Simon's paraphernalia to my car.

"Hot date tonight?" David asks when he hugs me good-bye. I'm too distracted by the feel of his arms around me to answer immediately.

"Hmm. Oh, date? No. Not unless you count Simon here." I swallow and force myself to ask the fateful question. "How about you and the new lady?"

A shadow passes over his face. "We're going to the movies."

I can't prevent the sting I feel. I can't make myself indifferent to how much it hurts to hear that while I'm good enough for Saturday afternoon, I'm not good enough for Saturday night.

David shifts from one foot to the other. "But I'm telling her absolutely no ice cream afterward. That's your territory."

So what? New Girl doesn't need ice cream. She'll probably get something far sweeter on her lips by the end of the evening.

"I'll hold you to that."

"You'd better."

And then the weirdest thing happens. Neither of us leaves. We're just standing there in the parking lot of Melrose Lanes, a few inches apart, as traffic whizzes by on Franklin Road.

I try to think of something, anything to fill the silence. "Hey, do you still have that tape of the makeover segment?" I ask. "My mom wants to see it. She says it will give her hope I may one day provide her with grandchildren."

Oddly enough, David turns a light shade of pink. "Um, actually, I think I erased it."

"Oh." I think I swallowed one of the bowling balls because it feels as if one has taken up residence in my stomach. Even at my cosmetological best, I'm apparently not worth a second look.

"Sorry," he mumbles, but he doesn't sound overly apologetic.

There's another long silence while even more traffic whizzes by. Finally, David releases us from the spell. "Well, good luck with your sermon tomorrow."

"Thanks. You, too."

And then he turns away. Simon Peter and I watch David get into his car and drive off. And then we do the same. Because no matter how much it hurts, I have to keep moving. I have a fish to care for.

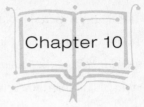

Chapter 10

Ever since I became a minister, my heart skips a beat every time the phone rings. Most of the time it turns out to be an ordinary phone call, not a crisis. It's my mom with her biweekly nag about my lack of a boyfriend or LaRonda wanting to bounce part of her sermon off me. Or Edna Tompkins calls to see if I've run the latest errand she's dreamed up for me. Usually, I get nervous for nothing.

But when the phone rings on Saturday night, it's never good. I'm settled into the cushions of my Salvation Army couch watching reruns of *Law and Order* when the phone rings, and I know my evening is about to take a departure from its expected course.

"Reverend Blessing? This is the emergency room at Vanderbilt Hospital. We have a Velva Brown here who asked that we call you."

The M&M's I've been binging on coalesce into a lump in my stomach. I thought the worst thing that could happen tonight would be David out on a date with another woman.

"What happened?"

"She lost consciousness and fell. We're running some tests, but it doesn't look good."

Of course it doesn't look good. The woman is ninety-four. Falling is not exactly a recreational activity at her age. But I refuse to believe that anything is going to happen to her. Not to Velva.

"I'll be right there."

I don't care that my hair is sticking up in three directions or that I'm wearing my tackiest sweats. I grab the car keys and my purse from the table beside the door and race into the night.

The emergency room is the great leveler of the human race. Rich, poor, black, white, English as a first language, and English as a second. Knife wounds, weed-whacker mishaps, flu, and broken bones. Everyone here is suffering.

After passing through the metal detector, I check in at the desk. The words, "I'm looking for one of my parishioners" are the universal pass code to get beyond the waiting room.

Velva's in one of the treatment bays with a curtain pulled partially around the bed. I wince at the sight of her hooked up to multiple monitors, an IV tube attached to her hand. The worst thing is that they've had to intubate her. An oxygen mask covers her face, and she's unconscious.

It hurts so much. I know I'm supposed to be professional and maintain my equanimity, but this is my Velva. I move to the side of the bed opposite the IV so I can take her free hand. Her fingers are cool and stiff in mine.

She rouses at the pressure of my fingers. Her eyes flicker open, and I realize she's regaining consciousness. She pulls her hand away to reach for the oxygen mask and the plastic tubing they've run down her throat.

"No, Velva. You can't." I grab her other hand and hold it in mine. Her eyes are two pools of pain. "I'll get the nurse."

But before I can call for help, the nurse is there. She whisks the curtain back with no-nonsense efficiency and examines the mysterious tubes and dials on the IV stand. "She's a tough one to keep under. Is this your grandmother?"

"No. I'm her pastor."

The nurse purses her lips. I don't have the time or the inclination to take umbrage at her disapproval of my profession. She can purse all she wants as long as she keeps Velva from pulling that tube out of her throat.

"Is she going to be okay?"

"I'm afraid I can't tell you that." The nurse's hair is slicked back into a merciless ponytail, but she's about twenty years too old to have any hope of the hairstyle making her look younger. "HIPAA, you know."

I'd like to get my hands around the throats of the fools who wrote the so-called Health Insurance Portability and Accountability Act, the new federal guidelines for sharing patient information. It's hard to get permission to disclose medical information from a sedated woman who's got a tube shoved down her throat.

"Please. I won't say you told me anything."

The nurse takes pity on me, perhaps because my hair actually looks worse than hers. She glances back over her shoulder to see if anyone is listening. And then in a conspiratorial whisper, she says, "We're waiting for the results of the MRI. She's having TIAs, and her hip may be broken."

She confides the information as if she's telling me the best place to score heroin, but I don't care. It's so unfair. A broken hip at Velva's age can be deadly, and the TIAs, or ministrokes, mean she'll only be that much more unsteady if she does manage to get back on her feet.

The human body doesn't give way with dignity or ease. It's as if Velva's body is getting revenge for having been kept alive so long.

"Can you give her something to put her back to sleep?"

The nurse scowls. "Gee, why didn't I think of that?"

I know the woman's tired. She works long hours, and patients generally give her the same kind of trouble parishioners give me. But Christian forgiveness is not exactly what's flowing through my veins right now.

"Just help her. Please."

She does. After five more minutes of struggle, some doctor authorizes an increase in the medication. Velva slips into a chemically induced sleep. The ER buzzes around me, a typical Saturday-night festival of gunshot wounds, vomiting teenagers, and wailing mothers. I pull up a rolling stool and claim my spot by Velva's bed. The staff can shoot me as many dirty looks as they like. I'm not going anywhere.

Around 1:00 a.m., two orderlies arrive to move Velva to a regular room. She's been admitted to the hospital. At 2:00 a.m., the floor nurse orders me out of the room and tells me to come back tomorrow. At 3:00 a.m., at home in my own bed, I drift off to sleep, with a vague remembrance that I have to preach in the morning.

The alarm didn't go off. I can't believe this. Why in heaven's name didn't the alarm go off?

I scramble from my bed forty minutes before the early service at Church of the Shepherd is scheduled to begin. I'd planned to spend my Saturday night carefully laying out my clothes, pampering myself with a bubble bath and a loofah, and going over my sermon. Instead, I spent it in the ER, and now I'm flying around my bedroom, digging out my black pumps from under the bed, and yanking my funeral suit from the overstuffed closet. My shower lasts approximately thirty seconds, and there's no time for six styling gels and a straightening iron to achieve my hottie hairstyle. Instead I let my curls go wild. There's not even time for coffee. I'll have to make do with the battery acid they serve in the fellowship hall.

My car rolls into the parking lot with fifteen minutes to spare. I clutch my sermon manuscript in my hand and race to the sanctuary to make sure the deacons remembered to prepare Communion and to do a sound check on the mikes. The silver trays rest reassuringly atop the communion table, and for once the microphones have decided to abandon their fondness for feedback. I fling my sermon manuscript onto the pulpit and make a mad dash to the sacristy for my robe.

Back in the sanctuary, I switch into minister mode. "Good morning. Good morning." The early service file in, and I make the rounds, greeting each of them. It's the golf-and-Depends crowd at this service, all thirty or so parishioners in a sanctuary that will easily hold five hundred people. You would think they'd all sit at the front, huddled together against the vast emptiness of the arched ceiling and the echo of the stone walls, but no. They space themselves evenly throughout the pews as if they're afraid of catching a disease should they come into close contact with one another.

On my second Sunday here, I had the brilliant idea of roping off the back half of the sanctuary for the early service. I couldn't believe no one had hit on this strategy before. Dr. Black smiled and nodded at me in an indulgent fashion, and I soon discovered the reason for his amusement. As the parishioners came down the aisle, they simply lifted the ropes, ducked under them, and settled into their accustomed places.

Mr. and Mrs. Christopher have claimed their usual spots on the back row in the corner. After the service they'll both complain that they couldn't hear the sermon. It will be all I can do not to suggest in a catty manner that perhaps if they sat closer to the front, they might improve the odds of their hearing aids picking up some sound.

The Judge appears in the narthex and, with all the pomp and circumstance of his former office, makes his way down the aisle to his place in the second pew. He has no reservations about sitting right under the preacher's nose. Most of the time when I preach, I expect to look up at the end of the sermon and see him holding a scorecard. Seven out of ten if I've done really well. Lower if I've stumbled.

I'm not ready, but it's time for the service to start. The organist sounds the chimes, and I step up to my seat on the chancel. There's no procession at this service, no choir in robes. Just the lonely sound of the organ echoing off the mostly empty pews.

We sing only one verse of the opening hymn at this service, and the prayer and Scripture reading are brief. I stand to ascend the pulpit, and when I look down at my feet, I realize I'm wearing one black pump and one navy one.

Too late I realize I forgot to put my customary cup of water on the little ledge below the lectern. Suddenly my throat feels dry. I bite my tongue to get the saliva flowing. But I bite a little too hard and taste the sharp tang of blood in my mouth.

Just breathe. Inhale peace. Exhale joy.

I place my hands on either side of the pulpit, cling for dear life, and open my mouth to begin.

Only there's a slight problem. My sermon manuscript is gone. Not again.

Panic surges through me, and I feel like one of Pharaoh's charioteers watching the inevitable wall of water loom over me.

"Good morning." I smile brightly to compensate for my panic. The congregants mumble back something that might be construed as a reply, but it sounds more like the three witches in Macbeth murmuring among themselves.

I search my brain, trying to remember the opening lines of my sermon. That's another thing I normally do on Saturday night—memorize the first thirty seconds of the sermon. I can't think of anything. What do I say? A joke. That's it. I'll tell that joke David sent me.

"How many women ministers does it take to change a light bulb?" I even deliver the punch line with a straight face.

No one laughs. In fact, the congregation looks at me as if I've just flipped my skirt up over my head. It feels that way to me, too.

In desperation I try another joke. One about Saint Peter and the Pearly Gates, but that one, too, sinks like a stone. And then my throat closes up, and I feel it coming. A coughing fit.

Relax. Breathe. Or, as an alternative, cough as if you've been condemned to a TB ward. This appears to be my choice.

It goes on forever, and each raspy hack echoes off the cold stone of the sanctuary walls. My eyes cross and water. There's probably something coming out of my nose. I can't stop.

"Excuse me," I choke out, and in humiliation, I step out of the pulpit. I'm headed for the water fountain, when I hear a resounding *thunk!* I look down at the second pew, and The Judge has disappeared. No, not disappeared. He's collapsed. Fallen over onto his side. Oh, heavens. He's having a heart attack.

At the late service I'd have my pick of a cardiologist, an internist, and an ER doctor. But this early I'm limited to a dentist and a podiatrist. "Call 911," the dentist shouts, and I fly down the chancel steps, out the side door, and to the nearest telephone.

I fling open the door to the sacristy. To my surprise, Edna Tompkins is there. She jumps when I enter. Her cheeks are flushed.

"911," I gasp.

"What?"

"The Judge! 911."

She stares at me blankly, so I shove past her and dive for the phone. You always see people on television calling the emergency number, but I've never done it before myself. My damp hands fumble with the buttons, and the receiver slips in my fingers.

"911 operator. What is the nature of your emergency?"

"I need an ambulance. Church of the Shepherd on Broadway. The sanctuary."

"I'm sorry. Can you hold, please?"

Hold? *Can I hold?* The operator doesn't wait for an answer. The line goes silent.

This is not how it works on television. About that time the sacristy door swings open behind me. When I turn around, the dentist is there, looking grave. Oh, heavens. I've killed The Judge. Or at least let him expire on my watch. They'll fire me for sure.

"It's okay, Betsy," the dentist says. "We don't need the ambulance."

My heart drops to my mismatched pumps. "Should I call the coroner?"

He smiles. "Not unless he wants to play a round of golf with the deceased."

"What?"

I charge past him, back into the sanctuary. Sure enough, The Judge is sitting up and laughing with the podiatrist. His shoulders and belly shake in unison. The dentist is right behind me.

"It wasn't a heart attack after all."

"What happened?"

"A common Sunday-morning malady. He fell asleep during the sermon."

My sermon manuscript never does turn up, but we spend the time allotted for the sermon telling the paramedics we don't need them after all, so no one ever knows I didn't have anything to say. Fortunately, the rest of the service proves uneventful. During the Sunday-school hour, I dash to my office and print off another copy of my sermon, so the late service goes off without a hitch. I spend the afternoon in the ICU waiting room at the hospital, visiting Velva for fifteen minutes every two hours. She's still in a medically induced coma, but at least she's stabilized. I leave the hospital at suppertime and go home to collapse.

Monday morning turns out to be no better than Sunday. I go to the office to play catch-up, even though it's technically my day off. Velva's still medically critical, and Mrs. Tompkins is still critical verbally. She turns up in my office bright and early, demanding an immediate count of the offering. She's heard a rumor that someone's been skimming the cash out of the plates.

"I feel sure, Edna, that the cash box in the sacristy is secure. We've used that system for years, and it's never been a problem. Only the church treasurer and the money counters have a key."

Mrs. Tompkins purses her lips, just like the nurse in the ER. "Then there's only one explanation. The offering is down because people don't like a woman in the pulpit. You should resign now before you destroy this church."

I think about suggesting there might be a direct correlation between the offering sliding and the fact that Edna's so unhappy with my new role. But Edna's money would amount to far more than the bills that get slipped in the plate each week. You know, even Jesus would have a hard time loving this woman. But he would do it, wouldn't he? I sigh, and she shoots me a dark look.

"Is it too much for you, Betsy? I thought it would be."

I can't say, "No, honey; *you're* what's too much." Instead, I say, "If there is a problem with the offering, I imagine it has more to do with normal giving cycles than with a revolt among the parishioners. Unless you know something I don't."

Mrs. Tompkins sniffs. "Well, we'll see about that. I'm going to have to call an emergency meeting of the personnel committee. We're in difficult enough financial straits, what with having to pay Dr. Black through the end of the year. We can't jeopardize the financial health of the church."

I roll a pencil between my fingers. "Please do call the meeting. I'm sure the more minds we put to work on this problem, the sooner we'll resolve it." Besides, I want some witnesses to any further conversation I have with Edna about the matter.

"Fine. I will." She jumps to her feet with amazing alacrity for a senior citizen and stomps out of my office. I lean back in my chair and close my eyes.

"Reverend Blessing?"

I'm forced to reopen my eyes. Angelique's in the doorway, a frown on her face. She's holding another white florist's box at arm's length, as if it might contaminate her if she gets too close. "Here's another one." She walks over and drops the box on my desk.

"Great." Maybe Edna Tompkins is right. Maybe people are so outraged by my presence in the pulpit, even if it's temporary, that they would rather destroy their church. Maybe they're all like Matt Carter. Or the guy who's sending me the dead flowers. Maybe I'm deluding myself to think this can even be a temporary solution. Why don't I just give up and go work for a temp agency typing and filing until law school starts?

Once again I slip the ribbon from the box and lift the lid. I pull back the tissue paper, and, sure enough, a dozen more dead roses. You know, the first time had real shock value. This go-round, it just seems old hat.

"Toss 'em, Angie." I push the box back toward her.

Angelique makes a small moue of charming distaste that might work on most men in America but is lost on a tired, irritated female minister. With a sigh of resignation, she picks up the box as if it's a dead mouse and departs.

I reach over, open my lower-right desk drawer, and paw through the contents. Why did I ever clean out my candy stash? Health, schmealth. I should have foreseen an emergency like this. Maybe there's something I missed. An aged chocolate kiss from the Valentine's party we threw for the residents at Hillsboro Health Care, or a couple of stale jellybeans from last year's Easter-egg hunt. Alas, the only thing left in the drawer is soy nuts and sugarless gum. I unwrap a piece of the gum and plop it into my mouth, all the while knowing it won't satisfy my craving. Neither would the chocolate, actually, but at least I'd get a nice sugar rush to dull the pain.

The one bright spot in my day occurs when David calls.

"Hey, Blessing. What's happening?"

"Nothing. Everything." I tell him about the dead roses. About how worried I am for Velva. About the Judge's miraculous resurrection.

"Just the usual, huh?"

"Yeah." I'm grateful to pour it all out to someone who just listens.

Finally, when I'm done, he says, "Thanks for the chili dogs, by the way."

At least someone is being nice to me today. "My pleasure. I hope it was worth the sacrifice of my feet. I'm checking them daily for fungus."

David laughs that nice, rich laugh of his that's like the chocolate I'm craving. I savor it, letting it roll over me, fill me. It's more satisfying than anything I could ever keep in my desk drawer.

"What are you doing for dinner?" David asks. His innocent question causes my heart to shift into overdrive.

"I need to check on Velva, but after that I'm free. Committee meetings aren't until next Monday night."

Like David's laugh and a good piece of chocolate, a free weeknight is also to be savored. Hmm. Maybe my evening could combine all three? Bliss.

David clears his throat. "Why don't you come over, and I'll cook you something?"

Ack! Okay, David is fabulous, but his idea of a homemade meal is Hamburger Helper and a can of green beans. Think, Blessing. You want to move your relationship with this man to the next level. What would a normal woman do? Or, considering that you've never been a normal woman, what would a smart woman do?

"I'll cook." The words tumble out of my mouth before they can be sensibly restrained.

"Excellent. It's been awhile since I had Steak à la Betsy."

Steak? I don't remember offering steak. But David loves it, and truthfully, I like making it for him. Before, when David sat at my dining-room table making appreciative noises about my cooking, I always felt the satisfaction one finds when feeding a starving stray. Somehow, though, I think my satisfaction tonight will be of a different variety.

"All right, mooch. I'll see you at seven o'clock."

"I'll bring dessert."

"Make it chocolate."

"Yes ma'am. I have a surprise for you too."

"I've had enough surprises for one week."

"You'll like this one. You'll see."

I hang up and place the receiver softly in its cradle. I can deal with Mrs. Tompkins and the personnel committee. I can even manage my worry about Velva. I can move the sanctuary three feet to the left if necessary, or do just about any other impossible task. I can do it all, if I can have dinner with David. Maybe the fish was just a fluke. Maybe he's finally catching on to what I haven't been able to say.

Chapter 11

"Betsy? It's Edna Tompkins. I've scheduled the emergency meeting of the personnel committee for five o'clock today." *Click.* The voice message wastes no time, words, or personal warmth.

No, no, no! I ran to Kroger on my lunch hour and bought steaks, baking potatoes, and asparagus. I even dashed into Pier 1 for a few candles. With careful planning I was going to have time to soak in a bubble bath for half an hour before grilling the steaks.

I'm going to be optimistic and believe that I can bulldoze the personnel committee into the shortest meeting in the history of all personnel committees everywhere.

Of course, five o'clock comes all too soon and not soon enough. This time when I enter the boardroom, I'm the first one there, and I take advantage of that fact. I choose the chair at the head of the table. I plan to run this meeting, not be run over by it.

The Judge arrives promptly, as do Sweet Marjorie Cline, Ed the Engineer, and Gus Winston, the Barney Fife–like chair of stewardship. The only one missing is Edna, who called the meeting in the first place.

For ten minutes we exchange pleasantries. The Judge makes no mention of his Sunday-morning nap, and neither do I. Like any dysfunctional family, we simply refuse to acknowledge what we don't want to deal with. He does commend me for my words at Mavis

Carter's funeral. "You should spend as much time on your sermon preparation as you did on that funeral homily."

For the next ten minutes, we speculate about the weather and whether spring will arrive early this year. Still no sign of Edna. It's as if she knows I'm desperate to get out of here tonight and is tardy just to spite me. Finally, half an hour after our intended start time, she appears in the doorway of the boardroom.

"Sorry to be late." She brandishes a platter covered with aluminum foil. "I had to wait for the blondies to come out of the oven."

Edna Tompkins is famous for her butterscotch brownies. She's also famous for commenting on any excess pounds she perceives on my person.

"Betsy?" She smiles so sweetly that even I am almost lulled into forgiving her. "Could you get the coffee?"

Something in me snaps like a dry twig beneath a sturdy hiking boot. I'm surprised no one else can hear it. My mouth goes dry, and my pulse picks up. Tears sting my eyes, but I refuse to cry. The people at this table would see it as a sign of weakness, not the product of frustration.

"No, Edna, I'm afraid I can't get the coffee. This meeting is late already, and I have to be out of here by six."

Marjorie Cline gasps. The Judge scowls. Ed shifts uncomfortably in his chair, and Gus fiddles with his bow tie. Not only have I contradicted Edna, I've had the temerity to call her by her first name. Perhaps that snapping sound I heard was the steeple splitting down the middle after all. Jesus may come down in a cloud of glory next.

"But we have to have coffee with the blondies." For the first time in the six months I've known her, Edna looks baffled.

"Then feel free to make some. In the meantime, I'm going to ask Ed to call this meeting to order."

I can see her sugar-coating dissolve around her. Her face shrivels. "I called this meeting. I have to be here."

I wave my hand at an empty chair. "Then feel free to have a seat."

"I will." Her glare could cut diamonds. She takes the chair next to me, and I nod to Ed.

He clears his throat as if there's a significant obstruction lodged there. Finally, after some serious hacking, he finds his voice.

"We have a confirmed report from the money counters that the cash offering is down significantly the past two weeks. The question is, should we be concerned about theft, or is it simply a normal fluctuation?"

Edna defiantly unwraps the foil from the blondies and shoves the platter toward The Judge. "People are clearly expressing their displeasure with Betsy's presence in the pulpit. We have to do something now before she cripples the church financially."

Gus tugs harder at his bow tie. "I hate to disagree, Edna, but I'm not ready to leap to that conclusion. Perhaps we could devise some way to monitor the cash box in the sacristy. As a precaution. But I'm inclined to take a wait-and-see approach."

Marjorie takes a blondie as the platter passes by. "I can't believe people would withhold their offering because of Betsy. She's such a sweet girl." She smiles and then closes her eyes in reverence while she takes a bite of the blondie.

I'm twitching in my chair. How did a problem with the offering become a discussion about my competence or popularity? Strike that. I know how. Edna is the master of bait and switch. "I like Gus's idea of monitoring the cash box, but I'm willing to bet it's simply a timing issue. We've had a number of folks out of town the past two weeks. And there has been some restlessness because of Dr. Black's abrupt departure. We just need to give it time."

Ed the Engineer nods. "I agree. Shall we vote?"

Before Edna can object, he's taking a vote. She's the lone holdout against the wait-and-see approach, so the motion carries. It's almost six o'clock, and David will be at my house in an hour. It will take the potatoes at least that long to bake. And for me to work up my courage yet again.

"Shall we adjourn, then?" Like a farmer's wife with the hens, I shoo the committee from the room. I make a quick dash to my office and grab my purse from my desk drawer. With a quick wave to the night custodian, I dash to my car.

There's no time for a luxurious soak in a scented bubble bath. In fact, there's barely time to shuck my hose and sensible pumps and pull on jeans and a T-shirt. I shove the potatoes in the oven with alacrity and prep the asparagus. Then I realize I've forgotten to start the coals. Drat. And why did I agree to grill out in February? It's freezing. Fifteen minutes later I reek of lighter fluid, but the grill is going. I'm getting more nervous with each passing minute, and it shows in my fumbling fingers as they try to stuff the filets with blue cheese and pesto.

Five minutes to seven. I dart out into the cold to fling the steaks on the grill, then race around my living room lighting candles and stuffing old newspapers, catalogs, and library books underneath the couch and behind the stereo speakers. No, that's too neat. It looks like I've made an effort. I dig yesterday's paper out from under the couch and toss it onto my surfboard-shaped coffee table, a seventies relic I picked up for ten dollars at an estate sale.

David knocks punctually at seven o'clock. He's right on time, a personality trait I usually adore, but it doesn't serve me well tonight.

I take a quick look out the peephole and see two people standing on my porch. David, and a blonde who looks to be about sixteen. This is my surprise? He brought one of the kids from his youth group?

I open the door as if I'm about to encounter a couple of Jehovah's Witnesses. Like the ones who, when I introduced myself as the Reverend Betsy Blessing, asked me without batting an eyelash if I'd been saved.

"Hey, Betz." David is all smiles, and the girl with him is all hair.

"Hey." I manage to smile with just a touch of quizzical charm.

"Here's your surprise." David puts his arm around the girl, and they step through the doorway.

"My surprise?"

David has the grace to look a little sheepish. "I told you on the phone I had a surprise for you."

"Oh yeah. That's right." I stick my hand forward. "Hi. I'm Betsy."

The next thing I know the blonde flings herself at me and hugs me like a druid bonding with a tree. "Oh, Betsy, I'm so glad to finally meet you. David's told me *tons* about you."

I wipe hair out of my face and disengage myself as quickly as possible. "Really?" I shoot David my dirtiest look. "Sometimes he can forget to mention the most important things."

The blonde giggles. "He can, can't he?" She looks at him adoringly and tosses her hair. "I'll fix that, though."

Fix it? And since when do youth-group members look at their ministers like that?

David's gone a bit pink about the ears and neck. "Betsy, this is Cali."

"Cali?"

She laughs, and the sound resembles a very high-strung donkey. "Cali. Short for California. That's where I'm from."

At that moment a familiar odor reaches my nose.

"The steaks!"

I race from the living room, through the kitchen, and onto the small patio in the backyard. Shoot! The steaks are burning. With a quick twist of the barbecue fork, I flip the meat.

And then I just stand there for a moment in the cold night air.

I'm no fool. I know that girl's not a member of David's youth group. I know he's had a couple of dates lately. And I know I'm a coward with a pathetic lack of timing.

Deep breaths. More deep breaths.

I have to go back in there and face them. Or I could just make a run for it. Out the back gate and from there to freedom.

"Do you need any help?" The screen door bangs, and the perky, giggly voice behind me is like fingernails on a chalkboard.

I turn with the world's most fake smile pasted on my face. "No, just a minor meat emergency. Thanks, though."

"Sure."

I look back down at the grill. Two steaks. Two potatoes. Asparagus for two. Only the two for dinner tonight are David and Cali. Not David and Betsy.

"Why don't you and David make yourselves comfortable in the living room? I'll be finished up here in just a minute."

"Okey-dokey."

Okey-dokey? Oy.

The screen door slams shut behind her as she goes back into the house. I am a mature, competent professional. I will not cry.

And I don't, no matter how much it hurts. A few minutes later the steaks are more than done, and I shift them to a platter and head back inside.

David and Cali aren't in the living room. They're at the little café table in my kitchen. The one with only two chairs and no room for more. How fitting.

"I just need to do the asparagus, and we can eat."

David is oblivious. "Sounds great."

And I guess it does, if you're David.

After I drag a folding chair from the coat closet, we huddle around my little café table. The food situation resolves itself. Cali's a vegetarian, so she passes on the steak. David announces he's on a new low-carb diet, so he doesn't want the potato. We each get four slender spears of asparagus. And somehow we make it through the meal.

When Cali excuses herself to the restroom, David smiles ruefully and reaches across the table to take my hand. "Guess this wasn't the best way to spring it on you, huh?"

"When you said a surprise, I was thinking more in the range of a new preaching magazine."

David bows his head. "Blew it, didn't I?"

I have to play it cool. "No, not really. I just felt bad that I didn't have enough food."

"But that worked out okay." He pats my hand and releases it. I miss his touch keenly. And I know that with the advent of Cali, I'm going to miss it even more in the future.

It's too late now. And it's my own fault. I had my opportunities, and I blew them. Too much fear. Not enough faith.

"Give her a chance. I know she's young, but you'll like her."

"I feel like her baby-sitter." The words slip out, and I regret them even before I see the hurt in David's eyes.

"Are we really going to begrudge each other a little happiness, Betz? I know it's not perfect, but what is?"

We are! I want to shout, but I don't. Because if David doesn't know that, then we aren't.

"She just seems so young."

"She's twenty-three." He pushes back from the table and crosses his arms across his chest.

Cali comes back to the table, and she smiles at us both. "This is so great." She reaches over to hug me again, and I get another mouthful of hair. "Betz, I just know we're going to be BFF."

"BFF?" She's speaking some kind of hip code language.

"You know! Best friends forever!"

Years of practice keep the smile nailed on my face. I have smiled at parishioners while they criticized me, condemned me, and insulted me. Surely I can keep the expression through the exuberant offer of friendship from the near-adolescent love interest of my best friend in the world. Just because I'd like to scratch her eyes out is no reason to reject her.

"Oh yeah. BFF. Um, sure." I rise from my chair and avoid making eye contact with David.

David groans. "I forgot the dessert."

Of course he did. "No problem. I keep a little something on hand that I like to call Rocky Road Surprise."

Which just about sums up my evening so far.

The next morning LaRonda meets me for an emergency session at Starbucks. I arrive first and manage to spill my latte on a nun. And not even a nun in a black habit. A Dominican in snowy white. Rats!

"I'm so sorry." I dab at her sleeve with a recycled paper napkin, which only smears the stain.

"Please." She jerks her arm away and grabs her venti House Blend. "You've done enough."

If she only knew.

"I'm really sorry," I say to the back of her wimple as she makes a beeline for the door.

I slink to a table and try not to assume a fetal position while I wait for LaRonda. I pretend to read a copy of the *Tennessean* someone's left behind, but I couldn't care less about NASCAR results and how Metro government is going to cut more from the school budget so they can lure professional baseball to town. Priorities, priorities.

"Sorry I'm late." LaRonda slides into the chair opposite me. "Minor police emergency."

"Police emergency?"

"Okay, I got a traffic ticket. I can't believe I couldn't talk the officer out of it."

LaRonda's persuasive abilities should be immortalized in song and legend. They're the reason she's gotten as far as she has in the church, and why she's managed to stay there. I wish they were contagious, like the stomach flu.

"Guess you'll just have to cop to it and pay the fine."

LaRonda scowls. "No way. I'll try my luck with the judge."

"Forget it. I've tried, and it can't be done." My one and only appearance in traffic court felt like standing before God at the Last Judgment. The judge looked like Charlton Heston and only allowed you to plead innocent or guilty. You couldn't say anything in your defense.

"Guilty," I had to reply. When I tried to explain the circumstances, the judge had glared at me.

"Are you aware that sixty-five is greater than forty-five?"

"Yes sir."

"Then you're guilty, aren't you?"

"Technically, yes."

"Technically is all it takes, Miss Blessing."

LaRonda slips her purse over the back of the chair and settles in. "So, David showed up at your house with another woman."

"Yep. Some *surprise.*"

"Well, what did you expect? If he doesn't know you're interested in him, he's got every right to look around."

"But I tried to tell him."

"Trying isn't doing, Betsy. Good intentions will get you a dateless Saturday night and not much else."

"It's too late now."

LaRonda rolls her eyes. "Why is it too late?"

"Ronnie, he's with somebody else now."

"So? Do you want David or not?"

"But that wouldn't be ethical. I'm no man-stealer."

"No man was ever stolen who didn't want to be. You have to keep trying."

"But what about the other girl?"

"If David really likes her, he'll stay with her. No matter what you say to him."

"I don't know, Ronnie."

"That's fear talking, girl. Not ethics." She sips her coffee. "Did you get an invitation to the fund-raiser for the Nehemiah Project?" It's a charity near and dear to my heart that provides transitional housing for struggling families trying to achieve self-sufficiency.

"I mailed in a check and trashed the invite."

"Well, you'd better dig it out. 'Cause you're going to invite David to go with you. Nothing like a black-tie 'do' to inspire a little romance."

"You want me to invite him to the fund-raiser?"

"No, I'm *telling* you to invite him to the fund-raiser. And we are going to make you so gorgeous that he'll forget all about what's-her-name."

"It doesn't feel right."

"Betz, is this girl the woman for David?"

"No. Even if I didn't have feelings for him, I wouldn't be happy about this. She's too young and shallow. He'll be bored in a week."

"Then you have no moral dilemma." She swirls her coffee. "Now, let's address the really tough issue. What dress are you going to wear?"

See why I have LaRonda in my life? She makes everything so simple, while all I seem to do is complicate matters.

Chapter 12

Work used to be a refuge from my lack of a personal life. Now my lack of personal life provides no refuge from work.

I continue to visit Velva in ICU, and she's much the same—over-breathing the respirator, which is good, but not enough for them to take her off it, which isn't so good.

Another Sunday passes, less eventful than the one before, and once again the cash offering is very low. Now I'm beginning to worry without any help from Edna Tompkins. What if she's right? What if people *are* voting with their dollars?

Gus suggested finding a way to monitor the cash box in the sacristy. It's kept locked, and only he and the church business manager have a key. At least, they're the only ones we know of. But church keys are like bunnies; they reproduce at an alarming rate. People will give a copy of their church key to their best friend's sister's cousin's bridesmaid who needs to get into the sanctuary early for a wedding.

I absent-mindedly check e-mail as I wonder how, short of hiding in the closet with the clerical robes, we can monitor the offering box.

And then the answer appears before me, right on my computer screen.

Monitor anyone, anywhere, from any PC!

A Web cam. That could work. I even know who could help me.

David may be too cheap to pay for anything more than dial-up Internet access, but the boy does know his way around electronic stuff—except for his VCR, which for some reason mystifies him.

I push the Speed Dial button on my phone, and he answers just as quickly.

"St. Helga's. Pastor David."

"You have a good voice for a receptionist. Bet you don't know how to transfer me to voice mail."

"Hey, Betz." I can hear his grin. "Fortunately no one's asked me to do that so far this morning."

"Secretary out?"

"Her kid has the vomiting virus. She offered to come in and bring him with her, but I declined."

"I need your help." David's used to my abrupt jumps from one subject to the next.

"Personal or professional?" He sounds wary.

"Professional. I need you to help me install a Web cam."

"Who are you spying on?"

"It's not a who. It's a what. Can you meet me at someplace electronic this afternoon to pick out the camera? We'll have to come back to the church tonight after everyone's gone to set it up. I don't want anyone else to know about it."

David sighs the sigh of the long-suffering. "Is this in any way illegal or immoral?"

"It's the work of the Lord, hon. I think someone's raiding the offering."

"Ouch. Then count me in."

"Excellent. Circuit City at three?"

"Sure. And, Betz?"

"Yeah?"

"How peeved are you on a scale of one to ten about dinner last week?"

"Help me install this camera and all is forgiven." That's not true, but what else am I going to say? I'm supposed to invite him to the fund-raiser, so I have to play it cool.

"I know you don't approve of Cali."

"It's your life, David. I shouldn't have been so judgmental."

"I'm glad you feel that way."

I take a deep breath. "Do you think Cali would let me borrow you Saturday night? I need an escort for the Nehemiah Project 'do,' and since my only recent romantic entanglement has just been reincarcerated, I'm desperate."

"Sure. I'll even pull out my old tux for the occasion."

David looks like James Bond in a tux. It's so unfair. He's a preacher. He shouldn't get to resemble a young Sean Connery. I remember when we bought that tux at a consignment boutique. It was for his wedding to Jennifer. The wedding that never happened. Partly because he was the kind of guy who would buy a secondhand tux, and she was the kind of girl who wanted to register at Tiffany's because David's family is from New York City.

I try not to breathe my sigh of relief directly into the phone. I don't want to sound like my obscene phone caller. "I owe you. In fact, I'll spring for dinner. Somewhere nice."

"No chili dogs?"

"Definitely no chili dogs."

"You don't know what you're missing."

Oh, but I do, David. In excruciating detail.

I drop the receiver back in its cradle with a *thunk!* I had no idea it hurts this much to be in love.

In love! It's not that bad, is it? But it is. My stomach does a full-twisting backflip with a 3.0 degree of difficulty. Why didn't I see this before? It's not just about having feelings for David. About being attracted to him.

Dear Lord, I'm in love.

And I mean that as the prayer of desperation and panic it sounds like.

I manage to hide my newfound realization from David when we meet to buy the Web cam. And even late that night, when we rendezvous at the back door of Church of the Shepherd, I play it cool.

"Betz, you do have a security code for the alarm, right? If the police get called, they send in the dogs first."

David is wary of dogs because of an unpleasant visitation experience during field education in divinity school. How could he have known the house number in the church directory was a typo and that the reclusive homeowner kept a pack of dogs for running off door-to-door salespeople and pushy evangelists?

"I have a code. Don't worry."

We're both dressed in black. All we need are stocking caps and some coal blacking to smear across our cheeks.

Okay, we're about as stealthy as the Three Stooges. But I like the feeling of being co-conspirators.

"Ouch!" David bumps into me in the doorway when I stop to punch in the security code. I jump about a mile, and not just from the surprise.

"Sorry," he mumbles. He's pressed against my back, and I'm aware of every lanky inch of him.

"It's okay." With the alarm system off, we switch on our flashlights and make our way down the darkened hallways. Here and there, security lights help show the way.

The sanctuary at night is a scary place. I find that very ironic. In full daylight it feels holy, a sacred space that provides comfort and inspiration. At night, in the dark, it's just an empty cavern that could conceal any number of bogeymen. I'm glad David is right on my heels.

We slip through a side door and into the sacristy. It's a smallish room off the chancel area where the altar is. Mostly it's used to store sixty two-liter bottles of Welch's Grape Juice for Communion. An ancient refrigerator grates and whines, struggling like most of the parishioners to do its part for the church. The deacons come in on Saturday mornings to prepare the communion trays for the next day. Then they store them in the refrigerator. By Sunday morning, the grape juice has acquired a metallic bouquet with a saucy hint of Freon.

The offering box is a wooden structure about the size of an end table that sits in the corner. It has a slit in the top for the deacons to drop the bank deposit bag into after they've collected the offering. A large silver padlock dangles down its side.

"What's the best angle?" I ask David.

He runs the flashlight around the room. "We don't want it to be seen."

"Up high?"

"Probably. We're going to need a ladder."

"Great." I can picture us wrestling a fifteen-foot piece of rattling aluminum through the darkened church. We'd look like something out of an old episode of *I Love Lucy*.

"Couldn't we just stand on a chair?"

"Nope. Not tall enough."

"But all we have to do is stick it up there, right?"

"That's what the guy at the store said."

I run my flashlight around the room. "What if we stand on the counter?" There's a small cabinet covered with Formica where the deacons fill the trays.

"That might work if you do it," says David. "I'm way too heavy. It won't hold me."

And that's how I find myself clambering up onto the counter with David's help. His hands on my waist scorch me, but I pretend not to notice. Once I'm up on the counter, he hands me the camera. "Be careful, Betz. If you drop it, that's all she wrote."

Great. No pressure. It's not the only thing that's about to crack.

I reach up as high as I can, but even in the dark I see that the camera's going to be too obvious.

"No good. It's not going to be high enough."

I turn to climb down, and my right foot gets tangled with my left. With a yelp, I pitch forward and brace myself for a head-on collision with the tile floor. Instead, two arms and a formidable chest break my fall.

"Whoa!" David scoops me into his arms like a groom about to carry his bride across his threshold. I'm shocked he's not collapsing under my weight, but he holds steady, unlike my heart rate.

"Thanks," I say with a breathlessness usually reserved for preteen girls and asthmatics.

It's dark. I'm in David's arms. I can feel his breath on my face, and it's the movie theater all over again.

"Betz…"

Kiss him. No, wait, he should kiss me.

"Yeah?"

"Are you okay?" His voice is as mysterious as the darkness around us.

No. I'm not okay. Not when I'm this close to what I can't have. "Right now or in general?"

"Did you hurt yourself?"

It's so dark. It would be easy to blurt something out. Something approximating the truth. Then I'd know. One way or another, I'd know.

"No. I didn't hurt myself." Or maybe I did, but not because of the fall. I hurt myself years ago in divinity school when I pretended I didn't have feelings for him so I could be his friend.

Slowly, he slides me to the ground. I'm still clinging to him for support. It's so clichéd, and still so intimate. No wonder it's a stock device in all my favorite romance novels.

I think I know what's going to happen, but it doesn't. No lip-lock whatsoever. Just the opposite. He sets me on my feet, and his arms fall away. "Maybe we should get that ladder after all."

"Maybe so." My knees lock, and I think I'm going to keel over. I clutch the Formica counter for support. While we're fetching the ladder, let's see if we can find my sanity.

Twenty minutes later we find the ladder, but my sanity is still MIA. Another twenty minutes and two tries later, the Web cam is hidden behind some trimwork above a storage cabinet. You'd never see it unless you were looking for it. But I have a wide-angle view of the offering box on the PC in my office. Now I just have to hide out here next Sunday after worship and see who's been helping themselves to the first fruits of Church of the Shepherd. And do some mental self-flagellation for not helping myself to a little of David while I had the chance.

Am I getting on your nerves yet with my cowardice about coming clean with David? I know I'm getting on mine. So let's change the subject.

The next morning I head for the monthly meeting of the Greater Downtown Ministers' Association. I make this pilgrimage out of a desperate need for camaraderie. We gather at one of the downtown hotels for a rubber-chicken lunch, complete with guest speaker and senior-minister preening. The quality of the food never varies. Neither does the preening. The speaker's the only thing that might hit or miss. But we attend anyway, out of some strange compulsion to flock with birds of a feather.

The group usually numbers forty or so. We come from all different denominations. We're white, African American, Hispanic, Asian. A handful of us are women. About seven or eight of us are associate ministers.

David's there. He's huddled with the second-string group of senior pastors. Their steeples aren't quite as big as the first-string pastors'; neither are their congregations. At this meeting, size *does* matter.

Most of the associates are women. They're standing off by themselves. The whole thing reminds me of a junior-high dance. I head for the girls, cup of coffee in hand, with a feeling of relief. There's a delicious feeling of understanding among women in ministry that sustains us through our darkest hours.

But as I approach, I notice a thread of tension in the air. Barely perceptible, but it's still there.

"Hello, Betsy." Frieda Groos is the Christian-education associate from the Reformed church. Her smile is about as welcoming as the dogs that attacked David in divinity school.

"Hi." I'm suddenly nervous. Surreptitiously, I run my tongue over my teeth to check for anything unsightly wedged there. A quick glance at my shoes shows I'm not trailing toilet paper from the ladies' room. No run in my hose. I'm pretty sure my blouse is buttoned properly, but I'm not going to look now. I wonder what this is about. Probably the makeover. That seems to be causing me problems everywhere else.

"So, you're the new senior minister at Shepherd." Frieda says it like I've contracted a highly communicable and particularly distasteful disease.

"Interim only. And under duress."

So that's it. They think I've betrayed them. I look around the circle, past Frieda, to Nan from the Presbyterian church. She won't meet my gaze. Kelly, the Lutheran, smiles awkwardly. Kevin, the lone male who's a new associate at the Missionary Baptist Church, shifts from one foot to the other. The women's foreheads are virtually flat from bumping up against the stained-glass ceiling. Kevin's only doing his time until he gets offered a senior job. For men, being an associate pastor is a launching point. For women, it's pretty much the end of the line.

I want to tell them the truth. That I'm not finagling for the top spot. *I don't want the job! I'm going to law school!* I want to scream, but I can't. Because I know in my heart it's not true. So I paste a smile on my face.

"Who's speaking today?" With my luck, it will be a scintillating lecture on how to properly transliterate the Hebrew alphabet. The last interesting program we had was when LaRonda did a slide show on the school her church is building in South Africa.

"It's Fred Farnsworth today," Frieda says with grim resignation. "He's going to tell us how to plan for adequate parking."

I see LaRonda across the room. God bless her, she's standing in the middle of all the Big Daddy Rabbit preachers, and she's holding her own, though I do notice the laugh lines around her smile seem to come more from stress than amusement. Her church is as big as any of theirs, if not bigger, and her four-inch heels put her on par when it comes to personal height, but she still has to work twice as hard. I envy her ability to mark her territory and occupy it in the midst of the jungle, but I'm beginning to see signs of the toll it's taking on her.

The president of the association bangs the gavel on the podium up front, which relieves me of trying to justify my current predicament to my fellow associates. We move toward the rows of chairs and settle in the back row. Usually we continue our junior-high behavior by passing notes and rolling our eyes if the speaker says something particularly inane. Hey, everybody has to be bad sometimes.

Fred Farnsworth is on a roll, detailing the relative merits of parallel versus angled parking, when my cell phone rings. It's the call I've been dreading.

"This is Vanderbilt Hospital. May I speak to Betsy Blessing?"

"Just a moment," I whisper into the phone and start climbing over people to escape the meeting room. By the time I make it out the door and into the hallway, the nurse has already told me everything. Velva's no longer overbreathing the respirator, and she has an advance directive that specifies her wish not to be kept alive by artificial means. The same document gives me the power to authorize the removal of life support.

"I'll be right there."

After a week and a half, I'm on a first-name basis with the ICU nurses. Julie stops me when I come through the double doors into the unit.

"She doesn't look good, Betsy. Just be prepared."

I myself have said that line to families when I've been with them and their loved one in the last hours. Somehow it sounds far more patronizing when you're on the receiving end of it.

Velva seems to have shriveled overnight, as if her spirit's been extracted from her body. When I step across the threshold into her room, I can't sense her presence anymore. It's clear that whatever it is that animates us—call it a soul, a spirit, what have you—isn't inside her anymore. There's an absence that speaks volumes.

"Can I have a few minutes?"

Julie pats my back. "Sure. Let us know when you're ready. We've contacted her niece in New Jersey. She said she trusted you to do the right thing."

And there is a right thing to be done here. Velva had ninety-four wonderful, grace-filled years. She made her wishes clear. I take her hand, and the tears start to fall. Not for her, but, selfishly, for me. What will I do without her?

I lean down and kiss her cheek, as papery as always. "See ya soon," I whisper in her ear, and maybe I'm imagining it, but I feel the slightest pressure from her fingers in mine. The heavy rasping of the respirator punctuates the quiet.

I nod to Julie through the window that faces the nurse's station, and the medical personnel assemble to do what must be a routine but sad task. Their brisk movements are efficient, impersonal. They remind me of women in Bible times who prepared the bodies for burial.

"Into your hands, O Lord…" My words falter at first and then pick up strength. "We commit our sister Velva. Ashes to ashes. Dust to dust. In sure and certain hope of the resurrection in our Lord, Jesus Christ."

Without the tube, she strains for each breath. It goes on for several torturous minutes. And then, with one last exhale, her body comes to a stop.

Julie hands me a tissue, and I wipe my nose and eyes.

"She's gone," I say, as if everyone in the room couldn't tell.

Julie puts her arm around my shoulders and squeezes. "Yes, but she's okay. And you will be too. Do you need some more time with her?"

I give the nurse a watery smile. "Yes, but not like you mean."

Velva looks so fragile, her frail limbs covered by a hospital gown and a thin sheet.

"I'll contact the funeral home."

Velva has planned her service down to the smallest detail. We spent a lot of hours and many cups of tea picking hymns and scrip-

tures. She doesn't want any flowers but zinnias. Or she *didn't* want anything but zinnias. The awful reality of the past tense hits me. I hate that
part of loss, that moment when you realize you have to change the very
language you've always used to speak about the person you love.

Julie is tidying up the room. "Julie?"

"Yes?"

"Will they take her like that? In a hospital gown?"

"Probably."

"She'd hate that. Could we put her nightgown and robe on her?"

Julie stops what she's doing and looks at me. I see a trace of tears
in her eyes. "Sure."

It takes both of us to remove the hospital gown and replace it
with Velva's pink cotton nightgown and robe. Maybe this should feel
icky or wrong, but it just feels like love. I pick up a comb and fluff her
hair a little in the front. Just as Velva always did for Dottie at the nursing home.

Just like that, it's over. No more stealthy hand-offs of contraband
herbal supplements. No more birds outside the window or pots of
strong tea. No more wisdom. No more courage.

I cry now because I can't later. Later, I'll have to be a professional.
The service will be a comfort to all of us at Church of the Shepherd
who adored her. I will put everything I have into her eulogy.

For now, I put what's left into grieving for my own loss.

Chapter 13

I can't write about Velva's funeral. LaRonda and David were both there, in the back of the sanctuary. They knew that if they sat too close to the front, I'd take one look at them and fall apart.

Even Edna Tompkins complimented me on the eulogy. The Judge shook my hand rather than slipping out the side door, so I must have done well. I hope I did Velva justice. That's what you worry about when the funeral is for someone you loved so much. Did your personal feelings get in the way of your professional competence?

Later, after the graveside service, David and LaRonda take me to La Paz for shrimp enchiladas and a margarita. They're both treating me as if I might shatter in the act of dipping tortilla chips into the salsa verde.

"We could go to the movies," David offers after I've ordered my enchiladas. With a side of guacamole. The guacamole here is a sacrament.

"No, thanks. I'm not in the mood to see anyone get blown up." I'm also not up to sitting in a darkened theater with David again. Not while he's still Cali-fied.

"Why don't you come home with me?" LaRonda asks. "We'll deep-condition our hair and watch Meg Ryan movies."

"Y'all are sweet, but I need to be alone for a while."

After we leave the restaurant, I head home. The minute I step through my front door, the tears start to fall. I curl up in a ball on the couch and let the hurt work its way from my heart to my stomach, along the length of my limbs, up my neck, and over my scalp. Why does God make us love? I was right to hold back, to keep people at arm's length. Look where vulnerability has gotten me. Alone. On a Salvation Army couch. With nothing to dull the raw aching except a stomach full of enchiladas and guacamole.

The phone rings. I hiccup and sniffle, wipe my nose on my sleeve, and answer it. It could be a parishioner in worse shape than I'm in.

"Betz?" The familiar rumble of David's voice is like Gilead's balm.

"Yeah?"

"You didn't tell me what time to pick you up on Saturday."

The fund-raiser. I'd forgotten.

"Forget it. I'm not going."

There's a long silence, as if he's thinking through what he's going to say before he says it.

"I think you should go. I think you need to go. Life goes on, Betz."

"I'm fine with life going on. It just needs to go on without me for a while."

"No, it doesn't. LaRonda will be at your house at four on Saturday to help you get ready."

"David!" I don't know whether to feel comforted or outraged at his high-handedness.

"Wear something cute."

"You wouldn't know the difference if I wore a potato sack."

"Sure I would. You'd be the one who had *Idaho* written across your chest."

I can't believe David just referred to my chest.

"Okay, okay. Pick me up at seven."

"I'm expecting a great dinner."

"David, your idea of a great dinner is chili dogs."

"Shall I make reservations at the bowling alley?"

I'm smiling when I didn't think I could. Maybe love isn't a complete loss after all.

"I'm only doing this because I want to see you in that tux."

He laughs. "Should I have my mother fly in from New York and take pictures, like for prom?"

I shudder at the thought of being within ten feet of David's overbearing mom. There's a reason he didn't go back to New York after we graduated divinity school. "Why don't we let LaRonda do the honors?"

He laughs. "Bye, Betz."

"Bye, David."

I scrape myself off the couch and head for a long soak in my clawfoot tub. With a bit of luck and a new loofah, I can scrub away at least one layer of grief.

The rest of the week provides enough distraction to make me dwell less on Velva's death and my screwed-up love life. I practice using the Web cam so I'll be ready for my Sunday-afternoon stakeout. Angelique barges into my office a couple of times, and I quickly switch from the Web cam view to my Outlook. Subterfuge was never my greatest strength. I'm sure I look like a kid with a hand in the cookie jar.

Edna Tompkins drops by to deliver her weekly harangue. She perches on the edge of the chair across from my desk, and I feel as if I'm being pecked to death by ducks.

"You really should let The Judge look over your sermon for Sunday. He can steer you in the right direction."

I'm sure The Judge would be happy to steer me right over a homiletic cliff, but I keep that thought to myself.

"That would be great, but I haven't written it yet. I usually wait for Saturday-night inspiration."

Edna purses her lips. "I thought you were going to the fund-raiser Saturday night."

How does she know that? I narrow my eyes at her, and she has the grace to look the teensiest bit uncomfortable.

"Angelique must have mentioned it," she says, studying the books on the shelves over my right shoulder.

Which, translated, means she's been in the reception area for the last thirty minutes pumping my administrative assistant for any information she can get.

"I guess I'll hope for Saturday-morning inspiration. In any event, I think I can handle the sermon on my own."

I stand up and move around the edge of the desk. I learned this trick in my last church. If someone plops down in your office and doesn't show any signs of leaving, you get her out the door by simply getting up and walking toward it. Inevitably, the person will stand up and follow you. Most of the time she doesn't realize you've thrown her out. Sometimes, as with Edna Tompkins, I actually have to walk all the way to the outside door of the church office to get rid of my visitor. Once I had to walk a grumpy parishioner all the way to his car.

Edna continues to offer me helpful advice and inspirational tid-bits until I've literally seen her out the door. When she's finally gone, I lean against the office door and feel my knees start to go. Angelique laughs. "She was tougher than usual."

"She had a lot of wisdom to share."

Angelique's eyes narrow, much as mine did with Edna Tompkins, as she assesses me. "You aren't maintaining."

"Maintaining?"

"Your makeover. You're letting it slide."

Well of course I'm letting it slide. Who has time to use that plethora of hair products and a flat iron? Or age-defying foundation and three carefully blended shades of eye shadow?

"Don't think of it as sliding," I say. "Think of it as a sabbatical from the ridiculous demands of perfection our culture places on women."

"Was that a real sentence?"

"Does it have to be?"

We laugh, and it feels good. Some relief from the intensity of the week.

Angelique eyes me thoughtfully. "You need to make an effort for the fund-raiser."

"I don't know. I don't really feel like it."

"I have a dress you can borrow."

Why do those words scare me? I look at Angelique, at her big hair and her leather jacket. She puts it all out there, no holds barred. I could never do that. I don't have the courage.

"I'm sure I have basic black somewhere in my closet."

Angelique taps her talons on her desk. "No way. No black. You need a fiery red."

Or a neon sign that says *desperate*. That would probably be more flattering to my hips.

Well, despite my protests, Angelique shows up at my house late Saturday afternoon with a dress concealed in a long garment bag. LaRonda's already been here for a while, and I'm now plucked, exfoliated, irradiated, and illuminated. If my face were any shinier, I'd be a reflector shield in the next *Star Wars* movie.

"You're not shiny. You're glowing," LaRonda assures me, but I don't believe her.

"Wow!" Angelique pops her gum and turns to hang the mystery bag on my bedroom door. "Did you wax her eyebrows, too?" she asks LaRonda.

"After I pinned her to the floor. The legs were easier."

"Hmm." Angelique assesses me as if she's judging a heifer at the state fair. "Nice arch on the brows."

"Thanks."

"Hello! I'm here! I have ears."

"Of course you do, hon." LaRonda might as well pat me on the head. Then she turns her attention back to Angelique. "I couldn't decide on the hair. Up or down?"

The next thing I know, I'm shoved in front of a mirror while four hands pile my hair in thirty different directions. Finally, my personal beauty team decides on a loose chignon with lots of wispy curls hanging down.

If I thought Antoine and that masseuse were a nightmare, I'm far more frightened by LaRonda and Angelique. They don't even pretend to coddle me.

"Ouch!" I cry when they comb out my hair after washing it with three different shampoos.

"Don't fuss," LaRonda admonishes. What happened to all that Christian mercy stuff she's always spouting?

They won't let me look in the mirror. I know my hair required copious numbers of hairpins and my makeup is more than I'd ever apply myself, but at least they didn't slap on as much as those "Holy to Hottie" folks.

"Time for the dress."

Angelique slowly unveils her offering to the romance gods. But it's not a dress. It's a red scarf.

"Where's the dress?"

"You're looking at it, honey."

"Get out." There's no way. Time to dig out the basic black from the back of my closet.

"No, really." Angelique slips it from the hanger.

"What do you wear under it?"

She gives me a blank look. "Why would you want to wear anything under it?"

I'm sure there must be something in the lady minister's secret handbook about going commando to a charity function.

"Angie, I've worn underwear every day of my life since I was three, and I don't plan to change that now."

She *harrumphs,* rolls her eyes, and finally acquiesces.

"Okay, but only the minimum."

"I was thinking full body armor, but I'll scale back."

That compromise reached, they unzip the tiny little zipper at the back and order me to step into that siren's wrapper.

"It really is a scarf," I protest, even as I acknowledge that scarves don't usually have zippers.

The dress is soft crepe that drapes from tiny straps at the shoulders.

The neckline drops to a provocative-but-not-slutty V, and there's no back to speak of. The hem brushes my ankles.

"Better get the double-sided tape. I feel like J.Lo at the Grammys."

"No way," Angelique protests. "It'll stay in place."

I compare her bust to mine. "Yes, well, for you maybe, but some of us can't claim your assets."

LaRonda assesses the dress with a practiced eye. "No tape needed, Betz. It'll stay put."

And so will I. I've changed my mind. I'm not going.

"Look, maybe this isn't such a good idea—"

But before I can finish my protest, they whirl me around and open the closet door. I see myself in the full-length mirror, and my breath catches in my throat.

"Oh!"

Very eloquent. But it sums up their work quite nicely. I look amazing. More amazing than I did at the salon makeover, because this time I look more like me, not like some Hollywood version of myself. It's how I dreamed of looking for the senior prom. Hair upswept, with a few tendrils hanging down. Eyes bright, but a little mysterious, too. A dress that emphasizes every curve. Softer, less hip than my make-over look, but still glam.

"I can't believe it." No wonder the Cinderella fairy tale is so seductive. They've brought out my inner princess.

"David won't know what hit him," LaRonda laughs.

Angelique's ears prick up like a bloodhound that's caught the scent of a fox. "David? I thought he was just a friend?"

"He is. He is." I resist the urge to elbow LaRonda in the stomach. "We're just pals."

"That's what movie stars always say right before they have a love child," Angelique says sagely.

What is it with people thinking I'm going to have a love child? First Edna and now Angelique.

"There will be no love children in my immediate future." I pick up my evening bag from the dresser and start stuffing in the essentials. Lipstick. Tiny comb. Cell phone. Emergency M&M's. I force the snap to close because I'm not leaving any of the necessities behind.

"Where are you going for dinner?" Angelique asks. "Not 12th and Porter?"

"No. The Merchants."

Angelique nods appreciatively. "Sweet."

"Let's hope so."

LaRonda pats my shoulder. "You're going to be fine, Betsy. Tonight's the night."

"The night?"

"The night you come clean with David."

"Come clean with him about what?" Angelique asks, her eyes narrowing with suspicion.

"Um, that I took the interim senior-minister job," I fib—and shoot LaRonda a knowing look.

"Oh." Angelique is clearly disappointed.

Thankfully, LaRonda changes the subject. "Well, princess, I think you're ready for the ball. Make sure you put all this fairy godmother stuff to good use." She looks at me meaningfully. I know what she's saying. I have to confess to David tonight. No more stalling. Roll the dice and let the chips fall where they may, to mix my gambling metaphors.

I give her a hug, but a careful one. Don't want to crush the dress or the do. "Thanks, Ronnie." I turn to Angelique and hug her as well. "You've gone above and beyond the call of duty."

She gives me a quick squeeze and steps back. "Somebody's got to keep the church going. You people are a lot of work."

"Aren't we, though?" I smile back with tears misting my eyes. "Good thing we have you."

This time when David shows up at my front door, I'm not expecting another man, and he doesn't have another woman with him. Things are definitely looking up.

Also, this time he says the right things instead of acting shocked and appalled when he sees me.

"Wow." He looks me up and down, something I don't think he's ever done before. At least I've never seen him do it.

"Is that a good wow or a dear-Lord-why-did-I-agree-to-this wow?"

"The first thing. You look great." He's enthusiastic but also a touch bewildered. I think that's a good thing.

"Thanks. You don't look so bad yourself." Which is the understatement of the year. Again, I will remind you to picture a young Sean Connery in black tie. "I see the tux still fits."

He runs his finger around his collar. "Unfortunately. Otherwise I would have gotten rid of it a long time ago."

"I'm glad you didn't."

We stand there staring at each other, neither of us making a move toward the door.

Finally, David says, "I should have brought flowers."

I look in his eyes, and I realize we're both thinking the same thing. The evening has suddenly acquired date status. He could change that in a sentence if he wanted. He could make some remark about Cali. Or I could put the kibosh on the date vibes. I could ask about her.

Neither one of us does, though. Instead, David offers me his arm. "Shall we?"

"Sure."

I place my hand on his sleeve, and we step out into a night that suddenly sparkles with potential.

Chapter 14

My last few dates have taken on a certain surreal quality. There was the parishioner's grandson, the ex-con. Another guy just wanted to sell me life insurance. And the third seemed more interested in my shoes than he should have been. (Can you say "fetish"?) So dinner with David is a little slice of heaven.

We're settled into a cozy table at the Merchants downtown. It's housed in an old bank building and retains that charm of yesteryear. The exposed brick walls, snowy tablecloths, and divine food set a romantic mood. I abandon any pretense of tracking Weight Watchers points.

On our way upstairs to the main dining room, I actually see a couple of male heads turn to watch me walk by. A girl could get addicted to that. Angelique's red dress slides against me as I move, reminding me that I'm not a preacher tonight.

The waiter takes our drink order, reels off the specials, and leaves us to peruse the menu. I find myself strangely silent, which is not usually the case when I'm around David. We never run short of conversation, but tonight he's no chatterbox himself. At the next table a couple kisses and coos, in stark contrast to our uneasy silence. The man has caught the woman's fingers in his, and from the suspicious movement of the tablecloth, I suspect she's stroking his leg with her foot. Or else he has a mosquito bite he needs some help scratching.

"Do you want an appetizer?" David asks.

I frown and concentrate on the menu as if I'm deciphering the Dead Sea Scrolls. "Mmm. Maybe."

Somehow we're going to have to break this tension. But the last thing I want to do is acknowledge what we're both thinking. *Date*. My stomach flips worse than it did when I tried out for the high-school choir. I try not to remember that I didn't make the cut when it came to the alto section. Please let me make the choir tonight.

The waiter brings our drinks and stands there expectantly.

"How about some spinach artichoke dip?" David asks without looking up from his menu. What, we can't even make eye contact anymore? If I weren't so happy to be here with him, deliciously tormented by this date vibe, I'd make fun of the two of us.

"Sure." That seems to be the sum total of my conversational skills this evening. Ready to go, Betz? Sure. Want an appetizer? Sure. I hope no one asks me to write a five-figure check at the fund-raiser. In my current condition, I'd probably do it.

There's got to be a way to restore some normalcy to the evening without naming the elephant dancing through the restaurant.

"I'm ready for my surveillance tomorrow afternoon," I say once we've placed our order. Maybe we can talk Web cams.

"Oh. That's good."

Okay, David is not doing his part here to get the conversational ball rolling.

"I hope it's not anyone on the staff who's taking the money," I say to give him another opening.

"That would be bad," he agrees as he fiddles with his fork.

With a sigh I wad up my napkin and throw it on the table in

front of me. "You have to help me out here, David. I can't spend the evening talking to myself."

"What?" David's a million miles away. He looks up, brow furrowed.

"Maybe this isn't such a good idea. We both have to preach in the morning. Why don't we just have dinner and call it a night? They won't miss us at the fund-raiser."

He frowns. "You don't want to go?"

Okay, a jury of my peers, twelve single women, wouldn't convict me if I stabbed him repeatedly right now with my salad fork.

"If I wanted to go by myself, I wouldn't have invited you. If you didn't want to come, you should have said so."

It takes a moment for the meaning of my words to sink in.

"No, Betz. It's not like that."

"David, you've been monosyllabic since we ordered."

"I'm just thinking."

"About church tomorrow?"

His cheeks color. "No, not about church."

"Then what?" I take a deep breath and force myself to say her name. "About Cali?"

That's when David looks at me. Really looks at me. One of those looks that makes you feel like you've been sucker-punched in the stomach.

"I was thinking about you."

"Me?" I don't mean to squeak like a mouse.

"Yeah. You."

"What about me?"

The waiter appears tableside with two plates in hand. Two Caesar salads and the offer of some cracked black pepper divert David's critical reply to the question.

Of course, a moment like that is impossible to recapture. Once the waiter's gone, I'm not sure how to steer the conversation back to its previous course. David appears to have forgotten to answer. He tears into his salad like it's a chili dog and makes appreciative noises.

Some moments of realization break over you like waves. Others are like mists that rise from the ground and then work their way up to the heavens. This particular moment feels more like my world shifting six inches to the left, and my stomach is making an accompanying motion. Everything's the same, but suddenly it's all in a different place.

Because I see that David's afraid too. Afraid of what's suddenly happening between us.

A tingling washes through me, down my spine, and around to my belly. I don't mean to be cruel, but his fear is the best thing I've felt in a long, long time.

By the time the entrées arrive, we've found our conversational sea legs. I don't force the issue of his fear at dinner. Instead, I enjoy the delicious sense of anticipation that's developed in my midsection. It's better than the crème brûlée we split for dessert. Like a child who awakens at three o'clock on Christmas morning and hears shuffling noises downstairs, I'm aware something wonderful is about to happen. I've been given a gift of this one night, like Cinderella going to the ball. I mean to make the most of it—even if it all disappears when the clock strikes twelve.

The fund-raiser is at the Hermitage Hotel, so I've come full circle from the night when I first acknowledged my feelings for David. We descend the steps beneath the lobby's stained-glass ceiling, and I feel like visiting royalty. People are mingling while waiters in tuxedos circle the room with trays of drinks. The dancing isn't scheduled to begin for half an hour.

Since I serve on the board of the Nehemiah Project, I know a number of folks present. David and I mingle, greeting people and stopping to chat here and there. The whole time I'm aware of him standing beside me. Once, he puts his hand on the small of my back and scoots me forward to keep someone from bumping into me. If another man pulled something that proprietary, I'd resent it. But with David, it feels natural. It feels right.

"Betsy! Look at you." Greg Iverson, pastor of The Groovy Church (not its real name, but you know the type) slithers over and tries to slobber on my cheek. I pull away just in time to make it an air kiss. Greg is one of those preachers who uses his pastoral identity as an excuse to invade a woman's personal space. Apparently no one ever told him about the stand-eighteen-inches-away rule.

Greg's eyes run down my red dress and all the way back up. Ew! It's especially obvious since he's standing close enough to deprive me of necessary oxygen. Beside me, David bristles.

"Hi, Greg. Nice to see you." I turn to David. "Look. Isn't that LaRonda over there?" I flash Greg a toothy smile. "Excuse us, won't you?" There's no LaRonda, but it gets us away from Greg.

I begin to relax and enjoy myself. I am receiving actual male attention. Even better, the bulk of it is coming from the male I want to pay attention to me.

A jazz combo plays softly from the corner. Before the dancing begins, the executive director of the program makes a quick pitch for people to pry open their wallets. It's always struck me as ironic to get dressed up and spend a fortune on dinner and tickets so you can give more money to the charity du jour. On the other hand, I like a good party as much as the next girl, and I don't actually get invited to that many.

Finally, finally, they herd us into the ballroom, and the dancing begins. I've been waiting for this all evening—the chance to feel David's arms around me again. With a twirl he guides me onto the dance floor, and we're off. If men knew how easily women turn to putty in their hands on the dance floor, they'd be lined up outside Arthur Murray a hundred deep. I don't know why most women love to dance and most men don't. One of nature's little quirks. Or perhaps a curse coming out of Eden they forget to put in Genesis, along with men having to till the soil and women having pain in childbirth. In any event, I'm delighted that David enjoys dancing, judging by the way he executes a debonair turn and then pulls me close again. His breath tickles my ear. The music is from the big-band era, the kind my grandfather always played, and the female singer breathlessly tells how she's found true love at last. Boy, do I know how she feels. I just wish I knew more about what was running through David's head. Maybe he'll burst into song and it will all become clear.

Or not.

In any event, I'm content to rest in his embrace, moving gently around the dance floor, my breath slowing to match his until it feels as if we're one person lost in the music and the moment.

This is what heaven must be like. At least I hope that's what it will be like. Because I could spend eternity doing what I'm doing right now.

All too soon the song ends and we step away from each other.

Despite the buzz of conversation around us, it feels as if we're in our own world. David looks at me and I look at him. I'm surprised other people can't see the current flowing between us. It's just this side of tangible.

"Betz?" David's dark eyes are unreadable—hate that! I had a better idea of what he was thinking when we were creeping through the darkened sanctuary a few nights ago.

"Yeah?"

There's a long pause. He swallows. "Want to dance again?"

There's not enough room on my face for my smile. "Sure." Maybe there's something to this whole being-agreeable thing. Look where it's gotten me tonight.

I move back into David's arms as the band plays the opening bars of "You Made Me Love You."

For purposes of brevity, I will spare you the blow-by-blow of every dance we dance this evening. Suffice it to say that it just gets yummier as the night goes along. Twice I have to accept invitations to dance from big contributors. I'm as willing to do my part for the cause as the next woman, but I begrudge both the waltz and the fox trot. I fully expect David to find another partner. Instead, he stands on the side of the dance floor and watches me. Constantly. I don't think he even blinks.

By the time he comes to reclaim me, my blood's pounding through my veins. I slide back into his arms with familiar, frightening ease.

"Hi," he breathes.

"Hi," I breathe back. From our sophisticated conversation, you'd never suspect we both had graduate degrees from one of the top universities in the country.

"Betz?"

"Yeah?"

I'm all delicious expectation.

Suddenly he frowns. "No. Not here. Come with me."

His arms fall away, and he reaches for my hand. I comply without question when he leads me out of the ballroom. He looks around, then tows me down a hallway. I have no idea where David's going, and clearly neither does he. Is there not one private nook or cranny in the entire hotel? We go through a door that turns out to be a fabulous art deco men's room. I laugh. David spins me around and retraces our steps. Two more false starts provide no convenient hideaways for a not-so-innocent tryst.

"David."

"No. Don't say anything. Not yet." Frustration draws his shoulders ramrod straight.

"But, David—"

"What?"

He turns on me, his eyes all chocolate and sexy.

"That way." I keep myself from smiling as I point to the lobby. "There's an enclosed veranda on the other side."

"Oh. Okay." And he's off again, towing me like I'm a barge bound for the harbor. Why does intimacy turn perfectly normal men into imbeciles? And why doesn't a modern girl like me object to the contemporary equivalent of being dragged off to a cave?

Societies may advance, but instinct never changes, thank the Lord.

We step through the doorway into a long, window-lined veranda. Potted trees dot the length of the room. We head for a semisecluded corner. But once we're there, icy fear reclaims the length of my spine. We should have stayed on the dance floor where we could drift along in dreamy ambiguity.

David lets go of my arm but slips his fingers through mine. There's a settee against the wall, and he nods toward it. "Sit down."

But it's harder to run away from a seated position! I want to protest. But I don't.

"Betsy, there's something I need to say."

"Okay." Well, I've improved my vocabulary from one-syllable words to two.

"I didn't plan this."

"I know." I can't say, *neither did I.*

"We've been friends a long time."

"Yeah."

I wait for him to finish whatever he's trying to say. He looks up, looks over my shoulder, and finally exhales heavily. "We have to do this, don't we?"

"Do what?"

"Kiss."

The giddiness slides right out of me and pools at my feet. He looks as if he's preparing to eat rancid insects on *Fear Factor.* "No, David. We don't." Shame burns my cheeks. Well, I brought this on myself, didn't I? Now he feels obligated. I don't want obligation. I want attraction. Passion. Conflagration. Not stoic resignation.

I rise from the bench, and he follows, still holding my hand.

"I didn't mean it like that."

"Then how did you mean it, David?" I try to keep walking, but he stops. Since our hands are superglued together, I have to stop also. I turn to face him.

"I meant it like this."

And he kisses me.

He kisses me with desperation, resignation, and, yes, passion. He kisses me as if he can't live any longer if he doesn't. And I kiss him back the same way, as if every part of me has to be involved. Heart, mind, soul. I can't believe there's not steam rising off both of us. Or maybe there is and the hotel sprinkler system will kick in any moment now.

Then suddenly David's lips aren't moving against mine anymore. I can't feel his arms around me. The sense of aloneness douses me as effectively as any sprinkler.

Reluctantly, I open my eyes. I know from the contrite expression on David's face that Cinderella's clock has struck midnight.

"This isn't fair to you," he says.

"I'm not particularly concerned about justice right now."

"You should be." He runs his fingers through his hair, standing it on end. So much for the young Sean Connery look. "I swore I wouldn't do this. I wouldn't take advantage of your grieving."

"My grieving?"

"Over Velva. You're vulnerable right now, Betz."

"What makes you think you're taking advantage? What makes you think I didn't want you to kiss me?"

David looks me in the eye. "You're not one for a casual fling. You've never been interested in me before. Plus you're not the type to go for a guy with a girlfriend. I know you're hurting, Betz, but this isn't the answer. And our friendship matters too much to mess around with it like this."

"What if I'm not messing around?"

This seems to stump him. Confusion etches the corner of his eyes. "What do you mean?"

Men are so clueless. That's why God made Eve, so Adam would have someone to tell him what he wanted and when he wanted it. Okay, so the apple thing didn't work out so well, but you get my point.

"What if I want you, David?"

I can't believe it. I finally said it. Okay, I didn't say it as much as ask it, but still. I think this is a breakthrough. I just wish breakthroughs didn't have to be fraught with such a sense of impending doom.

"I don't think you know what you want right now, Betz." He sounds sad, which gives me hope, but he also sounds definite, which shakes the ground beneath my feet.

"You think I don't know what I want?"

"When have you ever?"

He lifts a hand as if to apologize for the harshness of his words, but he doesn't stop saying them. "You thought a small church would satisfy you, but when it got tough, you didn't fight. You ran. Then you thought being an associate was your call to ministry, but it turns out that's not it either. Now you agree to this interim thing, and you're throwing yourself at me. You're flailing, Betz."

Perspiration explodes on my forehead and under my arms. "I am not flailing! And for your information, I'm done with my so-called career in ministry. I'm quitting at the end of the summer."

David's face sinks into skeptical lines. "To do what?"

"To go to law school."

"Law school?" He rolls his eyes. "You're kidding."

"No, David, I am not kidding. I've been accepted at Vanderbilt."

He crosses his arms, his tux jacket tightening over his shoulders. Those shoulders I've been clinging to all night. "When were you planning to tell me?"

I duck my head the merest fraction. "When the time was right."

"As in 'right' before school starts? I can't believe you kept something like this from me."

"I knew you'd just judge me."

"No, you knew I'd tell you the truth. What I'm telling you now. You have no idea what you want. You have no idea what God wants for you. You're latching on to whatever is handy, hoping it will make you happy. I'm not willing to be the guy who's handy, Betz. We've known each other too long for that. You matter too much to me."

How can a guy telling you how much you matter to him make your heart break like mine is doing right now? I'm glad I'm wearing red so the blood won't show, because this hurts too much not to be an actual, physical wound.

"You don't want me." The words taste as bitter as they sound.

"Not like this. No."

"You'd rather have that airhead bimbo, Cali."

"At least she wants to be with me because she wants to be with me. Not because she's using me to hide from something."

"Oh, quit being such a grownup."

"But that's what we are now, Betz. We're grownups. The time for playing games is over."

I can't believe how quickly it all evaporated. There's not even a glass slipper left to offer me some small hope for my fairy-tale ending.

"I want to go home."

"Fine. I'll have them bring the car around."

I wipe my cheeks with the back of my hand. "No. Not with you. I'll get a cab."

"Aw, Betz, don't be stupid. I'll drive you home."

But I can't be near him anymore. I might possibly make it to the front door of the hotel and into a taxi without collapsing, but if I have to stay with David another moment, I'll lose any shred of dignity I have left. I shove my way past him.

"Betsy. Don't. It doesn't have to be like this."

But it does. I have to run for cover like a fox with the hounds on her scent. David *knows*. He knows how I feel, and it's not enough.

But it's never been enough. I've never been enough. Not for my dad, who wanted another lawyer in the family. Not for my mom, who doesn't understand why I can't land a man. Not for my first church that valued gender over competency, and not for Church of the Shepherd, where they put appearances before substance.

And definitely not for David, who wants me to be more like LaRonda. Decisive. Focused. Powerful.

The Bible is full of scriptures about fools, and as I hurry through the lobby toward the front door, I feel like every one of them. No makeover can cover up the truth. I am not enough, and I never will be.

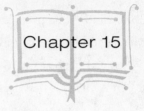

Chapter 15

I don't remember preaching this morning, but I must have, because both services are over and I'm sitting in my office watching the Web cam on my PC. Last night's fiasco with David sits like lead in my stomach, just below the lump in my throat created by Velva's death. If I weren't so numb, I think I'd be in a lot of pain. What else can I do, though, but keep moving forward?

So far there's no action around the offering box. I brought a salad from home to munch on while I keep my vigil, and the lettuce tastes like the spaghetti sauce I stored in the container last week. Like the rest of my life, my lunch is haunted by my past.

Or perhaps more to the point, my past has decided to take up residence in my present. Normally I can keep those ghosts at bay, but Velva's death and David's rejection, like my own personal kryptonite, have weakened my superpowers.

Someone looms in the doorway of my office, and I catch my breath, thinking it might be David. But it's Cali, of all people.

"Hi, Betsy." Her face is longer than one of Dr. Black's sermons.

"Hey, Cali." I mangle a greeting through a mouthful of romaine, then pause to swallow. "This is a surprise."

She drags herself into the room and drapes herself across a chair. "I needed to talk to someone about David. Someone who knows him.

Do you mind?" She peers at me through a tangle of streaked blonde hair like a cuddly animal hiding from a vicious predator.

"Now?" I peep at my PC monitor. Still no movement in the sacristy. "Um…it's not that great a time."

She looks morosely at my ancient Tupperware. "You're just eating, right? Go ahead. It won't bother me."

Out of the corner of my eye, I see a flash of movement on the monitor, but it's gone before I can see who it is. Cali is clearly not going anywhere until we've had our chat. I've heard of multitasking, but this is ridiculous.

"What's on your mind?" It's a question I've uttered countless times to the person seated on the other side of my desk, but I've never wanted to avoid the person's answer more than I do now.

"David broke up with me."

My fork stops halfway to my mouth. The lettuce plops onto my desktop.

"When?"

"Yesterday. We went bowling after lunch. He broke my heart in the middle of the seventh frame."

"He broke up with you?" My brain can't move past that fact.

"Right before he picked up the spare."

Why didn't he tell me last night? Another blur of movement on the monitor catches my eye, and I casually swing my head to the side as if I'm shaking my head no in disbelief. Again, I'm too late to see who it is.

"I knew the age difference would be a problem," Cali mourns, "but he won't even try to work it out."

"What did he say?" Why am I asking for details? It's like my love life is a terrible car wreck that I can't help rubbernecking. Cali assumes the lotus position in the chair as if she's settling in for an extended meditation session. I wonder if she's going to break out into Tibetan throat singing at any moment. Fortunately, she doesn't.

"He said it wasn't working. How could it not have been working? It was working for me."

What can I say to that? I look at her, really look at her, and see myself or any other young woman at twenty-three. She's naive, no matter how worldly she may appear. Her lack of experience isn't her fault, and the only way to gain the perspective she'll have in five years is by getting her heart stomped on. Repeatedly.

"That was his only reason?"

She plucks at the holes in the knees of her jeans. They're stretched wide due to the aforementioned lotus position, and her kneecaps are as bony as a child's. If I sat like that, I couldn't walk for a week.

Cali sighs. "I think there's someone else." Again, she peeps up at me through her bangs. "You would know, Betsy, wouldn't you? If he had someone else?"

A rush of heat suffuses my face. I'm sure the guilt is written on my forehead in nine-foot letters.

"He hasn't mentioned anyone."

As a minister you learn to tell the diversionary truth. Technically you're not breaking one of the Big Ten or other God-type rules. Don't think of it as a lie. Think of it as a method of nondisclosure.

"There must be somebody. Guys only leave if they have another girl lined up."

Is that true? Guys have never needed another woman in the wings as an excuse to break up with me.

"This has happened before?"

Cali nods her head, and I feel incredibly small. But what can I tell her? That I made a pass at David and he rejected me, too, after he'd dumped her? That would hardly make her feel better about herself. Or me.

A surprising thought occurs to me, and the fork falls from my fingers. Did David break up with Cali because of me even before Saturday night?

At that moment there's movement on the Web cam. This time I see it. It's a woman with white hair and glasses. She's bustling around the sacristy, a squirt bottle in one hand and a rag in the other. We have several custodians, so I don't know who—

"Betsy, what's that?" Cali's eyes have followed mine to the PC monitor.

"Mmm…overzealous parishioner, I think."

I wish I had something handy to drape over the monitor, but my coat is hanging on the back of my office door.

"What's she doing with that box thingie?" Cali asks and points.

At this precise moment I realize two things. First, that's Edna Tompkins on my computer screen. Second, she's got a key to the offering box.

"Hey!" Cali exclaims. "Is she supposed to be doing that?"

We watch as Edna reaches in the offering box and pulls out the bank deposit bag. With a stealthy glance over her shoulder, she unzips the bag and begins to pull out the cash.

I shiver as if I've been plunged into ice water. Then I flush hotly, adrenaline surging through my body.

Edna Tompkins, the biggest contributor to the church, is stealing the offering?

"Is she supposed to be doing that?" Cali asks again.

"Um…well, not really, but I'm sure she's just helping out the treasurer."

"Oh." Cali shrugs. "So, can you talk to David for me?"

"What?"

"Talk to David for me. Convince him we belong together. You see that, don't you?"

"Um…well…"

Cali's face falls, which distracts me momentarily from Edna.

"Look, Cali, I can't be the third side in this triangle. You need to talk to David yourself."

In a split second, her California sunshine darkens to New York black.

"It's you, isn't it? I knew it. You want him for yourself."

I can feel my face collapse into a guilty expression. "It's not that simple——"

"Yes, it is. You either want David or you don't. So which is it?"

Why is everyone asking me what I want these days? I turn away from Cali and watch as Edna stuffs a large wad of cash into her sensible handbag. Should I confront her now? Should I wait? No case study in divinity school ever covered this scenario.

I look back at Cali, whose demand for the truth intimidates me almost as much as the prospect of confronting Edna.

"Yes, yes. I want him, okay?"

"You made a play for him!" she shrieks. "I thought you were supposed to be all good and everything. I thought ministers had to be." She tosses her hair back and switches from hunted to huntress. "I'm going to tell on you."

What is this—third grade? But I can hardly argue with her because she's right. I made a play for her boyfriend, didn't I? Okay, technically he wasn't her boyfriend anymore when I invited him to the fund-raiser, but I didn't know that at the time.

"Cali, I'm sorry—"

"You're not sorry you tried to steal David. Like everybody else, you're just sorry you got caught."

I have no reply to that because she's right.

"Good-bye, Betsy. Some friend you turned out to be."

Cali storms from my office, and I sink back in my desk chair. On the monitor, Edna zips her handbag and scuttles out of the sacristy.

And in the office of the associate minister of Church of the Shep-herd, I engage in the only appropriate response I can think of. I cry. Because I don't know who I'm more disappointed in. Edna, who I know is evil. Or me, the one person I always thought would do the right thing.

Normally, life has a way of balancing itself out. For example, your job might reek, but you find a fabulous pair of shoes on sale to console yourself with. Or your outbound flight on your vacation gets can-celled, but the airline upgrades you, and eventually you travel where you're going in business class.

So where is the equity in my life right now? I've lost my mentor (Velva), my best friend (David), and the respect of an honest if naive young woman (Cali), and I have to confront my nemesis (Edna).

How did it all get so complicated? A month ago it seemed quite clear. I was leaving for law school and a new life where things would be refreshingly clear-cut. Now I'm further than ever from my escape.

That's what it is, of course. An escape. Velva was right about that. So was David. But as I discovered last night, I'm not enough for all this.

I wish I knew how other people figure out what they want. Velva's roommate, Dottie, knows what she wants—to live to be a hundred years old even if it means another eighteen months of pain and suffering. David wants to rebuild his church after the tornado, no matter how much conflict it causes in his congregation. LaRonda wants to prove she can be a big-steeple preacher, just like a man.

LaRonda. That's who I need right now. I reach for the phone. I've worn the Speed Dial button for her church smooth from frequent use. As I suspected, she's at her desk, using the Sunday-afternoon lull to catch up on the important-but-not-urgent tasks that get ignored in the daily grind of ministry. Things like prayer and Bible study.

"Ronnie? How about a latte?"

She sighs with relief. "Starbucks in twenty."

That's the extent of our conversation. It's good to know that even when my other major relationships are falling apart, my best girlfriend won't let me down.

Two seconds before I step out of my office, though, the phone rings. I debate answering it, but that niggling sense of impending doom that accompanies a preacher everywhere she goes won't let me walk out the door.

"Church of the Shepherd. This is Reverend Blessing."

It's the nurse from Hillsboro Health Care. Velva's roommate, Dottie, isn't doing so well. "Can you come right away?" the nurse asks.

No, no, no! I want to scream. I need a confab with LaRonda, not another emotional bloodletting. Dottie's not even my parishioner.

I guess this is why God made cell phones, so that ministers could break their plans with each other at a moment's notice. I call LaRonda to postpone as I'm getting into my car. It's not very Christian, but I *harrumph* all the way down Broadway and 21st Avenue to the nursing home. When I arrive, however, my personal pity party comes to a screeching halt.

"She's in the quiet room," the nurse says.

The quiet room? They didn't say anything on the phone about the quiet room. That's where they put you when you're ready to die and your roommate might object to your kicking the bucket in the next bed over.

I swallow the lump in my throat and follow the nurse down the hallway. Inside the room, Dottie's alone. Her pastor hasn't been to visit since Carter was president, and she has no family. Dottie's covered with a sheet. At least, what's left of her is covered with a sheet.

I move closer to the bed and hear her familiar whisper.

"Ninety-seven, ninety-eight, ninety-nine..." Her voice trails off at the critical number.

Easy deaths are a blessing. I've seen enough of the other kind to appreciate a good death. Sounds weird, doesn't it? But death is like life. Some people have fairly easy ones, and others suffer every step of the way.

I pull up a chair next to Dottie's bedside and take her hand in mine. It's more like a bird's claw than a hand; her fingers are gnarled into talons. I think of Angelique's violently red fingernails and realize that sooner or later even our hands succumb to the passage of time, manicures or not.

"Dottie? Can you hear me?"

She turns her head slightly, but her eyes remain closed. Her gray curls are matted to her head, which would have angered Velva.

"One…two…three…" Her voice is barely more than a breath.

I imagine Dottie was just as stubborn in life as she is in death. As physically deteriorated as she is, she's not about to let go until she celebrates her hundredth birthday.

"Dottie, it's Betsy."

Her lips curve slightly. "Nine…ten…eleven…"

That's the moment when inspiration strikes. At least I'm going to call it inspiration. Or mercy. It's just that so much has been wrong today. Edna's theft of the offering. My betrayal of Cali. And here's one thing, at least, that seems so clear-cut. God didn't intend for people to suffer like this.

"Dottie? I've come to see you for your birthday."

For the barest moment, her fingers tighten around mine.

"You're one hundred today, Dottie. Congratulations." I reach out and smooth her curls away from her forehead like my mother used to do to me when I was a child. I'm so inadequate in most areas of my life, but in this moment my path seems so clear. Dottie needs to be released from her suffering, and if she can't do it for herself, then it's my job to help her.

"It's okay," I whisper to her. "It's okay now, Dottie." On instinct I begin to recite the Twenty-third Psalm. "The LORD is my shepherd; I shall not be in want…"

As I recite the passage from memory, the quiet room grows quieter. Dottie's stopped counting. "Happy birthday, Dottie," I whisper in her ear when I finish, suddenly aware that if the nurse hears this conversation, she might not approve. I'm not even sure I approve, but I can only go with my instincts.

A moment later the nurse sticks her head around the doorframe to check on us.

"We're fine," I assure her. And when she's gone, I turn back to Dottie.

"You did it, sweetie. You're one hundred."

Now her smile is a little bigger, and her breathing is slower. And then even slower. For the next hour I sit beside her, holding her hand as she fades away. Maybe someone else would say what I'm doing is wrong. Maybe they'd say that any form of life is better than no life at all. But I say there's a rhythm to the dance of life, and God wants more for us than simply drawing breath. It's why I'm here right now, in this moment and in this place. Because someone has to do this work. Someone imperfect. Someone inadequate. But someone who shows up to represent God at a time like this.

I watch Dottie as she begins to change. The human will is an amazing thing. I think it's that part of God within each of us that motivates us to do things we could never do on our own. The Greek word for "spirit" is *pneuma* or "breath." I hold Dottie's hand as she draws that last bit of spirit into her lungs, and then with a whispering sound, she releases it. And releases herself.

The quiet room is completely quiet.

By the time I've finished talking with the staff at the health-care center and I've contacted the funeral home about Dottie, several hours have passed. When I finally meet LaRonda for coffee, I'm still pondering whether I can let God be God or whether I'll keep insisting on letting Betsy be Betsy. Am I as stubborn as Dottie? Have I spent my spiritual life counting over and over to one hundred without listening for a higher voice? Do I really have a call to ministry, or did I just want to have one because the church is supposed to be a safe place, the world's biggest come-as-you-are party?

"I ordered for you," LaRonda says and slides the latte across the café table to me. She looks as tired as I feel.

"You're a goddess."

"Tell that to my parishioners."

The discouragement in her voice jerks me out of my own woes. "What's up?"

I look at her—really look at her, instead of just giving her a cursory glance as I did when I came in—and see the dark circles under her eyes.

"The grapevine at my church has been functioning overtime."

"About you?"

She nods, her lips twisted too tightly for speech. Pain etches every line of her face, and she looks much older than her thirty-two years. I've seen more signs recently of the toll it takes on her, being a wunderkind of a preacher, but I assumed it was a temporary thing that would pass.

"What are they saying about you?"

I'm sure it's one of the usual rumors, the kind you learn to dismiss out of hand. That you're interviewing with another church. Or you're having an affair with a married man. Or you don't like men at all. Garden variety vicious gossip you just have to ignore.

LaRonda sighs. "A certain contingent has decided I'm not spiritually fit to be their pastor."

My bark of laughter causes several nearby heads to swivel toward us. Slumping down in my chair, I sip my latte and then sigh. "Honey, if you're not spiritually fit to pastor, what hope is there for the rest of us?"

LaRonda drains the dregs of her coffee and snaps the cup down on the table. "Evidently I'm damned for all eternity because I divulged the secret recipe."

Latte almost shoots out my nose. "What secret recipe?"

"The ladies auxiliary's sacred cow. The recipe for Death-to-the-Diet Brownies."

If LaRonda weren't so upset, this would be very funny. "Their sacred cow is a brownie recipe?"

LaRonda twists her cup between her palms. "They hold a huge fund-raiser every year. People drive in from Kentucky, Mississippi, Georgia—you name it. Since the ladies auxiliary won't give away the recipe, people buy dozens of brownies and freeze them."

"How did you give away the recipe?"

LaRonda looks away. "I sent it in for my sorority's alumnae cookbook. Under my name."

For a long moment we're both silent, because while I can understand what drove her to it, I can see we're both thinking the same thing. It was wrong.

She smiles, but there's no happiness or joy in it. "C'mon, Betz, you know what a lousy cook I am. I was desperate. All my sorority sisters are going to judge me on that recipe. What was I supposed to do? Send instructions for microwaving a Lean Cuisine?"

I don't know what to say, because LaRonda's never disappointed me like this before. "I guess you cut the wrong corner."

"Yeah. I didn't realize how serious they were about the secret part."

Okay. Technically, recipes can't be copyrighted. I learned that in my first church when the ladies auxiliary put together a cookbook for the church's one-hundredth anniversary. Two women submitted identical recipes for congealed carrot salad, and it was weeks before we sorted out the claims and counterclaims. LaRonda didn't do anything illegal.

"Okay, so you gave away a recipe. Not a great thing, but it doesn't make you a bad pastor. It just means you're human."

In LaRonda's case, or in the case of any female minister, you have to wonder how much of the ladies auxiliary's ire comes from the fact that they were betrayed by one of their own. If a man had divulged the recipe, would they have demanded his resignation? Or just been delighted that he exhibited an interest in baking?

"So, what will happen?"

LaRonda sighs. "It will blow over. Eventually. Until the next time I make a mistake. And then it will become part of the litany of my sinful ways." LaRonda rubs her temples with her fingertips. "You know, Betz, I'm tired of trying to live my father's life and my mother's life simultaneously. I feel like I'm the preacher and the preacher's wife."

LaRonda's always been so sure, so determined. It's disconcerting to see the uncertainty in her eyes.

"Will you leave your church?"

It scares me to think of LaRonda giving up. If she can't make it as a woman pastor, who can? But then I wonder why I care when I'm leaving the ministry anyway. I guess I want to know that someone can make it work, even if I can't.

"Actually, I'm going to South Africa," she says.

"Very funny, Ronnie."

"I'm serious, Betz."

And she is. She really is. I can see it in her face. The truth jolts me more than the added shot in my latte.

Her eyes plead for understanding. "I'm going to teach in the school for AIDS orphans."

"When did you decide this?" Hurt, anger, frustration all rise up from my stomach into my chest. "You had to have been thinking about this for a while. Why didn't you tell me?"

No, no, no! This can't be happening. First Velva, then David, and now LaRonda. It's too cruel. I ignore the niggling voice in my head that says I've been keeping my own secrets.

"You can't walk away," I protest. "It will prove them right."

"Prove who right?"

"Them. The ones who don't want us in their churches. The ones who are always waiting for us to fail so they can pick apart our carcasses like vultures."

"Do you seriously think male preachers don't have their own circling buzzards?"

"But you made it, Ronnie. You did it. Senior pastor. Large church. The 'in' group at the ministers' meetings."

"And it wasn't worth the price, Betsy. Not for me." For the briefest of moments, I get a glimpse of the real LaRonda, the one she's been hiding behind the fabulous makeup and the aura of power. Loneliness haunts her eyes, and responsibility has bowed her shoulders. "That was my father's ministry. Not mine. I'm not serving God to prove a point. I'm serving God to, well, serve God."

"And to do that you have to go to South Africa?" Panic takes up residence with the grief and hurt. "You can't serve God in the continental United States?"

"Don't judge me, Betsy. You haven't been where I am. When it comes to being a minority, I'm a double-dip. At least in the black community in South Africa I'll only have one strike against me."

"Oh, well, I see. Now the truth comes out. I thought we were equals, but apparently I've been second-tier all along because I'm not as successful or as oppressed."

"That's not fair."

"I'm not in the mood to be fair." I know I'm pouting like a six-year-old deprived of a treat, and I'm not proud of it. "Why didn't you tell me before?"

"I didn't want to tell you earlier because of Velva. I know you're hurting," LaRonda snaps, "but don't take it out on me."

"But you're leaving! What am I supposed to do?"

"That's the $64,000 question, isn't it?"

I hate it when LaRonda goes Zen on me.

"I refuse to answer that question on the grounds I might incriminate myself."

"That makeover's got to be more than skin-deep. You're going to have to figure yourself out sooner or later, Betz."

"Yeah, well, at the moment, later is an attractive option. I have enough to sort through in the short term. Besides, weren't you the one who told me I couldn't play it safe? That conflict is good?" I wish my tone of voice wasn't bordering on the hysterical.

LaRonda arches an eyebrow. "Did something happen with Velva's roommate?"

"Nothing. I mean, something did happen, obviously. She passed away while I was there."

LaRonda seems grateful for the change of subject. "Was it traumatic?"

Part of me longs to tell her the truth, to seek her advice about what it all means. But even though she's still my best friend, some-thing's changed in our relationship. I always thought of her as a big sister with all the answers, and now I'm realizing that she's just as human as the rest of us. She doesn't have any secret knowledge, no guarantees.

"Betsy, what's going on?"

"What do you mean?" When in doubt, act innocent.

"You've been acting funny for the past couple of weeks. Is there something you're not telling me?"

I screw up my courage. "Yes."

"And that would be?"

I hang my head. "That I'm leaving the ministry."

To my distress, I see something on LaRonda's face I've never seen there before, and it looks a lot like contempt. It feels that way too.

"I never thought you'd be a quitter."

That stings. "I don't think I'm quitting. I'm just correcting my course. And I can't believe you'd sit there and condemn me when you've just said you're leaving too."

"I'm not leaving, just refocusing. What happened to your call to ministry?" she says.

It's the scariest question one minister can ask another. Because if we're wrong about something as sacred as being called to be a minis-ter, how can we be certain about anything? The most threatening thing to preachers isn't personnel committees, declines in the offering, or even acts of God knocking down the sanctuary. It's someone deserting the ranks.

"My call? What happened to yours?" I snap.

"You've been pretty sure for the past eight years."

"That was before two churches convinced me otherwise."

"So just because it's not all sunshine and roses, you get to ditch the church?"

"You're leaving your church. Why can't I leave mine?"

LaRonda waves away my question. "We're talking about you now. Have you told David about this?"

"Yes."

"What did he say?"

Tears well up in my eyes. "Before or after he told me that he had no romantic interest in me whatsoever?"

"Ouch." She may be mad at me, but she's still sympathetic to my pitiful love life. "I guess last night didn't go so well."

"It's been a tough week."

She looks at me, and I see the pain in her eyes. "I didn't want to disappoint you," I mumble.

"Evidently, it's my week to be disappointed." She reaches down by her feet and snags her purse. "Look, Betsy, I'm sorry. Maybe it's better if I just go."

I try to catch her arm, but she slips by me. "Ronnie—"

"No, Betz. Not now. Maybe later." She chokes on the words, and I know she's about to cry.

"But—"

"I'll call you later."

And then she's gone. The last crossbeam in my shaky hut of a life.

Chapter 16

On Monday morning I limp back to Church of the Shepherd. Okay, I'm limping because I've donned the black stilettos for courage, but I'm limping metaphorically as well. If LaRonda can't cut the mustard, why should any woman try? I'm not trying, though, I sternly remind myself as I walk through the door to the administrative offices. I'm going to law school.

Angelique's on the phone, a frown creasing her face. "Yes, Mrs. Tompkins."

I meet Angelique's gaze and roll my eyes, but she doesn't answer in kind. The frown on her lips matches the lines on her forehead.

"I'll see what I can do," she says to Edna and then, after saying good-bye, she slowly places the receiver in its cradle.

I'm prepared for some very un-Christlike venting about what a pain in the neck Edna can be. Last night, when I wasn't replaying my fight with LaRonda or mourning the debacle with David, I was stewing about how to confront Edna. "What's up with Edna?"

"Didn't they call you from the hospital?" Angelique asks.

"The hospital?"

"Edna was attacked in the church yesterday afternoon. They had to take her to the emergency room."

I swallow the sudden lump in my throat. But Edna was gone,

wasn't she, when I left to meet LaRonda? I saw her leave the sacristy myself. "Is she okay?" I may not like Edna, but I don't hate her or wish her ill.

"Some guy pushed her down and dislocated her shoulder. He made off with the cash offering, too. I wonder why The Judge didn't call you."

I can't bring myself to tell her that last night, for the first time in five years of ministry, I unplugged my phone. After the showdown with LaRonda, I just couldn't deal with anything else. Just my luck my meltdown happened at the precise time I most needed to be a pastor. Because I'll never hear the end of this from Edna.

"Is she going to be okay?"

"Yes, but she's in a pickle. Is it okay if I take off for a few minutes? I'm going to go over to her house and help her with something."

My blood pressure skyrockets, and steam's probably shooting out my ears. "She called the church to ask you to come help her with something?" I guess my tone is a little bit harsh, but then that's my general attitude toward Edna, even when she's injured. "What does she need? A church staff person to pester at home since she can't leave the house?"

For the first time since she arrived at Church of the Shepherd, Angelique looks at me with disapproval. "Edna can't move her injured shoulder. She called to see if someone from the church could come over and hook her bra."

Laughter bubbles in my throat and then dies as quickly as it was born. I deflate like a helium balloon poked with a long, sharp needle. "I'll go."

Angelique looks at me in surprise. "You will?"

"Yes."

"Can you do it nicely?"

When Angelique first came to us, I was the wise one who had her life together and was glad to offer helpful advice to someone struggling to get through the day. Now our roles have flip-flopped, and I'm the one in need of wiser counsel.

"Yes, I can do it nicely."

She seems satisfied with my answer and sits back in her desk chair. "You better go on, then."

"Yep." Still, it takes me a few seconds to get my feet moving and headed toward the door. I hate having to be compassionate to a woman I'd just as soon despise. But I can't help myself. Basic human decency can be such an impediment to self-righteousness.

As I climb back in the car, it occurs to me to wonder about this mysterious attacker. I know Edna stole the money. Was there really a strange man in the church? I doubt it. Which means she injured herself some other way. More questions. More confrontations. All in all, I'm sorry I didn't call in sick and tired today.

Edna lives in Belle Meade, the old-money section of Nashville. In these elite environs, the speed limit never goes above thirty-five miles an hour, the country club is referred to simply as "the club," and the city recently, in a gesture of thoughtfulness, put out benches for the maids to sit on while they wait for the bus. I'm biased, you say? Resentful? I guess it shows a little.

Edna's maid, Alice, answers the door of the Tompkins's French provincial mansion. Alice's snowy white uniform contrasts with her dark skin, but her smile is the brightest thing of all. Now why Alice couldn't hook her bra I don't understand, but I'm sure in Edna-world there's a perfectly sensible reason for asking someone from church to drive fifteen minutes across town to do what someone ten feet from her could easily have accomplished.

"Good morning, Reverend." Alice has worked for Edna for thirty years. Whenever the women's group meets at Edna's home (which is frequently), Alice is an ever-present figure. I'm always more than willing to help Alice in the kitchen so I can escape the endless debates among the women about where to send twenty-two dollars in outreach money. Really, the World Bank ought to hire these ladies to straighten out the global economy, given their obsessive attention to detail.

"Hello, Alice. I think Mrs. Tompkins needs my help with something."

One of the things I like best about Alice, in addition to her raspberry scones, is her loyalty. Surely she knows about the bra dilemma, but you'd never know it from her expression.

"She's in her bedroom," Alice says. "I'll walk you up."

I've never been to Edna's inner sanctum. The farthest I've traveled beyond the living room is the kitchen, and I've certainly never been invited upstairs. Alice leaves me at the door to Edna's bedroom. I knock softly. "Edna? It's Reverend Blessing."

"Well, don't just stand out there. Come in."

So much for Edna gaining any humanity from her recent suffering.

I open the door and slip inside. Her bedroom is the size of my entire apartment and has more furniture in it.

"Good morning, Edna," I call out when I don't see her in the bedroom.

"I'm in here."

I follow the sound of her voice to a walk-in closet a Hollywood star would envy. Row upon row of clothing on padded hangers, racks of shoes, drawers upon drawers—it's an impressive collection.

Edna's standing in front of a full-length mirror in her half-slip, her bra wrapped around the front of her but hanging loosely at her sides. She's so thin I can see every one of her vertebrae. Age spots and freckles mottle her skin. The back of her hair is mashed flat, and she looks like what I so often forget she is—a frail, elderly woman. Her injured shoulder is unwrapped, her arm stiffly clutched to her side. I see a sling waiting on the shelf next to her.

My chest feels as if someone's lassoed me and pulled the rope tight. Standing there in Edna's massive closet, I'm suddenly humbled. This is my nemesis? the tormentor I've resented for her power?

I've stood silent too long. My gaze meets Edna's in the mirror, and there's a silent, uncomfortable connection. I know there's pity in my eyes. Her spine straightens. "Are you here to help me or not?"

I had planned to demand to know why Alice couldn't help her. I was loaded for bear, ready to give this woman a piece of my mind. I was primed for a showdown. Instead, I step forward and simply fasten her bra behind her bony back.

"Can I help you with the sling?"

"If you like." She says the words like a queen forced to address a filthy peasant. "Since you were nowhere to be found yesterday, you might as well make yourself useful now."

I swallow the sharp retort that rises to my lips and slip the sleeves of her blouse carefully over her arms. She waves away my hands when I try to button up the front and fumbles with the buttons herself.

The sling is a bit tricky, and she gasps in pain a couple of times as we settle her arm into it and I rig the straps around her shoulder and waist. It's the only time in the past six months that Edna and I have worked well together.

"Did they give you anything for the pain?" I ask her.

"I don't take pain pills." She sniffs in disdain and then winces as I tighten the last strap.

"Maybe you should. Just this once."

"Oh, very well. If you're going to pester me to death." She waves her hand toward a little silver bell. "Ring for Alice. She'll bring them."

It goes against the grain for me to ring for anybody. I keep thinking about Pavlov and his dogs. "I'll run down to the kitchen and get them. It's no trouble. Why don't you lie down while I go?"

Edna tries to shrug but flinches instead as her injured shoulder protests. She's obviously exhausted from the simple effort of getting dressed. A few moments later I have her settled on her enormous bed atop the threadbare spread. Why one of the richest women in Nashville should have a bedspread that looks as if a cat's been sharpening its claws in the middle is beyond me, but the ways of the truly wealthy are different from the habits and preferences of mere mortals.

It takes me a few minutes to find my way to the kitchen and Alice. She looks at me with quiet approval, and I'm ashamed of my earlier churlishness.

"It's you she needed, Reverend Blessing," Alice says, as if she hears my unspoken question.

I trudge back up the stairs to Edna's room with a cup of water and a couple of Darvocet. Her eyes are closed, her mouth slightly open as she dozes. A wave of tiredness washes over me. The last thing I want to do right now is confront her, but I have to. Because injury or no, Edna's responsible for the theft of a lot of money from yesterday's offering.

"Edna?"

She starts, looks confused for a moment, then realizes where she is and who I am. "It took long enough."

"Sorry." Wait a minute. Why am I apologizing to this woman? But that's her spiritual gift—keeping people on the defensive. I wish it were mine. Must be nice to operate from a position of power.

"Edna, we need to talk." After handing her a glass of water and her medication, I pull the little stool from her dressing table toward the side of the bed.

"I'm hardly in any condition for a tête-à-tête." She swallows the pills and sets the glass on her bedside table. The only other items on its surface are an alarm clock and a telephone. No family photos. No trinkets or mementos. I take a surreptitious glance around the bedroom. The furniture is of undeniable quality, but there are no personal touches there either. Since he retired from his medical practice, Edna's husband spends most of his time on a Florida golf course. They have no children, no other family nearby. For the first time I glimpse how lonely her life must be.

I clear my throat and mentally gird my loins for battle. Maybe the Darvocet will kick in and soften her up for this interrogation.

"We need to talk about the missing offering."

Not a smidgen of guilt shows on her face. "This is hardly the time."

"I think it's exactly the right time."

Once again our eyes meet, and I let her see the truth. I know what she did. And in that moment I also realize who's behind the dead roses and the prank phone calls. Edna blinks, and it's as if I can read her mind. She's trying to figure out how I caught her.

"I installed a Web cam in the sacristy, Edna. I sat in my office yesterday afternoon and saw everything that happened."

"Then you saw the man who assaulted me?" Butter wouldn't melt in her mouth. She could fool the FBI's best criminal profiler, but I know what I saw.

"I don't know how you were injured, Edna, but you weren't assaulted by anyone."

She purses her lips so tightly, I'm afraid they might pop off her face. "I can't believe you said that. Just wait until the personnel committee meets again. This is outside of enough. You should have resigned long ago, and next time I'll make sure you do."

I've been wondering why she did it. Whether the theft was a bid for attention. Or maybe her husband cut her off from their considerable finances. But with a flash I see the truth. She stole the offering to make it look as if people were withholding their money to protest my appointment as the interim senior minister.

"Edna, I saw you take the money. I saw you use the key you have to the offering box. I saw you stuff it in your purse."

She lifts her chin. "Well, then, that would be my word against yours, wouldn't it?"

She thinks she has me. For a split second I think she has me too. Then I remember I wasn't the only one in my office yesterday.

"Actually, I have another witness. There was someone else with me at the time."

I wait, letting the words sink in. Her expression shifts almost imperceptibly. She's calculating how to respond to this new piece of information.

"Who would this reliable witness be?" She glares down her nose at me.

I stop myself from saying, "A ditzy Californian with designs on my man." Instead, I say, "A friend of mine."

"A biased witness, you mean," Edna retorts.

I turn my head so I can roll my eyes without her seeing. When I do, I spy Edna's handbag on top of her dressing table. It's the same bag she was carrying yesterday. Is it worth a gamble to prove my claim?

"If you didn't take the offering, then you won't mind if I take a peek in your purse." I all but leap from the stool and snatch up the ancient but expensive black leather bag.

"No!" Edna tries to jump up as well, but she's old and injured, and I'm...well...not.

I have absolutely no qualms about unzipping her purse and pawing through its contents. Checkbook. Plastic rain bonnet. A roll of Tums. And then, yes, there it is. A thick wad of bills stuffed in the side zipper pocket.

"I can't believe you're violating my privacy like this." Edna tries to sound indignant, but her weak voice just sounds scared.

Even though I'm standing here with the evidence clutched in my trembling fingers, and even though my logical mind has already begun to piece together her motive, I have to ask. "Why, Edna? Do you really hate me that much?" I sink back to the stool, the money falling from my fingers to the floor.

Edna's eyes blaze. "It's not right. Ministers should be men. Especially senior pastors."

I grimace. "And it'll be a man again as soon as the search committee does its work. I'm a temporary fix." I sigh and run my fingers through my hair. "You couldn't live with a woman minister for a few months?"

"If it's wrong, it's wrong," Edna insists, but she's slurring her words. The Darvocet is working its mojo.

How many times have I had this argument? I decided several years ago that no amount of persuasion on my part was ever going to change someone's mind about women in ministry. Instead, I've focused on doing the best possible job I can, proving by my actions I do indeed have a call. Except now, since I've decided to leave the church, my actions aren't the effective testimony I used to think they were.

"Some people don't think it's wrong at all," I say. "Some very faithful, very Christian people." But my heart's not really in my words because how can I defend what I've chosen to abandon?

"If it was wrong in my day, it's wrong now."

"What do you mean—if it was wrong in your day?"

A slash of fear sparks in Edna's eyes. She clamps her lips shut and purses them.

Understanding cracks me over the head with all the force of Edna's fictional assailant.

"Edna, did you have a call to ministry when you were young?" It's the last question I'd ever have imagined myself asking Edna Tompkins.

"I don't know what you're talking about." Edna's looped enough to slur her words, but she also realizes what she's inadvertently revealed.

"You wanted to be a minister, didn't you?" I press her.

Unexpectedly, her eyes grow moist and two large tears drip to her cheeks. Compassion swamps me unbidden. Why didn't I see it before? This isn't the first time I've encountered strong opposition from older women whose own calls were thwarted. Self-preservation compelled them to buy into the notion that any call from God they felt couldn't possibly include the ministry.

"What did they tell you?"

I don't really expect her to answer my question, but she does.

"They told me I was wrong. That it was Satan tempting me away from marriage and motherhood. Well, I've had precious little of one and none of the other."

I'm so blown away by this unexpected discovery that it takes me a moment to absorb it all.

"They were right," Edna snaps—or at least snaps as well as she can while under light sedation. "I was wrong to think I should be a minister."

I could spend all day arguing the point with her, if she could stay awake. We could debate theology, pore over Scripture. Instead, I pull the stool closer to her bed, look her in the eye, and say, "Were you wrong, Edna? Were you? Or were they?"

This time I don't look away. I keep my eyes locked on hers and watch the play of emotions there. Frustration, anger, resignation. It's a wonder she didn't do something drastic years ago. Taking the offering is minor, given the circumstances.

"I already said. They told me to get married and be a mother."

But motherhood had never happened for her, obviously. And marriage had been a mixed bag at best. All that had been left was the church, which hadn't wanted the real Edna, the one with a call to ministry. Instead, the church had taken her money and let her take her frustrations out on others. So now Edna's just like the chair of the board in my last church that fired me. Human. In the midst of inflicting suffering on me, she's revealed her own humanity. I hate it when parishioners do that. It makes it so hard to feel morally superior.

I want to find out more about Edna's call, but the Darvocet has done its thing. Her head nods and then she's off to la-la land. And I'm left sitting on the dressing-table stool, a wad of stolen cash at my feet and my self-righteousness tumbling down after it.

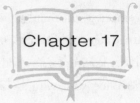

Chapter 17

You'd think between LaRonda's impending departure for South Africa and Edna's thievery, I'd have enough problems to keep my mind off the debacle with David.

Sadly, no.

To add insult to injury, the fish he bought me died. It jumped out of the bowl, as eager to escape my presence as everyone else in my life right now. I'd say it's an omen, but it's not much of one if it happens after the fact. More symbolic than prophetic.

At some point I'll have to face him again. David, I mean. Not the dead fish. I wish my problems with David could be disposed of with one flush of the toilet. Besides, I need to talk to him about this whole thing with Edna. LaRonda's too wrapped up in her impending move to another continent. And she's probably not the best person at the moment to help me come to terms with my ministry, given the vitriolic nature of her resignation letter. She sent me a copy of it via e-mail, and then I edited it for her, taking out the vitriol, before she actually turned it in. It helped when I pointed out she might need references to get another job in Nashville someday, and she might not want to burn every bridge.

So what will I do when David calls? Several strategies spring to mind. Pretense, as in pretend nothing happened. Denial, as in make a preemptive strike and say I was PMS-ing or something. The truth, the unattractive third option, is easily avoided for now.

After leaving Edna's house I can't bring myself to go directly back to the office, so I swing by St. Thomas Hospital to make a couple of pastoral calls. Nothing like a few IVs and heart monitors connected to your parishioners to take your mind off your troubles for a while. Especially when you make the rounds in stilettos, whose name must derive from the Latin for "please drive spears through my feet."

When I finally do return to the office, Angelique is nowhere to be found. She's probably off showing the sanctuary to a prospective bride. The stolen money burns a hole in my pocket, but it's too late to simply return it to the offering box. The retirees who come to count on Monday mornings will have finished and gone. So what do I do with this evidence of Edna's sins? A more Machiavellian preacher would head straight to The Judge's office and lay the groundwork for her disgrace. But every time my thoughts go that direction, I see her bony spine and her injured arm clamped to her side. I feel the pain of a bedroom void of any evidence of a personal life. And I think about how the church shamed her because of who God called her to be.

David would know what to do with the money. I should call him. And I will. As soon as the next ice age passes.

I open my office door, and to my surprise, Ed is sitting in the chair across from my desk.

"Hi, Ed. Did we have an appointment?" Angelique is normally so good at juggling my calendar. I'd be lost without her.

"We need to talk, Betsy."

"Oh."

A minister dreads those words. They could be the prelude for anything from "I was so moved by your last sermon, I've sold all my

worldly possessions and given the money to the poor" to "I'm here to
fire you." I've had more personal experience with the latter.

"Is there a problem?"

"It's about the offering."

"Yes?" Like Edna, butter wouldn't melt in my mouth. I force my
hand not to reach for the pocket of my khakis.

"Edna called me half an hour ago. She told me everything."

Again, it must be the Darvocet. "So you know what's been happening to the cash offering?"

Ed nods sadly. "Yes. It's a shame, Betsy."

I nod sagely. "Yes, isn't it?" I lean back in my chair, breathing a
little easier for the first time since Saturday night. "I'm glad I don't
have to keep the secret anymore."

Ed lifts one hand to fiddle with his bow tie. "Well, yes, I can see
where you'd be relieved at some level."

His tone sets off an alarm bell in my head. He twists his tie some
more and then gives it a final tug. "We can get you help, Betsy."

"Help? I'm not sure what you mean. My biggest concern is how
to return the offering with no one being the wiser."

Ed's nostrils flare. "That's not the attitude I expected from you,
Reverend Blessing."

I can't believe I'm indignant on Edna's behalf, but surely he
wouldn't want to expose his own sister this way. "I'm not willing for
this congregation to suffer for one person's mistake. Not when it can
be so easily rectified."

Ed's pale cheeks grow whiter. "I hardly see grand theft as a 'mistake,' as you put it. If you needed money, you should have come to
the committee."

"Excuse me?" The floor drops out from under me.

"I'm aware we were rather hasty in refusing to raise your salary to compensate you for your additional responsibilities. But negotiation would have been far preferable to theft."

My laugh comes out more like a bark. "You think I took the money?"

"Edna told me you confessed everything to her."

"Did she?" Clearly I overestimated the painkillers and underestimated the woman.

"She set a good example of Christian charity, Betsy. Told me we shouldn't call the police, not if you agree to resign and go quietly."

I resist the temptation to lean over my desk and see if Ed's fly is zipped. "I didn't take the money."

"It's too late for denials." He holds out his hand. "I think you'd better give me the money, Betsy."

"No." This time I'm not going quietly. I will not be complicit in the destruction of my ministry yet again. Plus, a felony conviction would really put a monkey wrench in my law career. "If you want the money, call a meeting of the personnel committee. I'll be happy to attend."

Ed sighs. "There's no need to make so many people aware of this mess."

"I think there's a great deal of need. And I think Edna should be there as well."

"That's impossible. She's still at home recuperating."

"Then we'll have the meeting at her house."

Ed's looking at me like I've sprouted horns and a tail and I'm hefting a pitchfork. "I never expected this of you, Betsy."

"Well, that's something at least. I'm glad to know my alleged kleptomania comes as a complete shock. At least your opinion of me was that high to begin with."

He shakes his head and pushes himself out of the chair. "Perhaps I should call Dr. Black."

I can feel the heat of anger rising up my neck and spreading across my cheeks. "If you call Dr. Black, I will file a lawsuit for slander. Are we clear on that, Ed?"

The mere mention of a lawsuit is enough to send him into a tail-spin. "Now, now, there's no need for that." He pats the air as if he's trying to soothe it. "I'll call the meeting."

"I'll see you tomorrow then."

And he's gone without a backward glance. I collapse into my chair. How easily it can all fall apart. It's just like the last time, only now I know exactly what's happening. I know Edna is the engineer of my demise. And this time I won't agree to put my tail between my legs and head for the hills. No, this time I'm going to fight. And I'm going to win.

The upside of the accusation against me is that I feel extremely empowered. The downside is that I have to call David to get Cali's phone number because I'm going to need her to corroborate my story. The Darvocet must have deleted that particular bit of information from Edna's memory. That or she thinks I'm bluffing—the spiritual equivalent of a round of Texas Hold 'Em.

With great reluctance I dial David's direct number at St. Helga's. To my simultaneous relief and dismay, I get his voice mail.

"Hi, this is David, pastor of St. Helga's Church. Leave a message and pray I remember to get back to you."

I can't believe he actually has that on his machine, but I'm sure his parishioners have become accustomed to his—shall we say "distinctive"?—sense of humor.

"Hey, David. It's Betsy. Give me a call." Just the right tone. Friendly, casual. No sign of the desperate spinster who flung herself at him two nights ago. "By the way, the betta died." Why did I say that? "Not that it's important. Or, I mean not that the information is important. Obviously the fish was important to me." I'm babbling and I can't stop. "Anyway, give me a call."

I hang up as quickly as possible before I can do any more damage. Then I sit back in my desk chair, fold my hands in my lap, and pray.

LaRonda would chastise me for this passive approach to my predicament. I choose not to think of it as passivity but as strategic delay. But I can't be strategic for too long. I only have until tomorrow to mount my defense.

Angelique reappears fifteen minutes later with a pink message slip in her hand. Ed's been true to his word and has called a meeting of the personnel committee for 5:00 p.m. tomorrow here at the church. Apparently Edna possesses remarkable recuperative powers. Motivation is everything.

Then, twenty minutes later, when my stomach's starting to protest its lack of a noon feeding, a taller shadow darkens my doorway.

David.

I'm so glad I'm sitting down. I'm even more delighted I was pretending to work on Sunday's sermon while I waited for him to return my call. I lay down my pen and close the commentary on Romans without actually having read a word of it. Given my current situation, it's hard to work up much enthusiasm for the pros and cons of circumcision among first-century Christians.

"This is a surprise." I wish I'd made some attempt this morning to apply makeup to go with the stilettos. And my hair looks more Bozo than Britney.

"Hey, Betz." He shifts from one foot to the other. "Can I come in?"

I hate this so much, this stupid awkwardness. All I want to do is spill my guts to my best pal. Instead, my stomach is in a tailspin over the surprise appearance of a man who makes me deeply aware I'm first and foremost a woman, not a preacher.

"Of course you can come in." I don't mean to bark the words. Great. Now I both look and sound like a terrier. Would it be awful if I excused myself long enough to run to the salon for a shampoo and style?

David slides into the chair so recently vacated by Ed. He swipes his hair out of his eyes (I'm usually the one who reminds him to get it cut) and rests one hand on each of his thighs. It's a thoroughly masculine pose, and I can't help it if I melt a little.

"How've you been?" he asks.

"Um…fine." Is this a trick question? Does he really think I'm going to part with that kind of classified information when it revolves around him?

"Look, about Saturday night—"

"Edna Tompkins has accused me of stealing the offering." Betsy Blessing, master of the diversionary bombshell.

"What?"

"She said I stole the cash offering."

David leans forward in his chair. "And Edna's the real culprit, right?"

"Very astute. You've been reading your Agatha Christie again."

"So the Web cam worked?"

"Yep. Only it's pretty much my word against hers. Except for…"

"Except for what?"

"Except for Cali." I rush the words out of my mouth, wishing I could duck for cover under my desk.

David scowls. "What does she have to do with Edna stealing the offering?"

"Cali came to see me yesterday. She's my corroborating witness."

"She saw Edna steal the offering?"

"Yep. I need her to come to the personnel meeting tomorrow and tell them what she saw."

"Will Edna be there?"

"Yes. Better than a lineup."

David's gaze suddenly intensifies. "Why was Cali here in the first place?"

I'd hoped to avoid this line of questioning. "Oh, just girl stuff."

"She wanted to talk to you about me, huh?"

"Yes."

"Specifically?"

I'm about to do the verbal equivalent of a Bolshoi ballerina pirouetting around the stage. Wonder how fast my words can dance around the truth?

"She told me you broke up with her."

David slouches down in his chair. "I had to, Betz. She was way too young."

"Apparently she didn't take it well." I stifle all the "I-told-you-so's" fighting to escape my lips.

David rubs his right shoulder. "I wasn't expecting violence."

"She hit you?" I don't know whether to laugh or go after her myself.

"Maybe I deserved it. I shouldn't have asked her out in the first place."

No, you moron, you shouldn't have. You should have asked me out instead. I also refrain from saying these things aloud.

"Will you call her for me?" I ask, wishing I had some actual feminine wiles to employ.

"I can't, Betz. She'll think I'm trying to get back together with her." He leans over the desk, picks up my pen, and scribbles a number in the margin of my sermon notes. "You can call her, though."

"Great." Which is the exact opposite of what I actually mean, but that seems to be my MO with David these days.

"Betz?"

I look up from contemplating the phone number. His luscious brown eyes are focused on me. Forty-eight hours ago, I would have given anything for that. Again, I like the option of diving for cover under my desk.

"What?"

"We have to talk."

"No, we don't. Not really." I pick up the pen from where he left it and open the commentary. "I prefer to pretend Saturday night never happened."

"If we don't talk about it, how can we get past it?"

"You mean you're not over it?" I am so Edna-like in this moment that it's completely frightening. And what I wouldn't give for a couple of Darvocet to dull the pain right about now.

David pushes himself up out of the chair. He towers over me, clenching the fingers on one hand in frustration. Someone who didn't know him as well as I do might not catch that telltale sign. "I'm not going to keep banging my head against your walls, Betz. Call me when you're ready to talk. Real talk. Not this weird denial stuff."

"David—"

"When you're ready to talk. I swear you can run away even when you're sitting still."

"But—" Okay, now I'm scared. I've never heard that tone of finality in his voice before.

"Bye, Betz."

"Bye," I whisper in return, but he doesn't hear me. He's striding out of my office, and I wonder if it's the last time I'll watch him walk away. Because that's what it feels like.

"Cali? It's Betsy."

"Oh. Hello. What do you want?"

It takes me twenty minutes of groveling to convince her to come to the church at five o'clock tomorrow. The only card I can't play is the one where I promise to help her get David back. But I'm at the point of offering her cash when she finally capitulates.

"Oh, all right. If you promise never to call me again."

I think I know how to finesse Edna on this one. If I'm lucky, I won't have to use Cali at all tomorrow. Her mere presence should get the job done. But she's my ace in the hole, and I'm not going to go gently into Edna's good night.

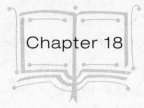

Chapter 18

I spend Tuesday morning shopping for a reconciliation present for LaRonda. We came to a truce while editing her resignation letter, but things really aren't back to normal. I can't let her leave without some attempt at closing the distance between us. I have no idea what you buy someone bound for a semideveloping nation, but I finally decide on a potpourri of helpful items from CVS: sunscreen, lip balm, insect repellent chock full of DEET, and some bandanas in neon colors.

I'd buy David something too, but I don't think a tube of lip balm is going to set things right between us. Plus, after kissing him Saturday night, I don't think he needs it. I'd buy Edna some compassion and human decency, but they don't carry those things at CVS. Unless they have them stashed behind the pharmacy counter.

By the time five o'clock rolls around, I'm a bundle of nerves. The extra latte I picked up at Starbucks was meant to fortify me for the confrontation with the personnel committee. Unfortunately, it has me on a caffeine buzz that could fuel a jet engine.

Again, I have the good sense to arrive at the boardroom early. The committee members file in one by one—Ed, The Judge, Sweet Marjorie, and Gus Winston, who carries an accounting ledger. Edna makes her grand entrance last with the aid of a three-legged cane. Why she should need a cane when her shoulder is injured, I have no

idea. Unless she plans to use it to beat me about the head and shoulders. She must have had her hair done this morning because she's
back-combed to within an inch of her life. Ed's looking squeamish,
Marjorie looks bewildered, and The Judge has clearly been to Florida
because his courtroom pallor has been replaced with a nice tan.

Ed clears his throat. "Shall we begin?"

My pulse accelerates. Cali's not here yet, but I don't want to say
anything because it would tip off Edna.

"Betsy, would you begin with prayer?"

Even though he thinks I'm a probable felon, Ed would rather
have me pray in public than do it himself. Pollsters say people fear
public speaking more than they fear death. I think people fear pray-
ing in public more than both of those things combined.

"Almighty God…" I begin as my mind races. I'm going to have
to pray for all I'm worth, because I have to stall until Cali gets here.
"From the beginning of the world, you have loved us…"

I proceed to work my way through the entire biblical narrative,
point by point. Creation, the flood, the patriarchs, Moses. The others
are beginning to get twitchy, but there's still no sign of Cali. I really
hope God doesn't mind this slight abuse of privilege in the interest of
truth and justice.

Finally, when I've passed the prophets and the rebuilding of the
temple and am contemplating throwing in the Maccabees, I hear a
noise in the doorway.

"…and so we thank you for your guidance. Be with us in this
meeting. Amen."

I look up, and Cali's standing there, thin, waxed, and tan, and
clearly unhappy to be darkening the doors of the church.

"Come in, Cali. You can sit here." I pull out the chair next to me.

Ed clears his throat. "This is a closed meeting, Betsy."

"It's okay, Ed. I invited her for a reason." I look at Edna to see if any of this is registering with her, but she's too busy looking triumphant to perceive Cali as any kind of threat. The Darvocet must have punched some potholes in her memory.

The Judge shrugs. "Betsy's friend can stay. This won't take long."

"No, it won't," I agree. I reach into my pocket and slap the stolen offering on the conference table in front of me. "Because I know who's been taking the offering."

Edna smirks. "We all do, Betsy. Your confession comes a little late. What we want is your resignation."

You'd never know that yesterday I was helping her with the simple task of dressing herself. Edna's momentary lapse into humanity evaporated as quickly as it appeared.

"I do have something to say, but I'm not going to resign." I swallow past the sudden dryness in my throat. I've been so busy being furious for the last twenty-four hours that I'd forgotten to be nervous. The enormity of the situation hits me at the worst possible moment. Now.

"Hey," Cali says, "isn't that the woman who—"

I step, ever so slightly, on her foot. The enormous table disguises the action.

"Ow!"

"Is your trick ankle acting up again?" I ask innocently, but I can see she's gotten the message. She settles back for a good sulk. I lick my lips and start again. "I know who took the money. Obviously, it wasn't me."

"That's not obvious to anyone," Edna snaps.

"I'm aware of that. But nevertheless, I didn't take it." I look her straight in the eye. "But I know who did."

From the tote bag at my side, I pull out the Web cam I took down this morning. I set it on the table next to the wad of bills.

"I've been monitoring the sacristy from my computer. I saw the culprit take the money Sunday afternoon."

Edna snorts, Ed looks intrigued, Gus looks up from his ledger, and The Judge leans ever so slightly forward. Marjorie continues to knit the fluffy pink sweater she's making for one of her multitude of blonde granddaughters.

"It was a church member, but I'd rather not say who. They've returned the money to me, and I feel sure it won't happen again." I look straight at Edna.

She thumps her cane on the floor. "Do you expect us to believe such an outrageous story?"

I stand up, place my hands flat on the table, and lean forward. "What I expect is to be trusted as the senior pastor of this congregation. You all selected me to fill Dr. Black's shoes, and now I want you to honor that choice." I look Ed in the eye, then The Judge and Gus, and finally Marjorie, who has actually laid down her needles. "You all know I didn't take the offering. For pastoral reasons I'm not willing to expose the person who did. I believe in second chances, and I'm willing to forgive the culprit and give him or her a new start." I pause for effect. "I think that's what Jesus would do."

Cali taps her french-manicured nails on the table. "Can I go yet?"

"Why is she here?" Edna snaps. "This is a private matter."

"Cali was in my office when the culprit took the money. She saw who took it, just as I did."

"Yeah, it was—"

"As I said, Cali and I both know who it was, but we're not going to reveal that information right now."

Edna pales beneath her pancake makeup and rouge. "Well, if it wasn't you, Betsy, it must have been the man who attacked me."

Very smooth, Edna.

"As I said, I would rather not name any names. I believe in forgiveness, and I'd like a chance to practice that." Again, I look Edna straight in the eye while I'm talking. It's like being locked in a battle to the death with Darth Vader but without the funny breathing, the big black mask, and the *whooshing* of the cool light sabers.

There's silence for a moment as the other committee members try to puzzle out exactly what's going on between me and Edna. I don't think it's occurred to any of them she's the thief, because why would the biggest contributor to the church turn around and steal it back?

Ed looks at Edna. "Does this mean you're withdrawing your accusation against Betsy?"

"Does this mean I can go?" Cali hisses.

I look around at their faces to gauge the mood of the group. They're confused, but even more they're relieved that we've avoided a major scandal.

The Judge, the smartest person present, clears his throat. "It appears to me an unknown person stole the money and attacked Edna. The property committee needs to look into improved security, but I see no matter for this committee to act on." He pronounces his judgment as solemnly as if he were behind the bench, bailiff at his side.

Relief slides through me like the rush from a really good piece of chocolate.

Ed twists his bow tie. "Then we can adjourn, I guess."

"Wait." I hold up my hand. "There's one more thing we need to address." I turn to Cali. "Thank you for coming. We won't keep you any longer."

Cali flips a strand of blond hair out of her eyes. "It took all this to figure out that the only thing you're capable of stealing is my boyfriend? Jeez." She pushes back her chair, stands, and makes an exit that rivals Edna's cane for dramatic effect.

The Judge takes a pocket watch from his vest and makes a point of studying it. I get the hint. I also sit back down, take a deep breath, and go to war.

"This whole offering incident has made me aware that we need a more structured agreement about my new role as senior minister." I pause to let the words sink in. "I would like for this committee to pass a vote of confidence in my ministry. I would also ask for a twenty-five percent pay raise, commensurate with my new responsibilities. And I want a one-year contract."

A what? Did I just say that? This is way worse than when I babbled on David's voice mail. What am I thinking? What about law school?

Ed's stroking his chin. The Judge crosses his arms. Gus has shut the ledger. Marjorie's gone back to her knitting, and Edna's opening and closing her mouth like my poor fish must have done when it took its dying breaths.

"And I'd like a decision on this right now," I add for good measure. The power surging within me makes me feel like a Christmas tree lighted up for the holidays. I should be appalled at my impulsive decision—part of me *is* appalled, actually—but I suddenly know with all my being that this is the right course of action. Ministry is what God wants for me. Maybe the Big Kahuna has just been waiting for me to quit playing it safe and stand up for myself. Which is exactly what Velva had been trying to make me see for the past six months, but I didn't have the ears to hear. Like Dorothy, I've been trying to find the magic I need to get me home anywhere but in the ruby slippers on my feet.

The Judge nods at Ed, Edna thumps her cane again but doesn't say anything, and Marjorie takes a pair of scissors out of her bag and clips a strand of fluffy pink yarn.

"Well, that's done," she says and pats her finished work. She looks up at me and smiles. "I think Betsy's requests are reasonable. As the largest contributor in this congregation, I'd suggest we do as she asks."

I swear the floor shakes. Sweet little Marjorie is the anonymous donor responsible for the financial well-being of the church? While Edna's been fooling us, allowing us to believe it was her?

For a long moment, nobody says anything. We're all wearing identical looks of astonishment.

And then, "All in favor?" Ed asks.

"Aye" is the answer, even from Edna who looks as if she's sucking a dill pickle when she gives her assent.

"Well, then..." I'm not really sure what to say next. I'm as surprised as any of them by what's just happened. I've just committed myself to Church of the Shepherd for the next year.

"Meeting adjourned," Ed says, and everyone stands up.

"Congratulations, Betsy," Marjorie says and winks at me.

I'm still feeling all empowered when I get home that evening, a com-
bination of the lingering effects of the latte and my victory in the
committee meeting. A Lean Cuisine and half a can of Pringles later,
I'm ready to tackle another confrontation.

I pull on my Vanderbilt Divinity School T-shirt, paper thin from
years of spin cycles in cheap Laundromats, and a tattered pair of jog-
ging shorts. With a deep breath, I stride into the bedroom and fling
open the closet door.

The first things to go are the leather pants and see-through chiffon blouse. Along with the deathly black stilettos. Next, I purge the
most unflattering elements of my wardrobe. Shapeless dresses, worn
khaki pants, sweater sets whose pills have pills. Item by item I stuff
them into paper grocery bags. It takes long enough that I work up a
pretty good sweat. Does that count as my exercise for the day? Every
so often I'm tempted to rescue something; I should have rounded up
the hosts of *What Not to Wear* in case I got cold feet.

I stick to my guns, though. When the dust settles and the carnage
is complete, there's not much left in my closet. Three pair of pants
that look as if they were purchased after the turn of the millennium,
not before. Two white Oxford shirts and my navy interview suit from
Ann Taylor Loft. And one summer dress that can pass for fashionable.
It's a good thing the personnel committee just gave me a raise, because
I'm going to need every penny. Right now I own approximately three
days' worth of clothing.

After purging my wardrobe I start pitching the makeup. Experts
say you should purchase new mascara every six months. I'm approximately two years behind. Powdered eye shadow that started out life as
cream follows the mascara. Expensive foundation—the wrong shade

but so pricey I couldn't afford not to use it. And, finally, all the lipsticks I have bought in search of that elusive perfect shade.

One by one I carry the bags to the trunk of my car to take to Goodwill. I dump the wastebasket full of old makeup into a garbage can and carry it to the street for pickup in the morning. And when it's all over, I collapse on the couch and try not to freak out over what I've just done.

One thing the "Holy to Hottie" makeover did show me: I don't have to settle for dressing like my mother. And I figure there's got to be a happy middle ground between frumpy and fashionista. The next day, clutching my credit card, I head for Ann Taylor. The real thing; not the cheaper Loft store. I've made an appointment with a personal shopper, and I can only hope this one has some experience with sizes in the double digits.

Sure enough, she does.

"I think pale blue would be a great choice," she advises as she hangs several garments in the dressing room. It's been years since I've actually shopped for clothes rather than order them from a catalog. I never much cared about cut and fit, but I see now that I can look fabulous and still be comfortable. This is my kind of makeover. Just normal Betsy, a young professional who has discovered what she really wants.

I'm admiring the pale blue suit when the personal shopper brings me something I wasn't expecting. It's a pink slip-dress, trimmed in lace. Just to humor her, I slip it over my head. It should look like a nightgown, but it doesn't. I should look ridiculous in it, but I don't.

"It's perfect," the shopper and I say at the same time, and we both laugh. But I can't really justify the expense for something so impractical. It kills me, but I pull the dress over my head and return it to its hanger.

"I'd better not," I say, and the personal shopper looks as disappointed as I feel.

"Are you sure?"

"That's a dress that needs an occasion. I really don't have anything coming up..." I trail off because I suddenly realize I do indeed have a special event in my near future. David doesn't know it yet, but he and I have a date with destiny. I finally know what I want from life, and if I can face the personnel committee and make my needs and wants known, I can do the same thing with David. In theory, anyway. With this dress, sufficient preparation, and perhaps a few of Edna's Darvocets.

"I'll take it," I tell the woman, and she's ecstatic. I'm a little ecstatic myself until I see the total for my new purchases on the charge slip.

"Is there a problem?" she asks.

"Oh no. Not really." I'm glad they don't have debtor's prison anymore, or else I'd be hauled off like some poor woman in a Charles Dickens novel. All I know for sure at this moment is that who I have become now fits into two Ann Taylor shopping bags. Tailored, but not stuffy. Colorful without being over the top. Womanly without being wanton. Well, okay, only a little bit wanton. Just me. Betsy. Trying to be faithful the best way I know how and no longer afraid of what the church might do to me. In fact, now the church might want to be afraid of what I might do to it.

Touché, Edna.

I giggle as I stow my new wardrobe in the trunk of my car. And so it is that, armed with two shopping bags and a new outlook on life, I head home to plan how to tell David I'm irrevocably, irretrievably in love with him.

Chapter 19

"You want me to lock you and David in where?" LaRonda asks. The contents of my peace offering—everything from Band-Aids to bandanas—are spread across the café table at Starbucks.

"It's for a good reason. So I won't try and run away."

"What were you drinking when you thought of this?"

"Diet cola."

"Couldn't you do things the normal way and just go talk to him?"

I sigh. "LaRonda, when have I ever done things the normal way?"

"I see your point."

LaRonda is so happy that I've maneuvered myself into a commitment with Church of the Shepherd. You'd think she'd be more supportive of my trying to make a commitment to David.

"It's a symbolic gesture," I argue.

"It's crazy," she replies. She rolls a tube of the lip balm between her fingers, stacks it on top of the bandanas, and sighs. "Oh, all right."

I try to keep the triumph out of my smile. "Can you do it this afternoon?"

"Why the hurry?"

"Because I can't afford to let any other woman get her claws in him. I almost blew it with the whole Cali thing."

If LaRonda weren't such a good friend, I'd resent her smirk. "Is it true she threatened to take out a restraining order against you?"

An indignant protest leaps to my lips before I see that she's teasing me.

"I wasn't *that* bad."

"Well, between you and David, you made a good effort at humiliating the poor girl."

The truth of her insight subdues me somewhat. I didn't mean to buy my own happiness at the expense of Cali's. At least David broke up with her of his own volition.

"What are you going to wear?" LaRonda asks.

"My secret weapon."

"The chiffon blouse?"

"Nope. I don't want to be holy or hottie for this. Just me. Just Betsy."

"Well, Just Betsy, you'd better get going if you're going to pull this off. What time do you want me at the church?"

"Four o'clock?"

"I'll be there."

I stop, look her in the eye, and smile. "You're a good friend. And I'm really going to miss you."

Tears well up in both our eyes. "I know, sweetie. I'm going to miss you, too. But I won't be gone forever."

"Yeah, but it will feel that way."

When we say good-bye, I hug her extra tight. A piece of me is going to Africa, and a piece of LaRonda will stay here. There's solace as well as sadness in that fact. That's what makes true friendship worth the cost.

I can tell Angelique is pleased with the turn of events at church because she's ordered me my favorite gel pens from the office-supply store. I've also got a fresh stack of pink legal pads and a new stapler.

"It's only temporary," I remind her. "The search committee will be looking for a new senior pastor. And then we'll see what happens."

The temporary nature of the arrangement doesn't seem to faze Angelique, though. "I guess we will" is all she says.

I try to spend the afternoon focusing on next Sunday's sermon, but the events of the past two weeks make that rather difficult. I'd rather daydream about David than study Paul's letter to the Ephesians in the original Greek.

Somehow the time passes. At four LaRonda appears in my office doorway. Together we head for the bridal dressing room at the back of the sanctuary. I have the pink dress in a plastic cover, and she's brought her cosmetic bag of tricks.

"Nothing heavy," I warn her, and she just grins.

"I found the perfect shade of lipstick," she says.

"What? Clergy Coral?"

"Nope. Neutral But Naughty."

That's the final confirmation. My best lipstick shade turns out to be the one that just brings out my natural color.

LaRonda arranges my hair in a casual but sophisticated semi-upsweep, and I slip into the delicate pink slides I found at Payless. Tiny pearl earrings and a matching bracelet later, I'm done.

LaRonda's beaming. "This is your best look yet, Betz."

I turn to face the enormous mirror that has reflected countless brides.

I'm not the hottie of my first makeover. I'm not the passive princess of the fund-raiser. I'm me. Sexy but sweet. A woman who's been called to a mostly male profession but retains some claim to her femininity.

"Wish me luck." All those butterflies that found refuge in the sanctuary after that last wedding have taken up residence in my stomach.

"Luck." LaRonda gives my shoulders a squeeze. "But you already have everything you're going to need."

"I hope you're right."

Yesterday, as I sat in the comfort of my living room, a diet cola in hand, the whole steeple scenario seemed like a stroke of brilliance. Now, though, as I climb the stairs to the sanctuary balcony and La-Ronda helps me up the ladder leading to a door high in the wall, I'm questioning the wisdom of my idea.

"Angelique knows to send David up here?" LaRonda asks. She guides my high-heeled feet from below, one precarious rung at a time.

"He thinks I need his opinion about a moisture problem."

"Is there actually a moisture problem?"

"I have no idea." I climb through the door into the steeple itself. It's like standing at the bottom of an elevator shaft. To my right a rickety ladder rises to a frightening height. Above I can see the trapdoor that leads to the next level.

LaRonda climbs onto the platform next to me. "Are you planning to go all the way to the top?" Church of the Shepherd is known for the exceptional height of its steeple.

"I think the first level is far enough."

LaRonda glances at her watch. "David will be here any minute."

"Right." I take a deep breath and wonder whether this would be the time to mention I'm afraid of heights. I forgot about that, too, in the excitement of my brilliant idea.

"Get going." LaRonda nudges me.

I swallow the lump in my throat and reach for the ladder. It's apparently held together with paper clips and baling wire.

"My first act as temporary senior minister is to order the property committee to build a new ladder for the steeple."

"Climb, Betsy."

"I can't believe I'm doing this."

How many senior ministers can say they've climbed their steeples in a dress and heels?

I thought I was afraid of the personnel committee. I thought I was afraid of telling David the truth about my feelings for him. Next time I think I'm too scared to do something difficult, I'll go climb the steeple to put things in perspective.

Rung by rung I make my way. It takes approximately three and a half years to get to the trapdoor. With one hand in a death grip on the ladder, I slide back the bolt and shove the door open. It flips back on its hinges with a thud and a cloud of dust.

It takes some wriggling, and one of my sandals almost slides off my foot to plummet to its death, but I manage to worm my way onto the platform.

"You okay?" LaRonda yells up to me.

"I think so."

"I'm going to duck out of sight."

"Okay." I wish my voice didn't sound so forlorn.

LaRonda disappears from below, so I swing my legs around and scramble to my feet. The platform is about fifteen feet square, with windows on all four sides. Wooden slats form a low wall beneath the windows. One or two feathered refugees have apparently found their way inside and left numerous white splotches as evidence of their occupation. To my dismay, I notice that we do, indeed, have a moisture problem. The slats let the air circulate, but they've allowed rain to seep inside as well. Some of the wood is rotting. In other places the paint is cracked and peeling. At least David can't accuse me of luring him up here on false pretenses.

There's not much to do but look out over the west side of downtown Nashville, so I pace, shivering in the cool March air. That works for a few minutes, until my cheap-but-fetching shoes start to chafe. I'd kick them off, but I don't want to step in the bird droppings.

For me, anticipation is always the worst part of any confrontation.

Finally, I hear the sound I'm both hoping for and dreading. Someone's climbing the ladder.

"Betz?" David's baritone reverberates from the emptiness below.

"Up here," I squeak, then stop to clear my throat and try again. "I'm up here."

The ladder creaks ominously, and with a flash of panic I fear I've lured David to an untimely death. *Please, God, not before I've had a chance to kiss him again.*

Fortunately, his head appears through the opening in the platform, and he hoists himself over the side. Looks as if I won't have to explain to St. Helga's why their pulpit is empty.

"Do you do this often?" He rolls to his feet and then stands, swiping his hair out of his eyes.

And then he freezes, because he sees me.

For a long moment, there's silence. Then he exhales noisily. "What's going on?"

"Would you believe I'm ready to talk?"

Ever so casually, I sidle over to the trapdoor and lean down to flip it closed. David frowns. "What's that for?"

"I don't want anyone to overhear us," I say casually.

"Who in heaven's name is going to overhear us up here?"

"Oh. Yeah. No one, I guess."

"And since when is a moisture problem confidential?"

I can't tell from his expression whether he's clueless about what I'm up to or being deliberately obtuse. Okay, this isn't going quite as I planned. David walks over to one of the walls and kneels down to inspect the slats, but the line of tension in his shoulders beneath his jacket tells me maybe he's not entirely oblivious to what's going on. For one thing, he hasn't commented on my dress at all, and I'm pretty sure he knows enough about women to know we don't normally wear pink slip-dresses to work.

He reaches in his pocket, pulls out a penknife, scrapes away some paint, and probes the wood underneath. "It's rotten all right." He stands up and turns toward me. "You spend a lot of time up here?"

"Not really."

"I didn't think so."

Okay, he's noticing the dress now, if not before. I can tell by the way he's looking at me and making a concerted effort to keep his gaze above my shoulders.

"You didn't need me to tell you that wood is rotten."

"No." I shift from one high heel to the other and resist the urge to dig my toe into the thick dust on the steeple platform like a kid who's been called on the carpet.

"Look, Betz, we don't have to do this—"

"Yes, we do," I interject before he can give me the out I'm scared enough to take. "We have to talk about this." I sound more like I'm trying to convince myself than him.

For a long moment neither of us says anything. And I wish desperately that it had never happened. That he'd never accidentally brushed my leg that night at the movies. That I'd chosen a different seminary in the first place. But you can't go backward. Only forward. I'm beginning to learn that, and I'm hoping to live it.

At that moment there's a sharp crack beneath the trapdoor.

"What was that?" David asks.

"Um…nothing."

"Betz?"

"Okay, it was LaRonda locking us in the steeple."

David rubs his closed eyelids with the thumb and forefinger of one hand, like my freshman English teacher used to do when I tried to diagram a compound-complex sentence. "Why is LaRonda locking us in the steeple?"

"Hey, David!" LaRonda calls from beneath our feet.

"Hey, LaRonda," he answers, but without the merriment she has in her voice. "Are you planning on coming back anytime soon?"

"About half an hour," her muffled voice replies. "Unless you want me to wait longer."

David looks at his watch. "No. I have to meet with the building committee at six."

"Okay," LaRonda says, and then I hear her climbing back down the ladder. It's quiet in the steeple except for the gentle sounds of the birds perched in the rafters above our heads.

David looks me squarely in the eye. "You have something to tell me?"

He's clenching and unclenching his fists again. I hope that means he's anxious, not angry. I hope he wants to hear the words I'm about to say, because if he doesn't, I may forgo the ladder and jump to my ignominious death.

"You were right." That's a good beginning, because men always like it when women admit they're wrong. "I shouldn't have run away on Saturday night, but…" I lose my nerve for a moment. Even with my newfound resolve, I still find it difficult to overcome eight years of not telling David how I feel.

David takes a step toward me. "I didn't handle it very well myself."

"Look, David, the thing is—"

"The thing is what?"

"Give me a second, will ya? Sheesh." I wipe my damp palms on my delicate pink slip-dress before I can stop myself. I look longingly at the trapdoor. David's eyes follow my gaze.

"No more outs, Betz."

I sigh. "Yeah. I know."

David moves another step closer, which does not help my nerves in the least.

"Look," he says, "if this is all about some early midlife crisis, just say so. I know you think I'm 'safe,' and maybe you just needed the nearest available guy for whatever drama's got you in its throes. I can't figure out whether it's the job or the makeover or what, but you have to deal, Betz."

"I'm not going through a midlife crisis!"

"Then what in heaven's name would you call it?"

Okay, now I'm angry. He thinks this is all some hormonally-induced drama?

"There is no drama," I screech, which kind of undercuts the point I'm trying to make. "You want to know what's going on? Okay, Mr. Smarty-Pants, here's what's going on. I love you, okay? I've loved you from the moment I tripped over your humongous feet at divinity-school orientation. I've loved you while you were engaged to Ms. Too-Good-To-Be-True What's-Her-Name. I've loved you for the past five years when we haven't even been in the same town. And now I still love you, and I kissed you, and everything is ruined."

I undermine the dramatic effect of this passionate declaration by bursting into loud sobs.

Now, this is the point at which he's supposed to sweep me into his arms, wipe away my tears, and declare his undying love for me.

Only, he's not doing any declaring. Or any sweeping, for that matter. Instead, he's looking at me as if I've lost my mind.

"And you were planning on telling me this information when? After we'd moved into adjoining garden homes in the retirement center?"

I realize that David is not flattered by my declaration. Believe it or not, he looks angry.

Okay, that's not what I was expecting.

"You're mad at me?" My question comes out with a fair amount of incredulity and frustration.

David puts both hands on his hips like a den mother about to scold a troop of Cub Scouts. "You've felt this way for eight years and never said anything?"

"Self-inflicted humiliation really isn't my style," I snap back.

"You were humiliated to have feelings for me?"

Honestly, sometimes men can be as thick as planks. "No, David. I wasn't embarrassed to have feelings for you. I'm just not a glutton for public humiliation."

"Meaning what?"

"Well, I couldn't very well put the moves on you when you were engaged, now, could I?"

"But you sat there, all those times in the student pub, and told me how to fix my relationship with what's-her-name."

No single woman would blame me for removing one of my shoes and stabbing him through the heart with the three-inch spike heel. But since I only paid fifteen dollars for them, I doubt they'd penetrate the chest cavity.

"I tried to be your friend," I say.

"But you didn't tell me you wanted anything more."

"I think you're being a little unfair."

"You could have said something after Jennifer and I broke up."

"It was graduation week. All of our parents were in town, and then before I knew it, we'd moved to different cities."

"We both had phones." David's not cutting me any slack.

"I don't think it's something you confess over the phone."

"You were afraid."

"Of course I was afraid!"

"Of me?"

"Of rejection."

"Yeah, I can tell you have a high opinion of my ability to handle women."

"It wasn't about you. It was about me." I say the words, and as I hear myself speak them, it's like a light bulb flicking on inside my head.

Heavens to *me,* it's the truth. It wasn't about David at all. All along it was about me.

"Then I'm confused," he says. "What's going on now? Is this what Saturday night was about? Some sort of revenge for my not reading your mind all these years?"

Okay, I'm not taking all the blame for this mess. Plus, he's sounding surprisingly defensive. "What about you, David?" I ask, turning the tables on him. "How do you feel about me?"

"Right now?"

"Right now in general. Not the right-now-because-I've-locked-you-in-the-steeple."

And then for a long moment he's quiet. Aha! So it's not so easy when the shoe is on the other foot, is it, big boy?

"Right now, in general, I pretty much adore you, they way I've adored you since the first day I met you. I just didn't realize it until that night at the movies."

I look at him long and hard because I don't know how to define *adore* here. Not enough context clues.

"Adore as in cute-little-fluffy-bunny kind of adore, or adore as in worship-like-a-goddess?"

His cheeks go bright red, and mine do too.

"The second thing," he growls.

"The second thing?" I stomp over to him, heedless of the pain my cheap shoes cause, and stab him in the chest with my finger. "What do you mean 'the second thing'? How long has it been 'the second thing'? Are you kidding me? Because I swear, David Swenson, if you are kidding—"

I can't finish the sentence because David covers my lips with his. And I was right. He doesn't need the lip balm.

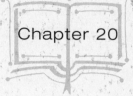

Chapter 20

Somewhere in the middle of the best lip-lock of my life, it occurs to me that LaRonda will return very soon. Reluctantly, I pull my lips from David's.

"Adore and worship? That's a bit cliché, isn't it?" I can't resist the urge to twist the knife a little bit. He deserves it, the rat, if he's had feelings for me and never said a word. And then made me feel like a coward for not spilling my own guts.

A pained expression crosses his face. "I'm never going to hear the end of this, am I?"

"No." But I may let him off the hook for now, since I'm feeling quite at home in his arms, and I'm not ready to stand on my own two feet again just yet.

Actually, I'm still a little miffed that David left me to swing in the wind by myself. "So all this railing at my cowardice was projection?"

"Pretty much." He looks past my shoulder and around the steeple platform. "Isn't there anyplace to sit down up here?"

"Not that isn't covered in dirt or bird droppings."

Over my shoulder, David looks at his watch. "We have eight minutes until LaRonda comes back."

I smile with what I hope is a hint of seduction. "We could practice our sermons on each other."

"Or not," David says and pulls me even closer. And when he kisses me again, I forget to lecture him about not practicing what he preaches.

My brilliant plan for LaRonda to lock us in the steeple has worked very well. There's only one hitch. LaRonda forgets to come back.

As David and I watch the sun set over Nashville, he fumes and I freeze. He's already missed the building-committee meeting. What's worse, he's in danger of missing *The West Wing.*

He's been holding my hand, but at some point, as the sun sinks farther below the horizon, his fingers fall from mine. The outdoor lights on the steeple provide us with enough light to see by.

"We're going to have to find a way out of here," he mutters, as if I didn't know.

"Well, if you'd remember to charge your cell phone, we could call for help." I say this with minimal inflection, but he bristles and shoots me a look that isn't hard to interpret.

"If you hadn't arranged for us to be locked in here, we wouldn't need my cell phone."

A classic chicken-or-the-egg situation all around.

"At least being locked in here made us open up," I offer helpfully.

His expression softens, his eyes going gooey chocolate, and he takes my hand again. "Yeah. That's worth missing a building-committee meeting."

I snort. "A root canal is worth missing a building-committee meeting for. Is it worth missing *The West Wing*?"

He takes a moment too long to answer, so I punch him in the shoulder.

"Hey!" he protests, but he's smiling. "Guess I should remember to set my VCR if you're going to be locking me up in steeples."

"It's sad that I'm the one bringing organizational ability to this relationship."

"Yeah, well, I still get to handle all the power tools." He might as well flex his biceps to prove his point.

"No problem." I have better things to do with my time than roam the aisles of Home Depot. Like pull my hair out by the roots.

David gives me a sidelong look. "I hope this part doesn't change."

"Which part?"

"The mutual torment and disrespect."

I smile. "No way. That's the fun part."

David leans toward me. "I thought this was the fun part," and he kisses me again.

Okay, I enjoy it for a moment, but then I shove him away. "We need a plan."

He moves toward me again. "I like this plan—"

"David. I'm hungry. Plus, I'm really cold."

He sighs and shrugs out of his jacket, which he wraps around my shoulders. "Okay. Got anything useful for getting us out of here?"

"Nothing on me."

David's eyes skim down my pink dress and back up again. "I'd have to agree with that statement. Not that I'm complaining, mind you. But I don't think you'd better try preaching in that getup."

"No, duh." I roll my eyes. "Empty out your pockets."

"My pockets?"

"Weren't you an Eagle Scout? Don't you have a flare or a mirror to send an emergency signal?"

David turns his pockets inside out and produces two quarters, a paper clip, some string, and a rubber band.

"How old are you anyway, eleven?" I ask with a laugh.

"You scoff now, but I'm better than MacGyver with this stuff."

"Who's MacGyver?"

"Don't you ever watch reruns on TV Land? He's the guy who can build a bomb out of a lipstick and a pair of sunglasses."

I frown. "We don't need a bomb. We just need to open that trapdoor."

David gives me a measuring look. "Tell you what. If I can get us out of here with what I have in my pockets, then you have to confront Edna."

"I did confront Edna."

"When?"

"At the specially called personnel meeting. I cut her off at the pass."

"No, sounds like you outmaneuvered her. Not confronted her. There's a difference."

"Okay, okay. I'll confront her." That's an easy promise since there's no way he can open that trapdoor with the assorted nothings from his pockets. "If you can get that thing open, I'll have my showdown with Edna."

"And you have to stay at Church of the Shepherd. No law school."

I can't believe I haven't told him yet about the personnel-committee meeting. It completely slipped my mind. I have to disguise the merriment I know is in my eyes. I sigh with dramatic gusto. "But law school was my ticket out."

"Was?"

"Um…I mean *is,* is my ticket out."

"You've already decided not to go, haven't you?"

Okay, there's going to be a downside to being romantically in-volved with someone who knows me this well.

"Yeah. I leveraged the personnel committee into a one-year contract."

David beams and holds out his hand for a high-five. "Now that's the Betz I know and love."

And then there's dead silence, because those words ring with authenticity. The love part, I mean.

In true manly form, David immediately changes the subject. "So, what changed your mind about law school?"

"Ironically enough, it was Edna."

"What'd she do?"

"She confessed she's always felt called to the ministry, but every-one told her it was of the devil."

"That explains a lot."

I stiffen. "But it doesn't excuse her behavior."

"No. You'll have to do that."

I hate it when David's right. Because he is, much as it pains me to admit it. I have to forgive Edna for what she's done, not just revel in my victory.

"I guess I'm not finished with her, huh?"

David grins. "Betz, you're not going to be finished with her until you officiate at her funeral."

Okay, that may sound mean, but he says it in a matter-of-fact way that preachers understand. Marrying and burying are part of our everyday reality. And if we grieve or rejoice at particular instances of those things, it goes on inside our hearts and heads, not publicly for everyone to see. At least, that's how it should be.

"Okay. You get us out of here, and I'll have a showdown with Edna."

"Don't think of it as a showdown. Think of it as a PMI."

"A *PMI?*"

"Personal maturity intervention."

And then he kisses me. So now I'm going to get unsolicited advice in addition to lip-lock. Mmm. Beats the previous setup hands down.

"Enough." I push him back. "To work, Mac-Whoever. We need to get out of here."

And wouldn't you know it? Fifteen minutes later he's fashioned a sort of fishing device with the paper clip for a hook, the quarters bound to the string with the rubber bands (as weights), and he's slipping the contraption down the crack between the trapdoor and the floor. His face twists in concentration, and he's never looked more adorable.

"I…think…I've…got it!" I hear a telltale click, and David's throwing the trapdoor open.

"You did it." Well, he can't remember to program a VCR, but he does have other uses.

"And you doubted me." He's grinning like a Boy Scout who just won the soapbox derby. Then he glances at his watch. "If we climb down fast, I can catch the last fifteen minutes of my show."

"You'll never make it. It'll take you half an hour to get home." David lives in an anonymous apartment complex down in Franklin, where rents are cheaper, but you pay for it with a half-hour commute up Interstate 65 every day.

David winks at me. "I'll make it, 'cause I'm coming to your house. It's the least you can do after trapping me in here and using your feminine wiles on me."

Hah! He knows I have feminine wiles. I'm so pleased with his acute powers of observation that I think I'll let him watch the rest of *The West Wing* at my house without interference.

After our escape from the steeple, I leave David alone with the couch and the remote while I call LaRonda.

"What happened to you?" I demand, half-mad and half-worried.

"Sorry. I got an emergency call from the hospital. Parishioner in cardiac arrest. By the time I remembered you guys, you were already gone."

"Well, luckily David does a good MacGyver impersonation."

"Mac-Who?"

See? I'm not the only one who doesn't spend all her free time watching TV Land reruns.

"Is your parishioner okay?"

"She'll be fine. Fortunately, she was already in the emergency room when she had her heart attack. Her grandson broke his arm earlier in the day." She pauses. "So, how'd it go?"

I giggle. It's completely junior high, but I can't help myself.

"Hallelujah!" LaRonda shouts so loudly she almost bursts my eardrum.

"Shh. He'll hear you."

"He's there?"

"Yes, but he's leaving right after his TV show finishes. Now that

Edna knows about Web cams, there's no telling what kind of surveillance I'll be under."

And so LaRonda and I celebrate on the phone as only two girlfriends can—with intermittent squealing and laughter. In fact, David has to wave his hands in front of my face to get my attention when he's ready to go. He can't leave without a parting shot, though.

"So you'll call Edna tomorrow?" he asks me between good-night kisses on the porch.

"Okay." I agree like a sulky adolescent who's been asked to take out the trash.

"Good." He steps back and looks at his watch. "If I hurry, I can catch my second-favorite show."

That catches me off guard. "You have a second-favorite show?" I thought I knew everything about David.

He smiles the slow, sexy kind of smile that makes me want to kiss him some more. "Oh yeah. It's called 'Holy to Hottie.' I watch the tape every night at bedtime."

"David!" I playfully slap his shoulder. "You told me you erased it!"

He moves back in for one more kiss. "I lied." His lips meet mine for a satisfyingly long moment. "So sue me. I wasn't going to part with it."

A warm flush rises from my toes. It's nice to know that I'm not the only one who's been experiencing these weird feelings over the past few weeks.

I give him one last, soft kiss. "Sweet dreams."

"No problem," he says as he disappears into the night.

So the next morning I have to pick up the phone and call Edna. But first, there's another conversation I need to have. I climb in my car and head for the Woodlawn Cemetery on Thompson Lane.

You'd think I'd have trouble finding Velva's headstone because this newer part of the cemetery only allows flat markers with a vase for flowers. But I walk straight up through the Garden of Something-Peaceful-Sounding to her grave. They've cleared away the flowers from the funeral, and the grass is freshly mowed. Lots of people bring plastic flowers because they last longer, but Velva would have hated those. Instead, I bring a different kind of remembrance I think would make her happy.

I kneel down in the grass and let my fingertips trace her name and the dates of her birth and death. There's nothing here to tell about what kind of woman she was, who she loved, and who loved her. No list of accomplishments. The only thing that will distinguish her grave from all the others will be the people, like me, who come to visit it.

"Hey, Velva." I feel a little stupid talking to a headstone, but that's the way they always do it in the movies. Besides, it feels better to say the words aloud, although I do glance over my shoulder to make sure no one's around to hear me talking to a dead person.

"I have something for you." I reach in my Kate Spade knockoff and pull out an envelope. The return address has the Vanderbilt emblem printed in the corner, and inside is the sheet of paper I thought was my ticket to happiness.

With appropriate ceremony, I lift the envelope in front of me as if I'm lifting the bread or the cup at the communion table. "I won't need this." And with great deliberation, I tear my law-school acceptance letter in half, then in half again. I continue a section at a time until the paper is shredded into postage stamp–size pieces. When I'm finished, I hold them in my two cupped hands and say a little prayer.

"Grant me faith, Lord." As if releasing a dove, I toss the future I never needed into the air. The wind catches it, and Velva and I are both showered by a gentle rain of providence.

Now I'm ready to confront Edna.

I stop by my house first to pick up something I forgot. I'm going to need it for this particular pastoral visit. I gather some papers and put them in a manila folder. I'm not calling ahead this time because I want to catch Edna unawares. As I've said before, the best defense is a good offense.

Alice greets me at the door. "Good morning, Reverend Blessing." She shows no surprise at finding me on the doorstep. I wish I had her discretion. I'd probably make bishop in a week.

"Good morning, Alice. Is Mrs. Tompkins at home?"

She smiles. "Let me tell her you're here."

Alice waves me into the foyer, and I wait there patiently while she goes to tell Edna the preacher's paying an unexpected call. Normally, it's an event that will make even the most seasoned parishioner quake with fear, but I'm sure it won't throw Edna off balance. I mean, we *are* talking about the woman who showed no qualms about framing me for felony theft.

Alice returns and leads me to the sun porch. Edna's there, en-sconced in a comfortable chair with the newspaper on her lap and a cup of tea at her good elbow. She's wearing the sling, which must make the newspaper a little tricky to handle. In the bright morning sunlight, she looks older and feebler than she did at the personnel-committee meeting a few days ago. Her back-comb droops from its once-formidable heights.

"Good morning, Edna."

"Betsy. This is a surprise." A surprise akin to having an emergency appendectomy, judging from the way her lips are thinned.

"I apologize for not calling first."

She makes a face that indicates she's not shocked at my lack of manners. "What more do you want from me?" she snaps. "I would have thought you'd be home gloating."

To my surprise, a stab of compassion pierces my midsection. As unpleasant as Edna has been to me, I know I'm probably the one person at Church of the Shepherd who understands what it's like to be shamed for who you are. For better or for worse, Edna and I are joined in a bizarre form of spiritual unity.

"I wasn't aware I had anything to gloat about."

She rolls her eyes. "Let's not pretend here, Reverend. You have what you want. And you have Marjorie's support, so why shouldn't you be feeling a bit smug? I think I would, in your place."

Well, at least she's honest. She probably would.

"I don't think my ministry is a competition," I say instead. "At least, I don't want it to be."

"Then why are you here?"

"I've brought you something." I take two steps toward her and hand her the folder. She takes it from me with her one good hand and lays it in her lap.

"Thank you."

"Aren't you going to look at it?"

"I know what's in it. A request I resign my membership from the church, with a possible admonition to be grateful you're not turning me in to the police."

Okay, that shocks me. "You're kidding."

Edna glowers. "I never *kid*, Reverend."

A fresh wave of sadness washes over me. In Edna's mind, that's how church works. And maybe in a lot of places, that's true. While I can't change what happens in other churches, I think I can change Edna's view of ours. At least I'm going to try.

"It's not a request that you resign your membership."

"Then what is it?"

"Look and see."

She frowns, shoots me a dark look, and then opens the folder in her lap.

"These are some sort of application forms."

"Yes."

She studies them for a long moment, and I let her. To my surprise, her hand, fingering the forms, shakes visibly.

"This isn't funny, Reverend."

"No, it's not," I agree.

And then an expression crosses her face that I usually see only when someone's child or spouse has died. Tears pool in her eyes, but she's not about to let them trickle onto her cheeks. Her shoulders begin to shake like her hand.

"It's too late," she whispers.

I close the remaining distance between us and kneel by her chair. "You know, Edna, I've only just learned it's never too late."

Her eyes meet mine, and I can't feel anything but compassion for the pain I see there.

"They'd never let me," she says.

"On the contrary. They'd be thrilled to have you." I cross my fingers behind my back, a little prevarication for a good cause.

"I'm too old."

"You're the voice of experience."

"I'm not smart enough."

"On the contrary. You've chaired almost every committee in this church, run the women's auxiliary, and served as treasurer. Anyone who can do what you've done at Church of the Shepherd all these years has more than enough brains for this. Trust me. I speak from experience."

"I'll look like a fool."

I smile at this and pull a tissue from the box on the table next to her. "Well, you'll be in good company. Everybody does there at one time or another."

She's quiet for a long moment. Then, "There's one more problem."

"What?"

She inclines her head toward her injured shoulder. "I can't write until I get my arm out of this sling."

"Not to worry." I laugh and dig in my purse for a pen. "I can be your scribe."

And that's how I came to be sitting in Edna Tompkins's sunroom, filling out her application forms for Vanderbilt Divinity School.

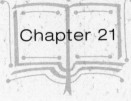

Chapter 21

All around me candles blaze. This time it's the scent of lilies, not roses, that overpowers the congregation. The men wear dark suits rather than tuxes, and I see far fewer hats. The vaulted ceiling of Church of the Shepherd still soars above me, though, as I stand at the foot of the chancel, David by my side. I drink in the scene, linger over every detail, and my knees quiver. A deep breath does little to calm my nerves.

Next to me, David stands tall and handsome. The organ swells as the pipes ring out the last notes of "The Wedding March." It's the lifetime commitment I've always wanted. A deep connection through all the "slings and arrows of outrageous fortune." No more loneliness. No more isolation. I look up to keep the tears from flowing.

David shoots me a lazy, thrilling smile, and it's all I can do not to melt into a puddle at his feet. How unfair that a man can have this effect on me whenever he chooses. My only consolation is that I'm pretty sure I have the same effect on him.

Who'd have ever thought I'd be standing here at the front of the church with David? Certainly not any of our parishioners. Because it's the first "mixed" wedding Church of the Shepherd and St. Helga's have ever done.

I return David's smile and then take a deep breath. With a calm demeanor that doesn't reflect my inner turmoil, I open my officiant's book and begin.

"Dearly beloved…"

No, I'm not performing my own wedding ceremony. David and I are sharing the honors for the couple standing before us. Lisa's one of David's parishioners, and Kevin is one of mine. David and I are currently locked in a struggle to the death over whose church gets the newlyweds. It only occurred to us a day or two ago that the couple in question might want to have some say in the matter.

I'm amazed, when I think back over the past few weeks, how my life has changed in such a short time. The folks at the law school seemed relieved by my decision not to matriculate there. Evidently they had such a high acceptance rate this year, they don't know where they're going to put all the students.

I've already taken Edna over to visit the divinity school and meet a few of the professors. It took me a week to get her past the fact that so many seminarians now sport multiple body piercings.

I drove LaRonda to the airport and have already exchanged a couple of e-mails with her. And I'm doing well with maintaining my new look in my own way, although some of my church members still think I should be covered from head to toe like a kid wearing a bed sheet as a costume at Halloween.

As for David, well, let's just say we're trying to figure out how you go from being best friends to boyfriend and girlfriend. For one thing, I've learned that he no longer takes my helpful criticisms in quite the same spirit.

Will there be a wedding for us? you ask. I don't know. I hope so. At thirty I don't want to wait forever. But I'm just getting on my feet at Church of the Shepherd, and that's my focus right now. Okay, it's not my only focus, because David and I see each other every day. But I'm trying not to turn into the pathetic, clinging sort of girlfriend who text-messages her guy thirty times every hour.

This wedding may turn out to be my best one yet. I finish with the Declaration of Intent and hand it off to David for the wedding homily. Since we've been working on it together, I pretty much know it by heart.

"Marriage should be a challenge," David says, barely looking at the text in the notebook as he delivers the words in his delicious baritone. "But it should also be a comfort." Ironic that two unmarried people are standing up here preaching to a congregation full of people who have actual experience with the subject, but we do our best. That's all any minister can do. I finally figured that out. You may never be enough for everybody, but from time to time, you're enough for somebody.

I take over and do the vows. All the other pieces speed by, and it flows so easily between the two of us. I'm having such a good time, the bride and groom are a mere afterthought. Until I accidentally say my name and David's in place of Lisa and Kevin's.

Oops.

Oh well. I always tell brides that every wedding has to have at least one significant gaffe, or the marriage won't last.

David and I follow the wedding party down the aisle as the organ sounds out the recessional. We reach the gathering area just outside the sanctuary, and David takes my hand in his. "Come with me," he whispers, and I follow willingly.

We'll resurface in time for the reception. I promise. And this time I won't be going alone.

David pulls me toward the side corridor that leads to the baptismal dressing rooms. It's perhaps the first time these walls have witnessed this kind of light ministerial misconduct.

With any luck, it won't be the last.

You are cordially invited to enjoy

Betsy's Wedding

Coming Summer 2006 from WaterBrook Press!

After years of lonely Saturday nights—interspersed with excruciating blind dates—I, Betsy Blessing, am about to be courted by the man of my dreams.

It's enough to make a grown woman giggle. Or purr. Or both.

I can't believe we're here at LaPaz, David and I, being escorted to our table by a hostess barely old enough for a training bra. Fortunately, I know David well enough to know he won't give the teen's budding figure a second glance. The menu, now, that's another story. Until he's dithered sufficiently over his choice of entrée, he won't pay any attention to me—which may be a good thing given that I'm sure I still have some tinges of toner around my hairline. Once he's settled on his choice for dinner, though, he'll focus all the charm and intelligence in those big brown eyes right where they belong. On me.

Let the games begin.

"Your server will be with you in a sec," chirps the hostess as she cuts her eyes at David. She's regarding his clerical collar with interest—not an unusual occurrence, I'm afraid. When David and I were just best friends, as we've been for the past eight years since divinity school, I laughed off the female fascination with his "uniform." But now that we've found true love and are officially on our first date, I don't find it quite as amusing as I used to.

"Mmm," David mumbles as he peruses the list of quesadilla options, oblivious to the hostess's last, lingering look. Even if I wore a clerical collar—and in my denomination, we don't—men would never find it as sexually appealing as women seem to find David's.

Figures.

Rule No. 1 for Women Ministers: All of the work; none of the perks.

"What are you having?" David asks, peering over the top of his menu. I scramble to open mine and give it a quick once-over. The truth is, my stomach is so tied up in knots, I'm not going to be able to eat a bite. A real date with David at a normal restaurant. Just like all the other couples I've been envying all these years. I know David is the one for me, but I'm not in any rush to the altar, despite what my mother likes to refer to as my "advancing age." I'm barely thirty, and as old-fashioned as it may sound, I want to be courted. Heaven knows I've waited long enough for a little romance.

"I think I'll have the shrimp enchiladas," I say, and David nods sagely, as if I've just translated a tricky bit of the Dead Sea Scrolls from the original Aramaic.

Then he frowns. What does that frown mean? My heart skips a beat. These days it seems to go into overdrive with every nuance of his facial expression.

"Or maybe I'll have the taco salad," I say weakly. Yuck. I hate that note of uncertainty in my voice. Just because David and I are officially an item does not mean I have to turn into an echo chamber for his opinions and preferences. Not that David would want me to. It's just something women seem to fall prey to in the early stages of a relationship, no matter how liberated they are.

Our waiter appears, and I'm forced to interpret the subtext of my entrée choice on the spot. "The shrimp enchiladas," I say, deciding it's better to begin as I mean to go on. I may be in love, but I remain a complete, worthwhile, and independent person.

Really.

"I'll have the steak fajitas," David says without any existential qualms whatsoever and hands the waiter his menu. Then his attention finally, blessedly, turns to me.

When I'm with David, I should carry a voltage meter, because I'm sure the electricity that shoots through me would register at an impressive level. For years I kept it under wraps, since I didn't think he felt the same way. But then recently, a miracle occurred, and David and I became an item. Let the congregation say "Amen!"

I try to ignore the angel chorus singing hallelujahs in my ears and turn my attention to David.

"How was your day?" I ask. It's a question I've asked him a million times, but it has a different ring to it now. A proprietary tone. I have the vested interest of a significant other in his response.

"Great. It was great." He's glancing around the restaurant like a fugitive on the FBI's Most-Wanted list. David's not normally a nervous type of person, so I have to tell you that little prickles of apprehension begin shooting up my spine. What if he's already decided this was a dumb idea, risking our years of friendship against the uncertain promise of a romantic relationship? What if he wants out already? Is the courting over before it's even begun?

"Are you looking for somebody?"

"What?"

"You seem a little nervous, like you're expecting to see somebody."

"Oh? Really?" He tries to look innocent, but that telltale flush creeps up his neck. David's a terrible liar, and everyone knows it. Especially his congregation. His neck is like a giant truth thermometer that can be read at ten paces.

"David? Is something going on?"

The flush overshoots his neck and spreads across his cheeks. He laughs like a bad actor in summer stock.

But he doesn't deny it.

So it's true. He's going to dump me on our first date.

And I was so looking forward to the courting.

The knots in my stomach would make Houdini blanch. "Listen, David, you know, I've been thinking—"

But before I can summon up the words to cut and run before he does, the strangest thing happens. David gets up out of his chair, comes around the corner of the table, and drops to one knee beside me.

"Did you lose a contact?" I try to ask, but the knot in my stomach vaults into my throat, and my words come out in a high-pitched squeak more suited to Alvin and the Chipmunks.

"Betsy," he says and takes my right hand in both of his. All around us, the other diners have swiveled their chairs to take a gander at the spectacle at Table 11.

"David? What's going on?"

His hands are sweaty but warm, and I don't think he would publicly humiliate me by announcing to the whole restaurant that he's decided I'm too repulsive to date. Then one of his hands leaves mine, and he puts it in his pocket. When it re-emerges, it's holding a black velvet box.

Oh, Lord, have mercy on me. A Little. Black. Velvet. Box.

I'm hyperventilating. I swear I'm hyperventilating. The knot in my throat drops to the floor, somewhere in the vicinity of David's knee.

"Betz, I know it's our first date, but I don't see any point in putting off the inevitable." He smiles—that smile I feel right down to my toes every time he trains it on me—and for several enjoyable moments I'm mush.

"The inevitable?" I repeat.

Around us, the other restaurant patrons are murmuring excitedly among themselves. As if in slow motion, David brings the box up to my hand so he can use the fingers wrapped around mine to open the lid.

"Ouch!" I protest when he accidentally catches the skin on the back of my ring finger in the hinge.

"Sorry." He raises my hand to his lips and kisses it, and it's all I can do not to slide off my chair into a puddle on the floor.

"Betsy, I know it's our first date, but I don't need any more time to know you're the one I want to spend the rest of my life with." He turns the box so I can see the contents, and nestled on the velvet is a small diamond engagement ring. A pear-shaped diamond on a wide gold band, surrounded with little pink things that look as if they came out of a gumball machine.

It's the most hideous ring I've ever seen.

"Betz, why don't we just go ahead and do it?"

He looks at me with those big brown eyes, like a puppy that has just learned not to piddle on the carpet. And a hole the size of Cleveland opens up in my midsection.

This can't be happening.

"Betz?"

Does my horror show on my face? I need to smile. I must smile. So I do, but it feels as if my lips are being pried upward with a cattle prod. The ring just sits there in the middle of the velvet box in all of its Technicolor glory. David's hand shakes a little. He's been on that knee a long time. The other diners start to murmur.

This should be the happiest moment of my life, but the tears that start to fall have nothing to do with joy. It's what I wanted, but it's definitely not the way I dreamed it.

"Beggars can't be choosers," I hear my mother's voice whisper in my ear. She said it when Harold Grupnik was the only one who asked me to the prom, and I'd resent her for it still if it hadn't had the death knell of truth behind it.

For heaven's sake, I'm getting *David* out of this deal. What does it matter if the details aren't perfect?

I blush and hope David will chalk it up to embarrassment, not shame. A fine distinction, but an important one at the moment. I'd much rather he think I'm shy about accepting his proposal in front of all these people than realize the depth of my disappointment.

"Compromise, Betsy," my mother's voice adds in my ear. *"You don't have your sister's natural beauty, but your intelligence is very attractive, in its own way."*

David leans forward, and now he's looking concerned. And there's such love in his eyes that I feel like a complete idiot. What am I doing? This man loves me. That's more important than the most fabulous courtship in the history of courtships. He doesn't need to woo me; he's already got me. As usual, I'm so busy getting in my own way that I can't accept what's being offered.

"Of course, David. Of course I'll marry you."

He smiles and relief washes across his features. At that moment I realize he was actually worried I might turn him down. A wave of warm affection washes over me, and I resolve to put my momentary doubts behind me.

"Kiss her!" a man two tables over calls out, and David grins.

"Why didn't I think of that," he murmurs to me as his lips move toward mine. I smother a giggle—or rather, David's lips do—and everyone in the restaurant breaks into applause.

A lot of applause. Really, more than there should be.

When David lifts his head from mine, I look over his shoulder to see that the doors to the party room have been thrown open, and wave after wave of familiar faces flow forth. My parishioners. David's parishioners. Friends from divinity school. And then I see my sister. And my mother. And right behind her, my father. I'm stunned. My parents haven't been in the same room since their divorce fifteen years ago. Even when my sister, Melissa, had her daughter, our parents took turns coming to the hospital.

"Mom? Dad?"

"It's an engagement party, honey!" My mom, always a great one for stating the obvious, practically shoves David out of the way so she can pull me out of my chair and hug me. Her hair is even blonder than the last time I saw her. A cashmere sweater set and modest pearls give her the air of old money—an air she cultivates without any actual financial backing to support it. "Are you surprised?" she asks.

Surprised? How about stunned? Appalled? My dad reaches me a split second after my mom. He's so tan, he's almost orange. Tracy, his new wife, must be dousing him with that spray-on stuff again.

"Nobody's ever going to be good enough for you, Sunshine, but I guess he'll do," my dad says and plants a peck on my cheek. My mom scowls.

"Not now, Roger," she snaps.

"Don't you mean 'not ever,' Linda?" he fires back. "You may not like it, but I plan to be a part of this wedding every step of the way."

And then, over the din, I hear the strident voice of David's mother, Angela Swenson. "Over here, Jeremy. I want a shot of this." She pushes past the well-wishers with her Lee Press-On Nails and a shake of her Farrah Fawcett hair.

My folks recede into the crowd, and a flashbulb goes off in my face.

"David, get down on one knee again," Angela orders him. "We missed that shot."

A shadow passes over David's face, but he does as he's instructed. I'm too stunned to do anything but passively cooperate. The flash pops again.

"Now, take her hand. You forgot to put the ring on her finger."

David slips the ring from the box and shoots me an apologetic glance.

"David, what's going on?" I hiss.

"It's a surprise," he whispers. "My mother wants to—"

His explanation is interrupted when Angela calls out another set of instructions, and the photographer continues to snap away. I feel like J.Lo at a movie premier—minus the fashionable clothes, hair, and makeup—when David's mother finally spills the beans.

"Isn't it great, Betsy? How many girls would give their right arm to be featured in *Budget Bride* magazine?" David's mother beams. "Lucky for you your future mother-in-law is the managing editor."

David's fingers tighten around mine. "Please, Betz?" he says under his breath. "It means so much to her. And the magazine will pay for everything."

My eyes meet his, and with a sinking feeling, I know I'm going to agree. Not because I care that much about making his mother happy, but because I want David to be happy. That's how it is when you love someone. I have David now. I can afford to be noble and gracious.

Also, I'm afraid of what will happen if I say no. You see, I knew David back when he was engaged before. To Jennifer, the Cindy Crawford look-alike. I know he can do better than me.

"It's fine," I whisper. "Really. It'll be great."

The lines on David's forehead dissolve into relief. "Thanks," he says, and then zooms in for another kiss. The flashbulb is popping again, but at the moment, I don't care. The whole world can be as imperfect as it wants as long as David keeps kissing me.

"It came from eBay," Angela informs me amid the bustle of my impromptu engagement party. The photographer snaps a few close-ups of my garish engagement ring. "Such a steal," Angela purrs.

Her words douse the faint flicker of hope that I might find a gentle way to suggest to David that we exchange the ring for something more, well, tasteful. I can't believe I'm going to spend the next forty-plus years of my life wearing an engagement ring that looks like an Easter basket. I bet the person who sold it to him is still laughing.

"It means a lot to me that he picked it out himself," I say demurely, because it's never too early to build a good bridge of communication with your future mother-in-law. No matter what cheap tabloid she edits.

"Oh." A brief look of consternation flits across her features. "Himself. Well, actually, I had my assistant Veronica do that for him. You know David. He's hopeless when it comes to shopping. Plus, Veronica's been scouring eBay for months for the cheapest ring possible. It's going to be a whole sidebar for the feature."

I try to ignore the stab of disappointment in my midsection. Probably a lot of guys have help buying their girlfriend an engagement ring. I just wish David's ring consultant hadn't been a twenty-year-old administrative assistant who thinks pink ice is the height of fashion.

"Please thank Veronica for me," I say to Angela, but what I really mean is, "A pox upon her and her unborn children."

Okay, that's probably a bit harsh, but I'm a little too overwhelmed at the moment to be a model of graciousness. I was expecting dinner for two, not a party of forty.

I see nothing of David for the next hour. Well, that's not strictly true. Since he's quite tall, I can see his head across the room. I'd hoped to spend a good portion of the evening in his arms. Instead, I'm spending it in the arms of the parishioners from his church (St. Helga's Lutheran) and mine (Church of the Shepherd). I had hoped to spend the evening enveloped in the combined scent of David's cologne and shrimp enchiladas. Instead, I'm surrounded by the smells of talcum powder (elderly church ladies) and Opium (David's mother, who buys it in bulk to save money). The closest I get to shrimp enchiladas are a few tortilla chips with some green tomatilla sauce. By the time I've received everyone's well wishes, I'm famished, my feet hurt, and my mother's driving me up a tree.

"A June wedding will be pushing it," my mom says to Angela, "but I believe it can be done."

June? Did David and I set a date without my knowing it?

"Look, Mom, this is all fairly sudden—"

"It's March, but I don't think it's hopeless," my mom continues, undaunted. "Betsy should have a little pull when it comes to booking the church." For the first time since I announced my intention to become a minister, my mother seems pleased with my decision. At long last, my profession has its use.

"Maybe we should all take a deep breath—" I don't get any further with that appeal than I did with the one before.

"Definitely June," Angela says. "My copy for the feature article will be due July 1, so we'll still be cutting it close. But that's the only way to make it into the December issue."

December issue? "Won't a summer wedding look strange in a winter issue of the magazine?"

Angela looks at me as if I've sprouted two heads. "Oh no, dear. It will be a Christmas wedding. We already have the theme: 'Low-Cost Winter Wonderland.'" She flashes her enormous smile—which is rather scary because of the gleaming porcelain veneers on her two front teeth—and brays a long laugh. "Isn't that great?"

"Great," I lie through my teeth and frantically look around for David. This is *his* mother; *he* can be the one to get us out of this mess.

But David's having his ear bent, twisted, and mangled by Obadiah Grant, the resident curmudgeon in his congregation. Obadiah doesn't look as if he's going to let up anytime soon. David's church is in the process of rebuilding the sanctuary after last year's tornado, and Obadiah has been making David's life miserable with his demands. Across the room of party-goers, our eyes meet, and I instantly feel calmer. Of course, he's not going to let his mother hijack our wedding, just as I'm not going to let mine use it as an occasion for vigorous social climbing. After all, we're the bride and groom. We're in charge. Everyone will calm down once the newness of our engagement has worn off.

"Regular trips to Goodwill," Angela is advising me, I discover, when I tune her back in. "Twice a week at least."

"Goodwill?" I echo, confused.

"Of course. You have to be in the right place at the right time. Because somewhere out there right now is a bride who's about to be jilted. She'll want to get rid of the dress. You have to be ready to pounce."

Ready to pounce? Doubtful. Ready to flee into the night? Absolutely.

In my wildest dreams, I'd never have dreamed my first date with David would turn into a wedding nightmare.